FAMILY PLANNING

Tim Parks's other novels include *Tongues of Flame*
(winner of the Somerset Maugham and Betty Trask
Awards), *Loving Roger* (winner of the John Llewellyn
Rhys Prize), *Cara Massimina*, *Mimi's Ghost* and
Europa. His non-fiction work includes the bestselling
Italian Neighbours and *An Italian Education*.

Tim Parks lives in Italy.

BY TIM PARKS

Fiction

Tongues of Flame
Loving Roger
Home Thoughts
Family Planning
Goodness
Cara Massimina
Shear
Mimi's Ghost
Europa

Non-Fiction

Italian Neighbours
An Italian Education

Tim Parks

FAMILY PLANNING

VINTAGE

Published by Vintage 1997

2 4 6 8 10 9 7 5 3 1

Copyright © Tim Parks 1989

The right of Tim Parks to be identified as the
author of this work has been asserted by him in accordance
with the Copyright, Designs and Patents Act, 1988

First published in Great Britain by
William Collins Sons & Co 1989

Vintage
Random House, 20 Vauxhall Bridge Road,
London SW1V 2SA

Random House Australia (Pty) Limited
20 Alfred Street, Milsons Point, Sydney
New South Wales 2061, Australia

Random House New Zealand Limited
18 Poland Road, Glenfield,
Auckland 10, New Zealand

Random House South Africa (Pty) Limited
Endulini, 5A Jubilee Road, Parktown 2193, South Africa

Random House UK Limited Reg. No. 954009

A CIP catalogue record for this book
is available from the British Library

ISBN 0 7493 9679 2

Papers used by Random House UK Ltd are natural,
recyclable products made from wood grown in sustain-
able forests. The manufacturing processes conform to the
environmental regulations of the country of origin

Printed and bound in Great Britain by
Cox & Wyman, Reading, Berkshire

For Michele and Stefania,
who always resist the best-laid plans

What follows is entirely fictional:
no reference to any living person
is intended or should be inferred.

HOME AT LAST

HOME AT LAST

Had they still been a possibility in England, Mr Baldwin would have sent his other children telegrams to announce his return. As it was, he felt unwilling, or perhaps in some psychological way genuinely unable, to get involved in phonecalls with all the scope they gave for direct and impromptu questions. One grew less and less interested as time went by in explaining one's own affairs, that was the truth of the matter. Letters might have been more congenial, but would have required the kind of time and effort that Mr Baldwin could hardly contemplate in all the bustle of winding up operations at the site and throwing things into packing-cases back at home. Especially since for the last couple of days or so Brenda seemed to be more concerned with placing her various cats with good families (were there such things, he honestly wondered?) than with preparing the Baldwin caravan. Raymond, of course, could not be expected to help, except perhaps after the most minute instruction backed up by extremities of promise or threat; as a rule one should consider oneself lucky if he didn't hinder. Anyway, there would be plenty of time to tell the rest of the family once they were safely back. That was the least of his worries. And when Brenda asked had they been told, he replied testily of course they had.

On the plane, which remarkably left Algiers bang on schedule, Raymond stayed an unreasonably long time in the toilet; not that this would have bothered Mr Baldwin in the slightest had it not been the occasion for one of Brenda's fits of hysteria. In the end he had to restrain her from going to the front of the little queue that was forming and demanding through the door what he thought he was doing in there. Mr Baldwin knew what she was thinking, of course, but unlike Brenda he saw such outcomes as the cut wrist or the makeshift noose as welcome releases. We should be so lucky, he told himself, hearing an old, cynical voice that had to be forever repressed in the presence of his wife. With no sense of logical consequence, he began telling her how much she was going to appreciate having Lorna close at hand again, or at least only a couple of hundred miles away. Not to mention the twins. If they had to live with their bad offspring, they might at least have the good ones (relatively good ones, he privately thought) in the vicinity to cheer them up from time to time. And three to one was a fair enough ratio when all was said and done. He'd been reading an article about a family where . . . Brenda, who suffered severely from ear trouble on planes, objected strongly to the word bad. A duty-free trolley was blocking her view of the toilet now. It wasn't a question of good or bad. How many times did he have to be told that?

'When exactly was the last occasion we were all together as a family?' Mr Baldwin was trying rather complacently, when all at once they both heard Raymond's raised voice arguing with the steward about not being able to get past the duty-free trolley. Despite the steward's replying politely in French, Raymond insisted with his pidgin Arabic. It was a disgrace that the national airline of a Moslem country sold alcohol on . . . Visibly relaxing, Mrs Baldwin stood up in the aisle and beckoned over the trolley, where no alcohol was to be seen. Smiling and as if addressing a tiny child, she held a finger over her lips in the direction of this hefty young man her eldest son, though when she'd finally got him back in the seat between them she began on a good telling off. Raymond said it was his fucking business what he did in the loo thank you very much. He seemed particularly belligerent. Mr Baldwin secluded himself at the window and, uninterested by canyons of flossy cloud below, began to list the pleasures in store for him back in Cleveleys: availability of English beverages, alcoholic and otherwise; availability of English television, radio and newspapers; availability of English cigarettes. And then no one could deny that it should be rewarding after all these years to have the family back together again. Or in the same country at least. Especially Lorna. He thought of Lorna with much fondness. What a nice surprise it would be for her to hear they were back.

It might have been a week later a youngish woman in her night-dress tore open a buff envelope.

'Dear Daddy,' she read in infant handwriting on lined paper, 'When are you coming back? It is Sunday afternoon. This morning we went to church. I wore my new lemon hat with the ribbons. Mummy wore her chocolate one. Now I am in Granny's room. She is still very sick and not speaking. Mummy says if she doesn't say something soon, she will scream. We are all looking forward to your coming back. Please come soon.

Love and kisses,
LORNA'

The folds of this letter were furry grey and the paper seemed ready to crumble apart in her hands.

After a shower and hairwash, dressed now in sloppy skirt and sweater, the woman sat down in front of her processor and opened a new file. For a moment she picked at the skin about her nails, then began:

January 18th   Fairfield Close
                                                         Finchley
                                                         London N12

Dear Father,
    Yesterday the postman brought the menus of the Steamship Adriatic, summer '63, tied in a blue ribbon and wrapped in what must be the original paper napkins. Today I got a letter I seem to have written myself a good twenty-five years ago; I suppose when we were still in Cleveleys and you had gone to Sudan. Both the envelopes are postmarked Lancs.,

so I presume you're back at last, which is good news, of course, very good news, and I do hope it will be for keeps this time, but don't you think a better way to announce it would have been to have written me a proper letter, rather than sending these scraps of memorabilia? Or you could have phoned. I do have a phone you know. What do you plan to do? Are you going to stay in Cleveleys and do up the house? What about Raymond? Is there any hope? And whatever became of Mother's dressmaking book? Nobody tells me anything.

As for your souvenirs, I hope you won't be offended if I tell you I chucked them away at once. There's no point in getting sentimental and nostalgic about our childhood (you've started cleaning out the dreaded back-room, I suppose). It was a rotten childhood. You were never there and Mum was always angry because she had too much to do. That doesn't mean I'm blaming you for anything, least of all for Raymond. Just that there's no point in getting nostalgic about something that wasn't much fun. Is there? So if you find any more old bric-a-brac, just chuck it away and get on with sorting out what you're supposed to be doing next.

Things are very much the same this end. Oh, except that Fred's career is taking off at last. They published his PhD thesis and everybody is interested in him all of a sudden (so you see it wasn't such a bad mistake us coming back to England after all). Meanwhile I'm plodding along ghost-writing an entirely superfluous book about an utterly inane pop group called Crackle. Fortunately we've found a good nursery for Kirsty, so I've got plenty of time. She is growing rapidly as ever. Her favourite trick at the moment is to climb on the living room table and try to pull the lightshade down.

As for the twins, it's a bit ironic; Graham phones regularly from his office two hundred miles away, while from Garry just a bus-ride down the road never a squeak. It's a shame. When we came to live here I thought we'd see a lot of him. I thought it would be nice to be living near one of the family again, and then the twins were always such a laugh when they were younger. But as it is he only shows up when he's short of money or needs a meal, then vanishes for months on end. God knows what he actually does all the time, plays politics I suppose. Anyway, I'll try and get in touch with him to let him know you're back and see if there's any chance of a swift reunion.

Best love Dad, and to Mum and Raymond. Do write a proper letter soon, or better still, phone. Call reverse charges if it makes it easier with the phone boxes. We can handle it.

Kisses,
LORNA

Dear Brother – she wrote on a separate sheet to Raymond – I'm so happy to hear you're back. Perhaps we can get together sometime soon. Fred is eager to meet you and I'm sure Kirsty is going to love her Uncle Ray very much. You should see her, she's such a darling little girl. Meanwhile, have fun rediscovering Cleveleys. I quite envy you all that fresh sea air. Remember when we used to play 'beat the waves' on our way to school?

Lots of love,
SIS

On the cold evening of that same day, from a call-box off the Edgware Road, a tall young man with jet dark hair, beneath which winked an earring, dialled the number of Colonel Gascoigne (retired) in Leeds. He stamped his feet and examined the strong brown fingers of his left hand. Thinking a thought though, he frowned. Then came the connection and, despite the fact that it wasn't his home, this young man's once identical twin answered rather promptly:

'Double four, double one, Gascoigne.'

'Hello, Graham, thought you might be there.'

'Garry.'

'Got you answering the phone now, have they? Sophy okay?'

'I like to make myself useful, you know.'

Cake in hand, cosy and warm, Graham's voice in suburban Leeds was stiffer, slower, plummier than his brother Garry's in seedy Kilburn, and anyway he was distracted by a television programme the Gascoigne family were watching. Unfortunately someone's parachute wasn't opening.

Garry was so used to implied criticism he never thought of doing other than ignoring it. Anyway, this was an urgent call.

'Look, Lorna left a message here saying the folks were back. I . . .'

'I know, it just so happens that I was down there at the weekend to give them a hand moving in.'

'You were? But they haven't been in touch with me at all. Not a word.'

'They probably thought you were too far away to be of help.'

'But you'd have thought they'd have had the decency to keep

me informed, wouldn't you? I mean. Anyway, what's the story? Tell me all.'

The story was that Raymond was as always; he hadn't taken his pills for months. Everything was as always. What did you expect?

Although there hadn't been more than ten minutes between their births, Graham's voice now seemed to carry a presumption of seniority, perhaps even a repressed exasperation. As if put upon.

'Violent?' Garry wanted to know.

'Quite probably. Mother was angling to come back with me to Leeds to visit, so maybe he was bothering her.'

'But she didn't.'

'What?'

'She didn't come back with you.'

'I haven't got any room, have I? I can't have Mother over here. I've done enough already, God knows.'

'And Dad has really retired? I can't believe it.'

'As of December 31st.'

There was the briefest pause while Garry took this in. Apparently it wasn't the easiest of facts to deal with. At the same time, from a corner of Graham's eye, the luckless parachutist hit the ground.

'But what on earth for? Couldn't he find some contract somewhere so God-forsaken Mum wouldn't follow him?'

Graham tittered rather than laughed, as if he didn't actually find this interpretation of their parents' relationship very funny. To anyone tapping the line it would have seemed there was a generation gap between these two.

'And how much is he going to get in the way of a pension for heaven's sake? I mean, he's only 62.'

'I have no idea. I asked him, but he just said, enough. Mother didn't know of course.'

'Right. So what's new? The old non-communication game.' And after a pause which Graham wouldn't fill, the London twin went on, 'No. I'm just a bit nervous. Obviously. I mean about whether he's going to keep sending money.'

There was another short electronic silence, before Graham asked pointedly: 'You did get the twenty quid I sent, I hope?'

'Of course, yes, thanks. Look, you're not going over there next weekend, are you? Perhaps you could put a word in for the, er, underprivileged side of the family. You know.'

'Well, Dad wants me to help renovate the main house. So he said to come over. They're living in the Broughton Street flat for the moment of course. But I can't go every weekend, can I? It wouldn't be fair on Sophy. So next weekend is out, I'm afraid. The weekend is the only time we . . .'

At which point the pips went.

'Call me back, bruv,' Garry asked, and quickly gave a number. He waited five minutes, but no call came. Because there was a queue forming he mouthed into the receiver while surreptitiously holding the cradle down with his left hand. After counting a further sixty seconds, he pushed the door, smiled at a bristling van driver and walked home.

Or towards home.

At the crossroads with Brondesbury Villas he did stop to consider. Amanda would be in the Prince Regent most probably, if she wasn't still at the Centre. There would be no visit from Mariangela for at least another couple of months. In the end, profoundly uneasy, yet equally profoundly sure he was right, sure of his worth, he dropped into the Cross Keys where friends had bought him drinks before. And for an hour and more here in the best of company Garry told jokes and laughed at jokes and complained about fare increases and enthused about a by-election result and likewise about a television documentary on police brutality and was entirely happy.

Two days later he received a letter first class in the livery of the Leeds Access Assurance Company. It was typed, though badly:

Garry,

I'm sorry, but how would it look if every time you phone me at Sophy's I have to call you back? It's one thing scrounging off me, but I really don't think I can just take the liberty of using their phone as I please. Can I? I'm sorry, but you know how it is. If you had a phone yourself of course I could call you from the office. Though until you get a job I suppose we'll have to rule that out.

As far as Mother and Father and Raymond are concerned, Father says he is looking into ways of getting him into a home and that he is willing to pay privately if he can't do it through the NHS. I think we should object to this <u>MOST STRONGLY</u> as it would eat up an enormous amount of money. Certainly not less than £200 a week – and with Raymond having a perfectly normal life expectancy you can imagine what that means in terms of a drain on resources. Anyway, I'm using what spare time I've got here to check up on the legal side of things and hope to come up with something soon. As always, the key point is that they can't force Raymond into a home permanently if he doesn't want to go (or at least not until he commits a major crime). But I'm afraid with the way he enjoys spending Father's money, he may agree to something private and comfortable. He's not mad enough not to know when he's getting a good deal.

I enclose another cheque for £20. It's all I can manage at the moment.

I hope we can get together soon. It was too bad I couldn't make it down at New Year but Sophy had her poorlies. Thanks anyway for the invitation.

Best luck,
GRAHAM

In the meantime, Lorna had received an unaccountably sticky photograph of herself and Raymond blowing eight candles out on a black-and-white cake (whose?), plus a speech-day programme from a convent school in Quito which named Lorna Baldwin in a long list of others as a prizewinner. This, however, was the last of the memorabilia, since by now Father must have received her letter and would be suitably offended.

'I can't see why it bugs you so much,' Fred told her in his strong New England accent. 'If he wants to remind you of the nice things in the past, why not let him?'

Like the good husband he was determined to be, Fred was forcing food through Kirsty's lips.

'He's old,' Fred went on reasonably. 'He wants to think he's been happy.'

Fred was tall and endearingly clean cut, if just a little overweight and sweaty. In loose floppy clothes, his wife had the most lovely blonde hair tied over a tall neck. Her face was without strong features but pleasantly creamy to look at and full of its own quick life. She said:

'He's 62. He might live till 80 and more. He just wants to make us feel attached so that we'll do things for him now he's back. When he never did anything for us but send money from abroad.'

Fred said he wished somebody would send him money from abroad. Although in a modest way of course, they were quite well off. And in an equally modest, tran-tran way, happy.

Not to mention the big breakthrough careerwise.

Saturday morning came as something of an upset though. This time the post brought a large card-backed yellow envelope; the postman had to ring the bell to hand it over as it wouldn't fit in the letterbox. And Fred was halfway up the stairs before he realized why there had been such a smirk on the postman's face. In thick felt-tip print, each line covered with a strip of sello-tape to prevent erasion, the envelope was addressed to: 'MISS DRIPPYCUNT SPERMSUCKER AND HER AMERICAN FUCK.'

'Which must mean yours truly, I guess.'

Inside were a few pages of the worst pornography and an article from the *Mirror* entitled: 'JEHAD THREATENS: WE'LL EXECUTE YANKS.'

'Don't,' snapped Lorna sharply, as Fred hovered a moment over a fellatio, 'let Kirsty see,' and she swept up cuttings and envelope together and had them in the bin.

So that their life, pushing the buggy down the High Road for Saturday shopping, seemed just an inkling less secure than it had done an hour before. As if a gust of the world you read about had been let in with the wind.

'Poor guy's just mad,' Fred commented, holding open the door of the International. 'Nothing new, is it? We've known that for ages.'

He remembered phones ringing at three in the morning and being hung up. An angry flatmate.

'Except that now he's back in bloody England.'

And later in the park, when Kirsty had trotted off to the sandpit, Lorna said. 'Poor Raymond. Poor Raymond. If you'd known him before, what a sweet boy he was. And now.' Her dazed eyes were shiny, wondering whether she wanted to cry.

Or laugh. Because there was the funny side too: thinking what the postman would be thinking.

'Makes normality seem so attractive,' said Fred, who had never doubted it. What other foundation on which to base success? His splendid thesis on metaphor.

Two hundred miles north a short, fat, bald man stood in the hallway of a large and apparently abandoned house. Red nosed. There must be something wrong with his gut, he thought. And the wall above the front door would need damp-proofing. 'Raymond!' he shouted.

The first thing to do would be to get the electricity turned on and bring in a kettle so they could boil themselves up some coffee of a morning.

'Raymond! Where in God's name have you got to?'

And a couple of comfortable chairs.

'Yessir. Ready, sir.'

A burly young man, hands thrust into the pockets of a tweed jacket, round head pushed forward, came quickly and heavily down the stairs, smiling facetiously, perhaps mockingly.

His father was tapping a cigarette against a blue packet.

'Measure the wall round the door, will you?'

Smoking, and with studied relish, he watched his eldest son work. Quite efficiently today as it happened. Life wasn't so bad. In small doses. Fairly peaceful in fact, once one had got him away from Brenda. Leave the boy alone was his line. Don't expect too much of him. At least one had a cheap pair of hands at one's disposal.

But on the way to the hardware store to stock up on a few basic essentials, Raymond said:

'I'm the only person you ever had the courage to despise, aren't I?'

Mr Baldwin was reflecting that in the twenty-five years or so he'd been away, English building techniques had deteriorated rather than the contrary. Which was to be expected, of course, since deterioration seemed to be the norm, though he was a little surprised by the absence of gables on some of these newer houses and the way the windows were quite flush with the walls. Had somebody forecast a change of climate? Did they plan to move the sea back?

Father and son walked along without looking at each other, the older man breathing in the fresh salt air as carefully and appreciatively as he had previously been smoking.

'Isn't that the truth? You're glad to have somebody around you can treat like a worm, since everybody else scares the shit out of you. Because you haven't got an ounce of courage or honesty in you. You need somebody who's no more than dirt, so that . . .'

'Oh for heaven's sake, do we have to put up with . . .'

But Mr Baldwin suddenly felt an elbow hard under his ear. He was flung sideways into a prickly hedge topping a low wall.

'What the hell's got into you?'

His burly son stood over him, breathing heavily, conveying an appalling tension. 'Big chief speak with forked tongue,' he said unaccountably, and equally unaccountably smiled. His face had a wan, glistening, stuffed-cheek look, the sort of thing you might admire the make-up artist for managing to scare you with in films. His brown eyes gleamed. Apparently he was triumphant. But nervous too, shifting his weight from foot to foot. And obviously dangerous.

His small father stood up, glancing around to see if anybody might have seen. He opened and closed his jaw, checking pain. There was dust to be slapped off his jacket.

'I told you I'd been to the police. Do that again and I'll have them take you away on an assault and battery charge.'

'Because you treat me the way you'd like to treat everybody else, like shit. Only you're too scared with the rest of them. You're scared they'd have your balls, you're . . .'

Mr Baldwin was already walking on down the street, caressing his neck and twisting his head from side to side. When his son caught up with him, he said in a low voice: 'Now listen, Raymond lad. If you don't start taking your medicine again, and above all, if you dare to lay so much as a finger on myself or your mother, then I shall go straight to the police and have them cart you away to cool down some place. For a good long time. Okay?'

'I'll kill you,' Raymond remarked. His fists in his pockets were forcing the jacket out of shape. The more so because the same pockets were stuffed with keys.

'Please do, I'd like to see who'd put up with you then. Ever thought about that?'

But of course this had been said almost daily for some years.

After the hardware store and despite the knot Mr Baldwin felt his gut to be tied in, they stopped in the Better Snack for coffee and a doughnut. Where Raymond began very earnestly:

'After we've got it really nice, though, we could persuade Graham and Garry and Lorna to come back, couldn't we? There's room for everybody. We could all live together again. All brothers and sisters together. The whole family.'

Squat Mr Baldwin looked up sharply from over a *Telegraph* he'd picked up.

'You'd like that?' he asked, not unkindly, though this combination of the spongy sweetness of his doughnut with the intriguing atrocities of the morning's news formed a pleasure he was usually loath to interrupt.

'I'd feel better,' Raymond told him in the most human of voices. 'I think it would help me get better.' He seemed sensibly enthusiastic, pushing greasy hair from his eyes.

'Well, we'll see.' Mr Baldwin went back to his paper. He licked thick fingers where icing sugar dusted nicotine. 'I've already asked them all to visit, of course.'

Which in his mind he had.

'But not Fred,' Raymond said now. 'Lorna will have to ditch him. I'm not living with any stinking imperialist big dick Americans.'

Turning a page, his father told him he didn't know what he was talking about.

'He'll just have to get lost, if Gaddafi doesn't nail him first. I've told them where he is.'

Do up, Mr Baldwin was now thinking, lifting his plastic bags, and sell up. Sell up and disappear. So that one fine morning they woke and he was gone. No more cheques, postal orders, car bills. No more generosity. No more responsibility. They'd be missing his memorabilia then. Oh yes. With Brenda? Perhaps. But equally well without. Untraceable. Australia, or better still Brazil. Ecuador again. Enjoying a quiet retirement. And without this constant attrition on the small pleasures that remained.

'You're an idiot,' he told his son as they walked back to the house. 'You know that?' He would see the doctor about his gut. Tomorrow perhaps. He could reasonably expect to go to the doctor's on his own, couldn't he? A little peace and quiet. Some tests even. Why not? Take a magazine and sit at the back of a long long queue. If the NHS was slow, whose fault was that?

Mrs Baldwin to Garry

Feb 28th

Broughton St
Cleveleys
Lancashire

Dear Garry,

Your father says he will send you money 'in due course'. But your father is a fool. It may have taken me thirty years and more to realize it, but nobody can say I didn't get there in the end. He is an ignorant, presumptuous fool. If you could hear him pontificating about England now he's back and trying to impress Harry and Mary with his Bougaa stories and wearing his safari hat in the rain! It's enough to curl your toes. Would that I'd had an inkling of good sense when I was young and men were two a penny. The Good Lord should have warned me against him while there was still time. But about the money: he says it won't do you any harm to scrape and save for a while, and of course we had to hear fifteen minutes' worth of how he had scraped and saved and how he'd never been out of a job since he was sixteen and so on and so forth. As if jobs were as easily come by now as they were then. As if I had never done any scraping and saving all those times his cheques didn't arrive. I can remember when I was shopping on credit in every grocer's between here and Blackpool and having to cart you twins round with me to stir up a bit of sympathy. But that's as maybe. Trials and tribulations are there to be borne, and I'm not complaining, even if Raymond is a greater cross than most families have to bear.

Anyway, let me say, as a mother, I'm proud of you for wanting to get involved in politics and not just taking the first thing that comes along like most people do. I think it's very brave of you, even if you will have to start earning sooner or later of course, but I'm sure you must realize that. On the practical side, I'm putting in twenty-five pounds in bits and pieces I've saved from shopping. I hope it will help. I'm sending the same amount to Graham too as I am sure he has trouble making ends meet and I don't want to show any favouritism. He came down at the weekend to get his car fixed here because he had no money to do it in Leeds. He's still on probation he says at the office and they're not paying him very well, so Dad got it done in return for the help he gave us moving in. I said I'd be happy to go back with him to tidy up his room and do a wash and cook him some decent food, but it was impossible because the landlord had the decorators in or something. Naturally enough, the mysterious little goddess Sophy didn't come. She had her period it seems (I remember moving mountains during my periods, when I still had them). She still shows no signs of marrying and making a home for him. He says they are not in a hurry to get married because they've decided not to have children in case they turn out like Raymond. But I'm sure this is just an idea her parents have put in his head because they don't want to lose her ladyship. And of course, it's all very nice for them, thank you very much, having Graham around all the time more or less as a servant. From what I can gather doing all their shopping and so on and cutting the hedge (he had blisters on both hands, poor lad), but the truth is, if she really loved him she would marry him, wouldn't she? And anyway, if they don't marry soon, it'll be too late, because it seems she's already thirty something, old enough to be his auntie. It's unnatural, if you ask me. Your father says, as long as nobody wants <u>him</u> to pay for anything, <u>he</u> doesn't care what they do. Because that is the kind of callous, shortsighted, selfish man your father is. His latest brainwave is for us to sell up everything here and disappear where Raymond can't find us. Meaning abroad again, like as not.

And meaning he just wants to escape from his responsibilities. I thought that when your father decided to accept early retirement it was because he was going to knuckle down to things here and sort out the house and garden and get the tenants out of the sea flats, find work for Raymond, give you boys a hand settling down and perhaps do some private business of his own. Not a teensy weensy bit of it. He goes to bed early. He gets up late. He mooches about in his dressing gown getting on my nerves reading the sports pages of the newspaper – your father who never kicked a ball or held a bat in his life! – and then he just goes over to Fleetwood Street and drinks coffee and bosses Raymond about without ever accomplishing anything as far as I can see. We're as far from having a decent home as we ever were. No, the only thing he's actively done since he got back is to rent a big colour television, even though your Uncle Harry said we were perfectly welcome to watch every evening at their place. So that's fifteen pounds a month we can't send to you or Graham.

But to go back to his brainwave: don't worry; he's not selling up Fleetwood Street, not over my stone dead body. I think it should be there for you children to inherit, just as it was for me. And poor Raymond will have to have somewhere to live. We are all in God's hands and there's simply no point in trying to make drastic changes just for one's own selfish sake. This is something your father has never understood. Raymond is our son and willy-nilly we must provide for him.

Still, I do think if you came up to stay you could have a good influence on Raymond. He needs to be persuaded to take his prescriptions and to try and get a job. And then you're probably the only member of the family he respects, since unlike Graham you have a degree and unlike Lorna you haven't married an American. I read in a magazine somewhere that his type of condition could be something to do with his thyroid, but he refuses to go to the hospital for the tests. Perhaps you could persuade him. Your father says I'm wasting my time, the doctors would have thought of it.

But if life's long enough not to leave any stone unturned, then why should we? God helps those who help themselves. Anyway, it would save you the rent you're paying in London. That doesn't mean that I agree with your father that you shouldn't have a decent place to live in and go on holiday every now and then. Why ever shouldn't you? If you don't do these things when you're young you never will, believe me. I know I never have. But it would be nice to have you back here and as I say useful for Raymond. In any case I'll do my best to make Mr Niggard send the money soon. His life won't be worth living till he does.

Love,
Mum

PS. I know it would be better if we could get a phone, but we are worried about Raymond using it all the time like he did in Algeria.

Oh, yesterday, Garry, I found such a darling little kitten mewing about in the bracken behind the shed, mottled grey with blue eyes. So I decided to keep him, or rather her, and call her Chiquita after the tom you twins found in Ecuador, do you remember, who sprayed in Father's briefcase! Good for him!

PPS. I'm sending you a parcel with an old suit of Raymond's. He's too fat for it now. But the cloth is still excellent. I made it myself.

While Amanda snorted over this letter, Garry tried on her husband's cast-off shoes. An excellent fit. And stylish. Which was more than Raymond's suit would be.

These two handsome young people stared at each other. Rather sulkily.

'I'll buy you lunch, Mummy's boy,' Amanda said. 'Where's it to be?'

In the Trattoria she took a pencil and notebook out of a handbag made of some synthetic silver material and asked, 'By the way, local Liberal achievements, how would you present them for best effect? Roger wants to do a constituency hand-out.' Her blonde hair sat almost too neatly about her head, helmet style. Specks of glitter came on and off about her eyes. Garry mooned over a lasagna.

'Caring for people,' he said. 'The old age pensioners' meal thing.'

'First?'

'Caring is the buzz word these days, isn't it?'

'What about the road plan? The new system? That was ours.'

'No, not that. It doesn't matter how you rearrange the traffic, there's always as many people pissed off as pleased.'

'It's just I was thinking we want to give people an image of a party that changes things on the ground, practical business things, not just giving away money.'

'Yes,' Garry said. He was looking at his old girlfriend as she wrote. He was looking at the fine wrinkles of concentration that gathered about the tiny bridge of her nose, like the most delicate ruffling of peachy silk. That flaxen, well-washed hair fringing all round.

'A sense of engagement,' she was saying, 'practical, tough. But fair too.'

'Being realistic though,' he objected, he was casting about for his meeting persona, since she had obviously assumed hers, 'there's not much you can claim when you've only got three councillors on the council.'

'Defeatism,' she said brightly, 'is our worst enemy.' She glanced up. 'And don't just keep staring at me like that, silly.' She laughed. Then frowned. He looked down and all at once began to tackle his lasagna with surprising gusto.

'Oh I don't know,' he muttered, his mouth half full. 'Probably you're right.' He ate almost ruthlessly.

'About what?'

'Defeatism I mean. Yes. It's just that with a family like mine, you tend to get that way.'

She had heard all this quite a number of times before, yet nevertheless said: 'In what sense?'

'Oh, you get a letter like that from your mother, not a word of sense in it, and you realize everything's always going to go on as it always has, not a hope of change or progress.' After a pause during which he sensed, rather than actually noticed, she was giving him her winsome expression, he said: 'I sometimes think that's why I didn't marry you, you know, so as not to land you with them.'

Making a wry face, she said, 'Give us a break, love, we've been through that.'

And into a difficult silence she said: 'Come on, tell me a joke or something. Any new ones?'

An hour later, having talked about anything but what most concerned them, this young couple parted with poignantly repressed lust at a bus stop in Maida Vale. She was my first love, he told himself, warming his hands at the radiator on top up front. He saw her pouted lips glistening lilac lipstick, those palest hazel irises trembling with life. My first love, he repeated out loud, trying to feel the full sadness of it. And he buried his face in his warm hands. Why was it taking him so long to get his career off the ground? Why had he bothered with the degree at all? Or if only the Party would give him a job. Everybody agreed he had deserved it.

One would have liked to have been a hero in some way. Really he would. Bob Geldof. Terry Waite. He fingered the earring she had given him. Or at least to have done something definite, shown courage somehow. He had been reading *Schindler's Ark*. But the world didn't seem to offer such opportunities. The world threw you back on yourself most terribly.

Marble Arch ground by, the bus swung into Oxford Street and the grey bustle of a wet afternoon. With a recognizably physical feeling of unease now concentrated about stomach and groin, Garry considered his course-book on computer programming and prepared to alight in those nearly-new neatly-tooled shoes. At least two months till Mariangela came again. Surely something would arrive before then. Unless they were determined to starve him back to Cleveleys.

Lorna was rather annoyed to find Graham on the phone. It was not that she didn't feel affection for her younger brother – a great deal actually – it was just that he, up at the Leeds Access, was so oily and relaxed and so obviously had so much chatting time on his hands, whereas she was faced with the tension of deadlines and no money if she didn't get on with things; so that every moment wasted made her more than ever desperate, at times even hysterical, wondering whether really she was any good at all at what she was supposed to be doing. Because it was proving far harder than she could ever have imagined to make Crackle seem an interesting bunch of boys who had something useful to say for themselves.

Graham called an average of perhaps three times a week, usually during his lunchbreak, since he saved whatever it was they were paying him by eating sandwiches in the office. And given that unlimited use of the phone was the job's only perk, he could rarely be got rid of in less than ten minutes.

He was trying to decide, he explained, whether to sell the few British Telecom shares he had. They must go down at some point. But what if they didn't?

Lorna was actually quite amused in a sisterly way and made an effort to take the conversation seriously, though this seemed to involve letting Graham do all the talking.

The point being that there was a strike in the offing, which would obviously bring the value down (workers would be workers at the best of times). Although perhaps the smartest thing would be not to sell now, but to actually buy more during the strike, if only he could manage to rustle up some cash from somewhere, count on its being short and then sell immediately afterwards when there was a false high with renewed confidence. Except that

32

if he waited that long it might be just as well to hang on for the dividends, seeing as . . .

Did he want to push up BT's shares simply by talking long enough on the phone?

. . . though again, given that everybody had earned so much just on the rise in basic value, perhaps they would keep dividends low so as to plough the money . . .

Lorna didn't appreciate that she had lost track of all this until she heard Graham asking how Garry was.

'How should I know? I never see him.'

'What I can't understand is why he doesn't settle for any kind of job, seeing as he's clearly never going to get what he was trained for. There must be some work of some kind around. There's always something in insurance. Except of course if one insists on wearing an earring one's hardly likely to get it.

'And this computer crap' – if she had meant to reply she was interrupted – 'is just pure pie in the sky, isn't it? How can he compete with the people who've studied computers at university?'

It had crossed her mind, Lorna agreed. Although at least it showed he was . . .

Didn't he realize what a drain he was being on the family as a whole and on family resources? Just the other day he'd had to send him another twenty pounds. And it wasn't as if he didn't have better things to spend his money on.

'Don't we all,' said Lorna, who had recently given Garry a hundred pounds, but didn't want to mention this in case it dried up the generosity of the others. Or got back to Fred.

'Or if he has to hold out for his blessed degree-related job, can't he at least go up to live in Cleveleys in the meantime and save on the rent. He could make his applications from there. They're crazy sending him all that money now they're back, when he could have a perfectly good home with them. Not to mention the Italian holidays.'

Lorna thought the dole people were paying his rent.

'Only half of it,' Graham told her, 'because the landlord only declares half. The other half has to come out of the money they give him for living. Anyway, if he went up to Cleveleys he could help Father with the house. It's going to take them years to make the place liveable, never mind saleable.'

'I didn't know they wanted to sell it.'

'They hardly need such a big place to live in, do they? When neither Garry nor I can dream of buying anything for years.'

Should she tell Graham she had someone at the door? Or would that be rather too blatant after the last time. On occasion it seemed to Lorna that there was no member of her family who wasn't just waiting to take offence.

'Sophy okay?' she enquired.

But Graham had already begun on another track: 'By the way, Father told me you were planning to go up for the Easter break.'

It took her a moment to connect.

'To Cleveleys,' he said.

'First I've heard of it. I told you he hadn't even been in touch.'

'Well don't in any case.' And lowering his voice to a conspiratorial whisper, as if the wires might be shouting to eager ears across all the wet countryside from Leeds to London, Graham explained that when he'd been over there the other week helping out, Raymond had made it pretty bloody clear that he really did have it in for Fred. In a big way. This anti-American mania he'd picked up in Algeria, partly in reaction to Father's pro-Americanism. The Islamic way of life was vastly superior and the Brits were in danger of becoming just a sidekick of the Yanks and the Jews. 'He's even thinking of turning Moslem.'

'In Cleveleys?'

Graham had a way of only half laughing, to show he had no use for humour.

'And you never know what he might do. Especially now that you have Kirsty. I mean, I don't know if she counts as American or English.'

When the phone wires hummed a pause, he added: 'You know how psycho he gets.'

These were just the kind of ideas she needed to spend a cool, clear-headed afternoon with her work, Lorna thought on putting the phone down. Her older brother massacring her daughter. Just the ideas that would help her sleep at night. And she reflected that she quite missed Kirsty daytimes since they'd put her in the nursery. You complained and got attached just the same. You said it had ruined your career and planned a second. Modern motherhood. It was quite as if she were in love sometimes, the way she missed the little girl's skin, her smiles, the smell of her small body.

On returning to the sitting room, Lorna discovered that the slightest flicker of the lights during their conversation earlier on had indeed been a power-cut, and the material she had foolishly left up front on the screen had disappeared. They must be working on the road again. Very briefly she cried, then prepared herself quite a complicated salad lunch with eggs and an avocado and two pieces of granary bread. Since when Fred came home she dieted to shame him.

It was curious that of the three of them it should be Mr Baldwin who, having been present so rarely during the years in question, was now the most interested in digging out the childhood memorabilia that lay at the bottom of a lifetime's bric-a-brac in the second bedroom of the small flat they were presently living in. When, after her mother's inchmeal death, Frank Baldwin had finally been unable to prevent his wife and children from following him to building sites in Beirut, Khartoum, Quito and Algiers, the family had rented out the main house on Fleetwood Street and the two flats nearest the sea, keeping the third, on Broughton Street, for their or their children's occasional returns. But with the tenants in the sea flats still paying rents established thirty years ago and then the main house falling into disrepair and unlived in now for the best part of a decade, Mr Baldwin's administration of the family property had not resulted in any significant accumulation of wealth; a failing that his wife Brenda lost no occasion to remind him of. At which Frank would inevitably remark that it had been her duty to stay behind and look after the property, the main house, after all, being hers by inheritance. Not to mention the world of good a stable home would have done the children. Well, she didn't know, she would retort, what a woman's duty might be, or might have been, if not to be beside her husband, nor what home could be considered stable without a man in it; and if they were talking about money, hadn't it been he who had made her give up her seamstress work when they married, work which had been rather more remunerative than his at the time if she remembered rightly. If she'd had her work still, she might have stayed.

And so on and so forth.

Because the Baldwins were perfectly capable of arguing for

36

hours, and heatedly, over decisions taken thirty years before.

And not only the big decisions. There was the time Mr Baldwin had drunk abundantly from and then repackaged the brandy intended as a Christmas gift for friends of hers, so that Brenda watched them unwrap a half empty bottle before her eyes and to her eternal shame; the time she had told everybody at a construction site party that poor Frank was impotent since he'd had the mumps (and if what she had really meant was sterile it hardly helped). Yes, these and so many other minor incidents from the fifties and sixties could still inflame the small hours of the late eighties, forming as they did both a shared past and a veritable charnel house of contentions to be picked over as they chose.

For in a very real sense, neither of these two parents had ever reconciled themselves to so much that had happened. And each for the other was a constant reminder.

The flat they kept empty for themselves when they left England was perhaps four hundred yards from the sea, round the corner from the main house, on a nondescript side street. Into it they had put all the furniture from their other properties that no self-respecting tenant would agree to live with, plus all the cast-off clothes, toys, utensils, appliances and other bric-a-brac they couldn't possibly take with them. And each time they returned for short holidays during the twenty long years of absence that were to follow, the Baldwins would bring back some souvenirs, gadgets, paraphernalia, books, magazines or whatever, and store them together with everything else that was getting in the way in what had now become the 'back-room' of the flat. So that on their final return this room was piled high from floor almost to ceiling with children's bikes, African masks, terracotta plaques, old gramophones and broken televisions, dress patterns, Spanish shawls, pots, pans, and plates, as well as heaps of anonymous cardboard boxes that might contain almost anything.

Although much had been ruined by encroaching damp.

Like everything else on their return, this pile of bric-a-brac now presented itself as an obstacle far greater than they could have imagined when contemplating their retirement from a small town outside Algiers. As far as any sentimental value was concerned, Brenda Baldwin would cheerfully, even vindictively, have emptied the lot into a skip and had it towed away to wherever skips do go. But imagining that so much in the way of material goods must be worth something, she was loath to throw it all out with the twins so much in need; there might well be some good old rolls of material in there somewhere; trousers or a jacket might be made. Her husband, on the contrary, cherished few illusions as to any money value involved, but pictured the Fleetwood Street house laden with trophies that testified to what others would see as an exciting and worthwhile life: Ecuadorian wallhangings, desert crystals from the Sahara, posters for Algerian films, a llama-skin – these were not things you could usually expect to come across in out-of-town Lancashire and would radiate a certain kudos. But that was for the future. Because for the moment, naturally, it was impossible to move anything over to Fleetwood Street, not until they had done up and decorated the place, and equally impossible to sort out the gold from the dross, as it were, in the cramped conditions of the flat. So that just as, while they were abroad, it had often seemed that they were floating in limbo, waiting for (sometimes dreading) the return to England for their real lives to resume, now it appeared that they couldn't consider they had really arrived and settled down until they had unpacked their lives, as apparently they were stored, in layers of damp and dusty memories in that room.

Ignoring (as he always had) his wife's scorn, Mr Baldwin spent an hour or so each evening picking his way round the room, rooting and rummaging, brushing off cobwebs and stamping on silverfish: partly because it seemed to be the only place he could expect to be alone and have a cigarette, partly out of genuine sentimentality, and partly because he knew that somewhere or other he'd hidden some photographs of himself and Trilling in a brothel with a couple of Sudanese whores, photos which it would be as well not to let Brenda or Raymond come across when eventually they emptied the place.

Although it was difficult to feel particularly worried or urgent about it.

Frank Baldwin strayed and mused, examined the joints on an old kitchen cabinet he'd made with his own hands, unwrapped a pair of worn-out shoes that had been stacked within, read the news from the sixties paper they'd been wrapped in, grunted over the loss of British prestige abroad. In a trunk there were letters from Brenda to himself, himself to Brenda, from the years when her mother was dying, before she came out with him.

He read one of his own: a bonus for laying foundations inside the deadline; a trip with Trilling to a nearby oasis (there was a photo of himself and his lanky friend standing by a bulldozer); the difficulties of obtaining alcohol; recommendations to the children to behave themselves. And one from her: the twins both had colic; her mother was refusing solid foods; the sea had washed over the wall in a spring storm and Mrs Howarth was complaining of dry rot in one of the sea flats – what was he going to do about it?

Nothing. With the rent they were paying he was going to do precisely nothing about it. What did they want? Blood? Had he ever in his life done anything but give, give, give?

Recalled eventually by the siren sound of *Coronation Street*, which seemed to offer, despite a niggling change of rhythm, one of the few points of contact with the past and all the British interludes in his exile, Mr Baldwin brought back with him a pack of old photographs. Many of the snaps were irretrievably stuck together, but others showed with startling clarity, Lorna and Raymond holding a twin each in their arms, Raymond with a trilby down over his eyes, holding an umbrella as if it were a rifle, Brenda before she'd started dyeing her hair, in a puffy summer frock, legs provocatively crossed over the parapet at Birkenhead, complacent smile showing how much she had always enjoyed being photographed. An odd one out, in sepia, showed a chubby little man, not unattractive, lightly freckled, trying to look taller than he was in ironed fatigues. Himself.

Unwrapping a toffee, Frank Baldwin sat on a long low threadbare red sofa which testified more or less to the date of their departure. Indeed everything in the room, barring the TV, would have taken a visitor back to the early sixties: the pale-blue patterned formica-topped table, the low veneered sideboard with its pretentious machined curves and ugly metal attachments, the angular armchairs with extravagant flower designs, a rickety standard lamp, white, a goldfish bowl with a little rockery inside but no water. Beside the boarded fireplace was a coin-operated electricity meter that had never got removed somehow when whoever it was was doing the rounds.

'Home!' Mr Baldwin sighed extravagantly, though it wasn't quite clear whether he mightn't have meant to be cynical. Or at least was begging the question. He popped in his toffee which distorted his voice.

'Take a look at this, Brenda.'

For Frank Baldwin had, as it were, kept the best for first, the one he knew would give the most pleasure. It showed Brenda herself, handsomely missionary in a safari outfit with large floppy hat – how she had loved to cut a figure – standing arm in arm with a huge and very black black. The black was wrapped in some extravagant golden material, for these were already the days of colour, and had a bone through his nose. Six or seven children pressed about his and Brenda's legs, while in the background, as if it had been planned as a caricature – or like one of those little sets photographers will put up on European beaches to lure their customers – was a mud and straw hut complete with curving palm tree.

'Oh,' Brenda lit up, rearranging her legs for the cat on her lap; she bent down and kissed it between the ears. 'Mafeking. Remember Mafeking, Raymond? With the bone through his nose and all those scars.'

Eating steadily through a pack of ginger snaps, their eldest son refused to look at the photos. Despite his closeness to the television he held a book on his lap, *Advanced Logic Systems*, and while apparently trying to read, kept rubbing the wrist of the hand that held the biscuit back and forth across his forehead. Tight in his trouser pocket, the other hand was clutched around a bunch of keys. One knee jerked incessantly. Occasionally he threw back his head to take greasy hair off his eyes.

'The clothes they wore too. What beautiful colours.'

Mrs Baldwin had begun to share the photographs with her husband, was almost in a holiday mood of oohs and ahs ('just look at Billingsworth, the old fraud!'), when, going through the black-and-whites on it must have been Blackpool beach, she was suddenly overwhelmed by the transformation from this darling chubby-cheeked little boy with his brilliant gap-toothed smile over bucket and spade to the monster Raymond had now become. Because it was precisely when she thought about, or worst of all was somehow brutally presented with, her life, past and present, that it all became too much to bear. She should never have taken her eyes off *Coronation Street*.

'Lorna. What a bobby-dazzler!' Mr Baldwin handed over another snap. The skinny girl was shivering on the beach, her first bikini top wrapped around nothing to hide.

'When was the last time you washed?' Mrs Baldwin demanded. The cat sprang from her lap to take refuge under the sideboard.

Raymond didn't appear to have heard, still gazing at the book that fretted on his knee, though it didn't seem he could have turned a page for some long time.

'You smell,' she told him, 'I suppose you do realize?'

Mr Baldwin sighed. 'Not now, Brenda,' he said vaguely, reaching for a cigarette. But he had already finished today's pack. He was rationed.

'Go and take a bath this instant, it's unpleasant being in the same room with you.'

'Fuck off.'

'Don't talk to your mother like that,' her husband now felt bound to come back. Though it was rather mechanical. Why didn't she just leave be? Why didn't she let him smoke as much as he wanted? 'And could you turn up the volume please?'

'We'll have the sanitary people to hose you down if you don't wash.

'Raymond,' she pleaded. 'Do be reasonable. For the love of God. If you won't do any tests you might at least keep yourself clean. Or do you want them to put you in a home?

'Please, Raymond, be my boy. Please. Look what a lovely child you were.'

And Brenda suddenly let out a moan behind which, the others knew, tears must soon follow. She wanted so much to love him, to have him her best boy again. Instead of this constant bereavement. There and not there.

'How can we have people over, how can we ever go out with

you stinking like this? We might as well be in Timbuktu still if you're not going to make yourself decent.'

Mr Baldwin strained after the TV dialogue.

'Walled up in our bloody tombs,' she shouted, 'the whole family.'

She stood up, already in her nightdress, which showed how much her body had rounded since the days of those photographs. Though not unpleasantly. She was still a handsome woman.

'In God's name,' she finished vaguely, tears pricking.

'Go and wash,' Mr Baldwin said with a sharp practical brusqueness that seemed to imply obedience was inevitable – the way he used to talk to coloured labour actually – though nobody in the room for one moment expected Raymond would move.

'I am what you two made me,' their son now announced one of his favourite lines with deliberate melodrama. And for the first time looked up at them. There could be no mistaking a mocking vindictiveness about his smile, an awareness of their usual agony.

'Personal hygiene is one of the things they look at when they come to check you up,' Mr Baldwin suggested.

'I'll wash then then,' Raymond said, perfectly reasonably. He returned to his book and took another biscuit from the pack on the floor. 'But I'm not washing for the likes of you. Watching this crap on television,' he added. 'Provincial yobs.'

If only he could, Mr Baldwin reflected in the moment's silence that followed. If only he could.

Mrs Baldwin was standing, on the brink of hysteria.

'Why don't you *do* something?' She turned on her husband now, who was amazed to notice the way her eyes had suddenly sunk away into dark blueness. Unless it was just the light from the television.

'Frank!' Pleats of wrinkles were working away at the corners of her lips. She was old of course.

'Brenda . . .' he began calmly, but with a hint of irritation. It was obvious why he didn't do anything. He didn't do anything because Raymond was bigger and heavier than he was. And violent.

'I can't stand it in here with him,' and she turned and fled, violently slamming a door that was anyway uncertain on its hinges. Plaster fell from around two plates of frosted glass that had been all the rage when Mr Baldwin built the place.

But she was gone, and the old man, as he liked to think of himself these days, wriggled down a little in his armchair. Now perhaps he could find out what they were all up to down the Street. Yes. Here we are. Two of the youngsters they'd brought in, whose relation to the few old faithfuls he hadn't quite established, were giggling over pints in an exaggeratedly public bar: smoke, beer, slops. Mr Baldwin wouldn't have minded being there himself. He tried to remember . . .

'Cunts,' Raymond announced.

But was unlikely to provoke his father so easily. Had it been Ena, or . . .

'Fuck, shit, cunts,' he insisted, 'cuntlickers', and with the suddenness with which his expressions could change, he seemed to be gloating now, as if *Advanced Logic Systems* had turned up a nude. It was disturbing how totally he could be engrossed, and then break off.

And how frighteningly in control of his madness he seemed to be.

'I know you put sedatives in my food. But you don't know I piss in yours.'

. . . who had died of cancer? Of the stomach?

'I SAID I PISS IN IT!'

But Mr Baldwin clung to his imperturbability: he would never lay claim to having been an ideal husband, or father, but would not accept that he'd been an especially bad one either. Hadn't he been one of the first men in Cleveleys to get his wife a washing machine and fridge, all those years ago? When others were still mucking about with soap sticks in freezing water. Hadn't he insisted on calcium and vitamin pills for the kids? Look how tall they all were. Not to mention the university fees, sending Ray and Lorna to the States. No, if it was a question of duty, he'd certainly done his. The presents he used to bring back for Christ's sake. So that surely, all things being equal, he and Brenda could have made a go of it: marriage, family, retirement. Life had let them down rather badly.

The credits floated up, born away on a signature tune he'd rather they'd never played around with at all.

'How about you staying on here, in the flat?' he suddenly tried. 'When your mother and I have moved into the house. Give you a bit of independence. Your own kitchen, your own . . .'

'You can't palm me off that easily,' Raymond rounded on him, as if he had been waiting for just this opportunity. It was an ambush he had set. 'Get that. You can forget your sneaky little plans on my behalf. You have a responsibility towards me and I'm going to make damn sure you fulfil it. I stay with you. I'm not going to be thrown out to the wolves.'

'Look, Raymond, come on, what are you now, thirty-two? You must appreciate that . . .' Despite the evident futility, Mr Baldwin could find no other alternative than to go on talking reasonably.

'Appreciate what, Baldy?' His cheeks were flaming.

He would go about his gut tomorrow. He could . . .

When Brenda Baldwin flew into the room and grabbed her son by the collar of his jacket. She wouldn't let him sink into degradation.

'Come on. Up. Wash. In the bath. I won't have you sitting round the house stinking. Even if your father doesn't give a damn.'

He resisted. Running water could be heard.

'Come on, up, move. It's for your own good.'

'Brenda, please, take it . . .'

And Raymond stood up suddenly, took her by the shoulders and heaved his mother bodily across the room.

'Of course,' Garry was saying that same evening, 'it was their fault. Look at the way they treated us.' He turned to Fred, warming to a favourite topic. 'He used to belt us. Really. You didn't even know why sometimes. Out came the belt and thwack. We'd interrupted his radio programme, for God's sake, he was trying to read the newspaper or something. Thwack slap. "Snotty layabout! Aren't we ever to have a moment's peace?" What a fascist! Which was when he was there of course, when he wasn't off somewhere new, sending sentimental letters home. "Wish I could tell you all to come now but am having trouble finding accommodation." It's a wonder I didn't turn Communist, never mind Liberal.' He laughed bitterly. 'Can you imagine.'

'When he was away,' Lorna put in, 'Raymond used to sleep in Mother's bed. Then when he . . .'

'And the pornography he'd leave lying around the place. There were always *Playboys* in his drawers, everybody knew. *Knave*, *Penthouse*. No wonder Raymond's fucked up. What kind of example did he have? If they'd brought us up decently it would never have happened. If they'd brought us up decently we might have made something of our lives.'

Speak for yourself, Lorna could have said, but was chewing crusty bread.

'Look at the time' – Garry poured himself another glass of wine – 'he took Graham and me to Leeds to start the university. Plane in from Algiers, hired car to Leeds. Seven o'clock in the evening, he thumbs through the classified in the *Yorkshire Post* over a half of Boddington's, makes a couple of phone calls comparing prices. Then we drive out to the most god-forsaken of suburbs, we didn't even know where we were, never mind where the university was. Two rooms on the third floor of a rotting old house run by a creepy Slav. He leaves a hundred pounds. "Take care of yourselves, boys." And he's off.

'To a brothel most likely,' he added and laughed. 'No wonder Graham ended up with a menopausal mother figure and surrogate family. Anything for security and all the better if they've convinced themselves they can't have children. And I mean, with an example of selfishness like that in front of you, of course I want to do something a bit on the altruistic side. You feel you have to atone, or at the very least do something different. You know what I mean?'

His sister smiled.

'Then if he's going to send me money,' Garry said, 'why can't he send it regularly, for God's sake? Why can't we agree tot a month directly into a bank account, so I don't have to keep running and begging and borrowing from everybody else? But no. It's always the odd postal order, yes, postal order, antediluvian, because he doesn't want people knowing his bank-account number – you know Mother has never known how much he earns, how much he's got in the bank – fifty pounds here, a hundred pounds there, a three month break. "Oh yes, Garry, I remember Garry, trying to heal the political divide, excellent cause, here's another eighty pounds." Shit, as if I'd been living on air in the meanwhile. The point is he wants to humiliate you. He'll give you the money, but only if you accept the implied dependence and run around doing things for him. Which is how he's always been, the only family relationship he can understand. "Daddy'll give you sixpence if you run out to the shops."'

'At least he does send some money though,' Fred remarked. He was noticing that for all his pennilessness, the disgustingly handsome Garry managed to dress a great deal better and more stylishly than he did. 'He could quite easily not send it.'

'Take a look at this, for example' – while Fred spoke, Garry had been signing with his great liquid brown eyes for his sister to cut him another piece of quiche. 'Just listen to this.' He unfolded a sheet of paper taken from his jacket pocket. 'Completely unprovoked. I haven't spoken or written to him for ages, bar a Christmas card.

' "Dear Son" – Great, no? Not "Dear Garry", "Dear Son";

typical conservative reinforcement of hierarchical structure that supposedly gives him authority – "Dear Son, when and if you ever reach some kind of mental-stroke-psychological maturity," ' – Garry read rather theatrically, exaggerating what he remembered as his father's pontificating style – ' "you will no doubt appreciate that one cannot expect one's progenitors to provide an inexhaustible supply of this world's goods. Unfortunately you were not born into the Getty family."

'I mean, why does he have to ironize? I'm not an idiot. If I didn't need his money I wouldn't ask for it, would I? I'm trying to make my way in the world like anyone else.'

'Go on,' Lorna encouraged, with just the faintest wink to let Fred know she agreed with all he was thinking. 'Read the rest.'

' "At your age, offspring mine, if I remember rightly" – yeeees, yes, yes – "I had already been working for some ten years, spent two in a prisoner-of-war camp and built the sea flats with my own bare hands" – Oh do give us a break, please – "My only advice to you therefore is that if you are unable to find gainful employment for yourself in London, you return here and help me with doing up the big house, for which I will be happy to pay you whatever your labours are worth" – sometimes you'd think he'd swallowed a government policy document, no? – "And should this new foreign girlfriend of yours deign to come and stay with us, then of course any consort of the Baldwin family is welcome here. We can put you both up in the first bedroom that gets finished. I don't think you could ever accuse me of being prudish or old-fashioned about such matters, and it will be all the more incentive for you to get some work done" – yes, Mrs Thatcher, thank you, Mrs Thatcher – "What I will not do, however" – listen to this – "what I will not do is pay for any more of your Italian lakeland holidays, your London love nest and your little aristocrat's tastes" – oh do come on! – "Nor, and I repeat, nor will I honour any more of your debts. Perhaps you could let the dear young lady know that, as I can promise you that what happened last time with the other girl is not going to repeat itself. Those days are over" – well, I can't remember them ever having started frankly. You'd think I'd been living in the lap of luxury.'

And he began to read very quickly.

' "I have noticed, by the way, since we've been back, a general reluctance of you children to come and visit, the excuse being, presumably, that Raymond is not the best of company. Remember, Raymond is your brother, just as much as he is my son. He is a burden the family should share amongst *all* its members, and it would be a great relief to your mother and I, old and often ill as we are, if you and Lorna and Graham were to come over occasionally to brighten us up. After all, one only has one mother and father in this world. Some time surely could be found for them.

' "I look forward to your arrival, when we can discuss your financial situation in more detail.

Affectionately,

FATHER' "

'Pompous old wanker,' Garry added.

'I rather admire the old guy's balls,' Fred grinned. 'What style. Let's all go up next weekend. Throw a party.'

'And have Raymond beat you up?' Lorna said.

'Oh I don't think it would come to that.'

'Or Kirsty. What if he goes for Kirsty?'

'But she'd never be out of our sight.' Wasn't that precisely what made life so difficult?

'It only takes a moment.'

As this fear rose to the surface and set there very evident on Lorna's round face, there was a silence which caught sister, brother and brother-in-law exchanging glances around the small well-laid table over the leftovers of their quiche. The fitted kitchen cupboards in simple stained pine, the dishwasher, the bright tablecloth and attractive cutlery, testified to comfortable middle-class life. With a touch of yuppy in the two bottles of Chablis.

As if in response to the mentioning of her name, a child began to wail in another part of the flat. Lorna pushed her chair back.

Fred remarked that he'd known it was too good to be true.

'But don't you agree' – Garry resumed as soon as Lorna was out of the room – 'that if I go back up to Cleveleys it's more or less equivalent to burying myself? What am I ever going to achieve with my life up there? I mean, if there is a useful outlet for

48

somebody who's studied economics, if there is a chance to really make something of myself, it's going to be down here in London, right? Not in seaside, souvenir Cleveleys. The place is more or less an old people's home out of season. Not to mention the contacts I have with the local party here just when things have really started moving for us. They're . . .'

'You could be a gigolo,' Fred suggested unhelpfully.

' . . . really bound to give me a job sometime, the amount of canvassing I've done for them. In research or something. I'd be ideal. Especially with this computer course under my belt. And once I'm in I can't see any reason really why I shouldn't get into Parliament in the long run, always assuming the party takes off. You know. And maybe even change a few things one day, do something useful. Except that now I'm supposed to throw that all away just because my scheming ignoramus of a father . . .'

Lorna came back with a screaming child who was rejecting every attempt to comfort her.

'A nightmare,' the mother explained, forgiving.

'I'd say,' said Fred. Child-beating of the fabled Mr Baldwin variety became so much more comprehensible when you had one of your own, though so far he had raised little more than a finger. Which was more than could be said for Lorna in her moods.

Kirsty was placed in uncle's arms and to the immense surprise of her parents shut up at once. And perked up.

'Give Uncle Garry a kiss,' Lorna said, and the little girl did. 'Say Uncle Garry now. Uncle Garry.'

'Unga Gawwy.'

'I hope she doesn't gob on your nice jacket,' Fred hinted. In fun, for it was months since Kirsty had got over gobbing. Garry, however, reached quickly for a serviette to slip over his shoulder. He really was most handsome, it appeared, when he was most in earnest and most making a fool of himself.

'Yes, it is a nice jacket.' Lorna had only half noticed. Now she smiled, for her brother was eminently teasable. 'Have I seen it before?' And she reached out to finger the attractive pale green cloth where Kirsty was nestling. 'Must have cost a bomb.'

'Someone gave it me.' Garry was already defensive.

'Who?'

49

'A friend.'

'Nice friends,' Lorna said.

'Yes.'

'Anonymous,' Fred remarked. 'The best kind.'

And he said: 'Want some bubbly with dessert?' He was already at the fridge. 'I'd like to make a toast.'

Lorna lifted eyebrows.

'To your old dad,' Fred announced. 'And the family's future.'

While they drank their champagne Garry very endearingly cuddled his little niece against his big chest and kissed her hair and tickled her feet and said things like, 'I'd eat you all up if I had half the chance, all right up. You're all made of sugar. Sugar and spice and all things nice.'

'Apart from the shits,' Fred remarked.

But Lorna was touched. 'What a good Daddy you'd make,' she told him. 'Really, you should get on with it. What about this Mariangela?' Because like all parents she was concerned that everybody should share her fate.

Until, finally relaxing, Garry began to laugh freely and be his better self and tell jokes. He had a fine line in dirty jokes.

'So this young priest is doing confession for the first time when a girl comes in and says she's given her boyfriend a blowjob. Well, he's a bit floored by that, he doesn't know what penance to give, so he slips out to talk to the older priest. "How much should I give for a blowjob," he asks. And the priest says: "Pass her a tenner, my son, if she's halfway good at it." ' He laughed as heartily as they did, though he must have told it a dozen times this week. 'Heard the one about the woman in the sperm-donors' queue?'

And some time later in the corridor, putting on his coat, Garry didn't even go into one of his huffs when Fred refused him a loan of a hundred pounds. On the contrary, he embraced both of them in almost a party mood before going out. 'Night, sis.' The squeeze of his big boy's shoulders was eager and intimate. 'Thanks for the meal, kids.' They could hear him whistling on the stairs.

'I hope you feel miserable,' Mrs Shaker now told her husband in the sudden silence of the two of them alone, 'letting him walk out of the door without a penny. And if you didn't rub him up the wrong way in the first place maybe he wouldn't spend the whole evening moaning like that.'

'I thought you agreed with me.'

'Of course I agree with you, but you don't have to show it the whole time. Why couldn't we just have a pleasant evening together.'

And after washing and teeth cleaning she was saying animatedly, 'The point is you can't just condemn people to their fate as if you had no part in it. Poor Father has . . .'

But Fred had suddenly burst out laughing.

'What's so funny, damn you?'

'I was just thinking, how on earth is he supposed to go into Parliament and so on wearing that stupid earring?'

'Oh everybody wears them these days. Haven't you noticed?'

'I suppose,' said Fred, settling down to sleep, 'it might distract some attention from the chip on his shoulder.'

'Dear Mariangela,' Garry wrote on returning to his room. He sucked his pen for some time.

'You are quite right. There's no point in my staying on here in London. There is nothing for me here.'

He considered the photograph of Amanda on the wall, stunningly leggy in that green costume of hers. One of the infuriating things about life was how realizing you were being ridiculous didn't make it any easier to change, any easier to be that brave purposeful creature one had always hoped one would one day wake up to be.

'Especially now that my father's refusing to send me any money.'

Why was it so hard to write to Mariangela?
He sucked.
Circumstances seemed to present a brick wall against which you could only batter yourself like an idiot.

'The point is, I've got to break out and change my ways, make something of myself. I'm getting to feel so down here, with so many people I'd counted on not helping me out. I need new faces, a new scene, new challenges.'

He tried to imagine her. He tried to feel how impressive it was that she was Italian and called Mariangela. 'My girlfriend, Mariangela.' There was a way she had of catching one foot behind the other when she walked that helped him to start. And of course the way she put a knuckle between her teeth to laugh. That was very sexy.

'So this time, after you come, let's go back to Milan together, like you suggested. I can always make some money somehow or other, teaching English or something. Then I could help with what you do for the Radicals. It would be useful to get a European perspective the way politics is going these days. We might have a really great time.'

In his pants a hand bunched his balls. He turned and looked out of a window he ought to clean down across Kensal Rise. There were dripping trees and damp houses in the sickness of city lamplight and beyond that lucky people driving out along Westway, going far perhaps.

He flicked at a torn fingernail on the desktop.

'You know I told you that my parents might be coming back. Well, they have. In fact, they're angling for me to go up to Cleveleys so they can stick me in a flat with raving Raymond once they've got the tenants out and so get him off their backs. And of course Lorna and Graham are siding with them and putting on the pressure, so that they won't have to feel they need to give me any more money. Everybody seems to want to plan out my life, in the way that best suits them. Naturally they're all convinced that if I haven't got a job in more than a year's trying, it must be because I'm lazy. As if I was the only person unemployed in the whole fucking country. There are only three million of us. And they seem to forget all the demeaning things I have done for money, like serving at the Orange Pee and delivering the Christmas post (with a bunch of complete yobbos) and now training to be a dogsbody computer programmer. The cynical superior Fred with his cushy university number is the worst of all. You can see he's just dying to go back to Uncle Sam and dump the Baldwin side of the family forever.

Anyway, I'm not going up to Cleveleys, not on any account. I'd rather starve. And what could I ever achieve there? Raymond's illness is obviously incurable and equally obviously the result of my father's fascist chauvinism and my mother's peasant lunacy. Being with them only makes him worse, and it would make me worse too. If you only knew what our childhood was like. Actually, I think the most sensible thing they could do would be to sell up and separate from him for good, before he goes and kills one of them in just revenge. Except Mother would never dream of that because she's spent the last twenty years imagining her triumphant return to Lancashire and how amazed Uncle Harry will be when they turn the big house into a palace (I'll believe that when I see it). My own feeling is that the only thing you can hope to do with your family is to keep away from all of them. Nobody ever got to be famous by staying at home.

Anyway, why don't you start looking around for something for me to do there, and then we can go back together.

I can't wait for you to arrive.

Hugs and squeezes,
GARRY.'

It started almost as a doodle on the reverse side of a rejection letter, but soon he was writing with sudden and blissful fluency. The cramped style of cramped sentiments lengthened out into long, smooth undulations that seemed to want to eat up the page.

'Dear Amanda,

I couldn't listen to any of those speakers last night. I couldn't give a damn whether we hold the balance in the next parliament. I don't care if Penhaligan is dead and I couldn't give a shit whether we've sacrificed all our principles on nuclear disarmament. The only alliance I care about is with you. The only consensus I want is yours. The only canvassing I'm going to do from now on is at your door.

Amanda, Amanda, why on earth have we allowed this to happen? I love you, I live you, I dream you. Why did we have to make it so difficult for ourselves? And why, why, why did you have to marry him? What were you trying to prove? I know he's well-off, but then so are you. I know he's got a job and direction and everything and your father liked him, but then your father's a conservative old fart, isn't he? And anyway, he likes me well enough too. And if I'm rather a flounderer at the moment, I won't flounder for ever, will

I? Something is bound to turn up. I know I've got it in me to really do something sooner or later. Anyway, haven't we always said that making pots of money doing boring jobs that are of no real use to anyone is not the be all and end all of life?

You can still change your mind. People do. It's no good hiding behind your marriage as if it were an uncrossable barrier. The divorce rate is 40% plus. You'll tell me not to be ridiculous, that people would laugh. But people are already laughing. They're laughing because you married him less than three months after going to Algeria with me. They're laughing because you still keep your flat in Hampstead and only go to Manchester at the weekends. They're laughing because they still see us together every night at the Centre, because they see us walking home arm in arm. Let's at least be spectacular and do something.

And these clothes of his you keep giving me. Why? I'm going to burn them. I'd rather go in rags. It's ridiculous giving me his clothes. Anyway he must notice: he can't have so many. What is he, stupid or something?

Amanda, do think. Do, do think. I feel this is our last chance before everything crystallizes, before we freeze into our roles. I think about my parents. They should never have married. The war took a great chunk out of their twenties and then they were in a hurry. And he's spent all his life trying to get away from her, away from the children, and she's spent all her life insisting on being with him, because she would never accept that she'd made a mistake, that they'd be better off apart, that she could find somebody else. Neither of them ever quite had the courage to be honest with themselves, to do the sensible thing, so that now they're just two old disappointed people who never do anything but argue and have ruined their children arguing, turning their frustrations on us, and on poor Raymond who bore the brunt.

Amanda, don't stay with somebody you don't love. You know you love me. How can you have children from anybody but me? Or me from anybody but you? I would love to have children from you. They would be so handsome. We are so suited to each other.

Please, Amanda, make the break and let's set things to rights. I really don't know how to see my life without you, where it's come from, where it's going.

Always your
GARRY'

Of these two letters, Garry found on re-reading the following morning in the kind of light that will sift through London cloud and condensation on greasy panes, that duty bound him to mail only the first, and to store the second (there was, after all, the problem of the rejection letter on the reverse side) in the lower right-hand drawer of his desk, with other memorabilia: the photos of Marion and Sue, the football team pictures and medals, Graham's letters when such letters had mattered, various folk objects from Ecuador.

Anyway he would be seeing her this evening. You couldn't write a letter to somebody you would be seeing this evening, could you? And what if she said yes?

In the green jacket, leather pants and Italian shoes, Garry left his room early to walk down to the Centre, where he was on duty from ten to twelve. And as he walked he whistled, feeling fairly carefree. It was the evenings that got to him.

Lorna experienced moments of real anguish when she didn't know what would become of her family. And this was not something new, but part and parcel almost of being Lorna Shaker née Baldwin. It had begun, most probably, when as a child in Cleveleys she had written letters such as the one her father had recently returned to her. 'When are you coming home, Daddy? We are so looking forward . . .' Almost the first words she had written, surely. It had developed, grown, with all her father's absences, Mother's fits, and then the frequent changes of school and language that had characterized her kaleidoscopic adolescence after they had begun, on Grandmother's death, to follow Father around. So it was an anguish coloured by Mediterranean skies, desert day trips, Quito cooking; an anguish that had to do with telegrams, letters, packing and airports; an anguish, finally, that had received its most tremendous confirmation the day, travelling down from Boston to New Haven, she had found Raymond like that in his room no better than an animal.

Beginning another letter now, occasionally picking at the skin around her nails, Lorna was vaguely aware of how one might truthfully say after all these years that everything and nothing had changed.

'Dear Mum and Dad,' she banished Crackle to some warm chip somewhere.

'You've been back two months now and you haven't written or phoned once, while I've written three times. Yet I see in a letter of yours, Dad, to Garry, that you are already complaining that we haven't been to visit. That's really not fair. It's term time. Fred's terribly busy at the university and I have an awfully tight deadline on this rubbish I'm writing.'

Lorna paused. On your own in a room at 19, 20, 21, as she had been before that visit to New Haven, you imagined you had escaped your family. You imagined, with your own key and small scholarship, that childhood and all its angst-ridden relationships were behind you. Nothing could have been further from the truth. And for all she had complained of the lack of help when Kirsty was born, her parents' absence in far-flung lands seemed so desirable now, removing as it had for so many years the pain of being forced to think, too often or too precisely, either of them, or of Raymond – and thus, from a certain angle, of herself and whatever might be in store.

These unhappy reflections with their hints of unthinkable obligations and responsibilities suddenly made Lorna Shaker feel brusque and very practical. It was 12 o'clock.

'You say in your letter that we should all come and help out with Raymond. I hadn't meant to tell you, Dad, since it seems pointless adding to your worries, but Raymond has started sending us threatening letters full of stuff like, "Death to the Yankee imperialists," and so on, accusing Fred of having written defamatory letters to his "girlfriend" in Algeria so as to dissuade her from marrying him. Some fantasy he's conjured up. With the result that I'm terrified, frankly, that if we come and visit there'll be a bust-up with Fred, or even worse that he'll do something to Kirsty.

Dad, I do wish I could help you with Raymond. I would give anything to be able to do so, but I don't see how I can. You know how much I tried at first when we were both in America and all the good it did. The only thing that would help, surely, would be some new treatment that actually works. Have you tried any new doctors since you got back? Isn't there anything? Perhaps if Fred agrees I'll come up alone one weekend to cheer you up.

Having said which, Pop, you really are a bit of a fraud. What do you mean, old and often ill? Come on. Reagan is 70 odd and he's President of the United States, more or less. Even Maggie Thatch is no younger than you. And I can't remember you or Mumsy with anything more than a cold or headache all your lives. Of course I know Garry is rather a pain the way he mopes about being unemployed and then rushes off somewhere exotic as soon as you send him some money, but surely this is just a problem of careful management. I mean, if you paid a small amount directly into his bank account, monthly, or better still weekly as he's always asking, he'd never be able to amass the sums needed to get away, would he? He's not capable of saving. As for the problem of honouring debts, you're right to tell him what you do of course, except that from what I've seen and heard of Mariangela there won't be much problem there. Her family aren't terribly well-off I don't think and she's not half as glamorous as her name suggests. Certainly nothing like Amanda. In fact, now I'm on the subject, you'd think if one was going to bother carrying on a long-distance relationship with an Italian, you'd at least have found one of those lithe Latin beauties with dark flashing eyes, etc. etc., but Mariangela's rather a scrubby blonde with an unhealthy complexion and plain face, quite sweet, but very bossy bossy (as was/is Amanda for that matter) and with all kinds of political ideas she's determined to explain to you in the most broken English. She's a "Radical" apparently, whatever that might mean. Anyway, she's all over Garry, or she was the only time I saw them together. Couldn't stop kissing him. Perhaps because he's the best-looking man she could ever hope to get. (I forgot to say, she's ever so small, which makes her look rather odd next to towering, broad-shouldered Garry.) He just loves the attention of course. Still, he is a dear, and at least he's idealistic, his heart's in the right place.

So, Dad, are you finally getting some gardening in? And are you happy, Mum, now you have all the ingredients to bake whatever you want? I remember you complaining so much about the shops in Algeria. Have you bought the new sewing machine you were always promising yourself? And what about the dress-making book? It would be nice to think you were having a happy retirement after all those years travelling, despite Raymond. I do hope all will turn out for the good.

Much love,

LORNA'

Obviously, she thought, as it printed off, obviously it would be nice to think they were having a happy retirement. Only that it was utterly improbable – and somewhere along the line, Lorna realized, she had allowed her letter to be sidetracked. Nothing material had been said. Nothing that got to grips with anything. Which perhaps explained why she wrote so often.

She pushed back her seat, walked to the window and rubbed off condensation with a towel. Fairfield Close appeared in its customary geometric order; over garden fences a breeze nagged at winter twigs. The next-door neighbour but one, in flat cap, was revving his Maxi for the usual half-hour a day before covering it with its blanket again. She wasn't responsible for her parents, was she? They had brought it upon themselves partly. Perhaps. That endless travelling, rowing, preaching. A case of family hubris really, followed punctually by inevitable downfall. Preston-born Frank Baldwin had been so determined to break out, to break into a new and prosperous world, so determined that his children would be the most advantaged of all their contemporaries. He had gone to the ends of the earth, worked shifts and weekends, posted cheques, had them live in compounds, cheap hotels, guest worker prefabs. Himself always on site, always busy. Thinking of their education of course. If he had wanted to drive his kids insane he could scarcely have done a better job.

And yet mostly it must just be chance. The other members of the family hadn't gone mad, had they? Or not entirely. She smiled. And frowned. If Father died, would Fred put up with Mother? And would Raymond ever leave them alone now he was back? ('Dear Professor Shaker, otherwise known as Mr Yank Sperm-fountain or Fred Fuckface, I am writing to inform you of your imminent execution following your much publicized crimes against the Libyan People's Jamahiriya. It is a matter of common knowledge that after raping my sister . . .') He was so helpless and so evil. You felt it must be a curse from the gods almost.

And when she could still remember the happiest brother-and-sister walks together along the seafront in Cleveleys, in Beirut — another paradise transformed into inferno.

She summoned Crackle: ' . . . while in their second hit, "Only a Nuclear War", the subtle interplay of Rod's thumping bass with the dazzlingly patterned bursts of treble that seem to spill from Elf's Stratocaster, brilliantly create the impression of . . .'

What impression? What had she meant to write?

If she worked with other people in an office, her mind wouldn't be such easy prey to all these worries. Would it? She could drink coffee, exchange gossip, and flirtations, observe tics.

Of a nuclear war? Surely not. Could she have sunk that low?

And Lorna decided it was time to do the shopping. She stood up.

Though at least that was one thing a mad brother saved you from worrying about. What a luxury to have only a nuclear war on your mind. Or AIDS. She wasn't the slightest bit worried about AIDS.

Or drug addiction. Or the crime rate. Or even the General Election. What a lucky person.

The phone rang. And why did phones always surprise her so, as if she had forgotten they existed? Why did she start? It would be Graham. After a moment's hesitation, Lorna slipped out with her purse and shopping bag, closing the door behind her with unnecessary stealth.

Mrs Baldwin stood at her sink looking out on flapping washing. She thought perhaps if he had had a girlfriend at some point, none of this would ever have happened. Perhaps even now if Frank took him to a prostitute, God knows he wouldn't have any difficulty finding one, he knew where to look. She rinsed mugs. Sex turned out to be so important, or so they told you, though she couldn't quite see it herself. Perhaps more so for men. She would mention it to the psychiatric social worker. The pornography he bought. Perhaps if he never had sex, one day he would just break out and rape someone. Or worse. There were so many stories like that in Frank's *Telegraph*. She read them with growing fascination. Perhaps there were even prostitutes on the National Health for people like Raymond. She'd heard about a scandal or something once. On the World Service in Bougaa. Though with all these new herpes and AIDS things about . . .

Mrs Baldwin watched a crow hopping on the black slates of the roof opposite. And she wondered which of the thousand ways they had been guilty it might have been. Or none of them. They couldn't be responsible for his thyroid for example. Except that probably she should always have known not to have children with a man like Frank.

She dried her hands to stroke the cat. 'There, pussy pussy. Chiquita, Chiquita.' Were there such things as schizophrenic cats? She thought not. The animal kingdom seemed so sane, so predictable. With no problems with sex either. She wouldn't have minded being a cat herself.

A MOTHER
TRAVELS

Some five years ago, having given up university and finding himself temporarily unemployed, Graham had agreed to spend a summer in Cleveleys with Raymond in return for the right to live off the rents from the tenants of the sea flats. His parents got a break from Raymond, he got the money. This was the arrangement. Ever since that time, however, Graham had constantly and adamantly refused to let his parents know his address, or even, if he had one, his phone number. And not only his parents, but his elder sister and twin too. His reasoning being that his father and mother had been utterly irresponsible to leave a twenty-year-old with somebody as mad and dangerous as Raymond, and thus deserved no better, and, further, that neither they, nor Lorna, nor Garry could be entirely relied upon not to give the address to one of the others, and so eventually to Raymond (the keeping of secrets not being a talent for which any of the family were especially noted). For towards the end of that summer Graham had spent three days in a Blackpool hospital with suspected concussion after Raymond had caught him on the temple, not at all comically for all the likeness to slapstick, with a heavy frying pan. In the days before that tussle, he had seen Raymond masturbate over some photographs Garry had left of Amanda and then rub them across his face and in his hair; he had seen him put a foot through a television screen, and he had seen him cut his own foreskin with a pair of rusty nail-scissors. All things which apparently did not make him committable, since Graham had also seen how perfectly polite and reasonable Raymond could be with authorities of any kind, how well he knew his rights and would insist on getting them, and how perfectly capable he was of explaining away every abnormality and seeming genuinely eager to be treated (if treatment was really necessary) on an out patients' basis. Raymond, after all, had always been the genius of the family, and genius had not deserted him in his madness.

So Graham was determined never to get caught alone with Raymond again, nor to be subject to unexpected visits or phone-calls (for the sake of communication he kept a box number at the post office). Yet all the same he did appreciate that his mad brother could not simply be ignored. One could not just not visit one's parents and enjoy the luxury of never facing the situation (this was actually a considerable mistake on Garry's part). For the family represented the only source of wealth that might one day put himself and his twin in a position to buy decent houses for themselves; hence it was crucial that one keep an eye on how Father was managing what was, at least potentially, their own and only money, and in particular, how he was managing it in relation to Raymond; since it would be typical of Father to try to spend his way out of trouble at the expense of everybody else and quite possibly for only the shortest period of grace (the others may have got their degrees, but they didn't appear to appreciate these things).

With the result that, despite what he had said to his twin, and despite Mr Baldwin's complaints, Graham at least of the children had been back to Cleveleys every weekend but one since his parents had returned (it was his duty, really, as the Gascoignes perfectly understood, to help his parents settle in), although never allowing his mother to return to Leeds with him as she always seemed so eager to, partly because he spent every evening at Sophy's anyway, and partly because it was so important to have the mental security of knowing his address was an unassailable secret.

Which was why it came as such a shock when, on a bright spring morning, leaning against a filing cabinet by the big window to light a cigarette, Graham Baldwin caught sight of his mother in her ancient green coat, looking up at the Leeds Access from across the street, a battered holdall in one hand, a wicker basket tucked into the crook of the other elbow.

At some point he must have made the classic mistake of telling them who he worked for.

'This can't go on,' he was insisting on the phone to Lorna the following morning, rather earlier than he usually called (otherwise she might have known not to answer). There was an earnest outrage in his voice that both the twins were so good at.

'You can't bring a cat into your son's office just like that with no warning. I mean, she comes marching straight in, starts joking with everybody, "Don't let me interrupt you," you know how she is, God, "I'm only an old woman come to see her hardworking son." She even started telling old Grimbledeston how important she thought insurance was and how happy she was they'd given me a chance to start a good career, what a blessing children were, and what a burden, if only you could know what they'd be like before you had them. You know the kind of thing. Talking as if I wasn't there, as if I was still a little boy. And why can't she dress better for heaven's sake, always in the same old coat with some ridiculous hair-do and pretending to be more Lancashire and working class than she really is just because she thinks it's colourful. As if times hadn't moved on while she's been away. Then the cat had to go and piss in somebody's post-tray of course. The point is, if it happens again, they'll probably fire me. I'm still on probation. I mean, you can't have your mother coming in paralysing the office for an hour, can you?'

'They probably loved it,' Lorna said. 'Everybody likes Mum. On first meeting,' she added.

'And after I've been down there every weekend to help. I mean, they could hardly accuse me of neglecting them.'

'You've been there every weekend?'

'Somebody has to. Don't they?'

'Yes, I suppose they do.'

Graham allowed the line to remain ominously silent a moment now, a trick Webb had taught him for dealing with difficult clients, then said very solemnly: 'Don't you think it would be much better, Lorna though, if she came down to your place? I mean, I don't even have a spare room, she's sleeping on the couch.'

Lorna hadn't quite understood why Mother couldn't go back to Cleveleys, if it wasn't convenient at Graham's. Cleveleys being infinitely closer. 'Though of course,' she hurried on, realizing she might be seeming ungenerous, 'if . . .'

'She's broken her arm.'

'What? Badly?'

'No, no. Her wrist actually. Just a break. Not badly enough not to be able to carry a cat basket.'

'Oh.'

'So she says she doesn't want to go back to Cleveleys till the plaster's off. In case people get the wrong idea.'

Graham put a lot of stress on these last two words, but somehow this didn't help Lorna to appreciate what the wrong idea might be; while for Graham's part her difficulty was just another confirmation of the fact that a university education didn't mean anything at all. He had done well not to waste his time.

'That Raymond might have done it,' he explained.

'Ah, I see. Yes. And did he?'

'No, no, it seems she fell over the same stupid cat she's brought here. Why I don't know. It ran across her feet on the front steps and she fell.'

'She says.'

It hadn't actually occurred to Graham that his mother might not be telling him the truth. He checked around the office a moment to see that no one was following the conversation, since people had started to troop back from the coffee machine now.

But then the idea was obviously absurd.

'No, if Raymond had done it, it would have been the perfect occasion to persuade them to put him in a home, wouldn't it? I mean, that would be criminal assault, they . . .'

'If she wanted to put him in a home.'

'But why wouldn't she?' he protested. And after a pause: 'I can't imagine there's a single person in the world doesn't want him in a home, barring the Chancellor of the Exchequer.' Which was something Colonel Gascoigne had come out with recently.

Lorna gave up. She found her brother very sweet, and it was generous of him to go to Cleveleys every weekend, but he did seem rather short on observation and psychology. Perhaps because, having been brought up in all those different countries and languages, and then studying economics of all things for just a year, followed by four years dogsbodying for a haulage company, he had never got any serious reading done.

'Look, tell her she's perfectly welcome to come here. We've got a spare room if we move Kirsty into ours. Or she could sleep in the sitting room. And the cat's no problem.' Obviously, Lorna thought, Mother knew that if she left the cat behind with Father she'd never see it again. Just as she knew that if ever she said she was willing to testify that Raymond had assaulted her, Father would be down the police station in no time.

'Right, that's just what I've been telling her, I'll . . .'

But seeing Grimbledeston shouldering backwards through the door to shield his coffee, Graham was obliged to hang up in indecent haste.

'How's your mum?' his boss wanted to know. 'Fine woman.' He was smiling and avuncular.

'Oh, very well, thank you.'

'What about lunch tomorrow?'

Graham was slow to react.

'I imagine you're seeing her lunchtimes. What about something down at the Rose? Celebrate the end of your trial period, discuss your future a little. You could bring your mother along. She seems a sociable sort. I'm sure she'll be happy about your contract and so on.'

Grimbledeston had one large terylene ham on the corner of Graham's desk.

'I'm sorry, I mean, no, she's leaving tomorrow morning. She's going down to my sister's in London.'

The older man sat there a moment looking at the new boy from over the steam of his fivepenny coffee.

Chubby cheeks he had.

Fred woke in the night and found he had to go piss again. And it wasn't the baby had woken him oddly. He brushed through the darkness, full of a sense of unease. Why, when he had the lectureship in the bag? That stuff on Stevens had been pretty damn brilliant frankly. Roll over Vendler. The cover wasn't so . . .

She had invited her mother to stay. Fred stopped over the bowl. Damn. Damn and damn. That was it. She had invited her mother to stay. Nothing to be done of course, without appearing grossly ungenerous, although seeing as the woman had broken her arm, mightn't she be better off at home? There was a line.

Unless Raymond had broken it? No, that was just a typically alarmist flight of the imagination on Lorna's part. The Baldwins revelled in drama was the truth of the matter, and a general determination to make things seem worse than they were, to create a sense of mystery. Typical response to empty lives. So the guy was mad. He got off on making threats. But he'd been that way for seven, eight years now and never done anybody any serious harm. Sometimes you even suspected a hint of humour in those letters: 'The undersigned has sworn an everlasting Jehad against all emissaries of the Stars and Stripes.' Indeedy! He should write for comic books. Or Sci-Fi films.

Looking on the bright side, there might be advantages if Mrs B was willing to look after baby all the time and maybe help with the housework. Yes, it could all turn out for the good; Granny watched TV with Kirsty in the sitting room; Lorna got on with her book at the screen in the small bedroom and he could read and make notes in their bedroom. There was no table, but . . .

Not if she had a broken arm. Oh fuck. It would end up with Lorna doing everything; she'd get even further behind with this Crackle thing, she'd blow the contract, three thousand pounds down the tube; she'd never get her career off the ground, all because . . . and there'd be tears and . . .

Not much of a piss that. More drizzle than drive. And he'd taken his time about it too.

Which now reminded Fred of other tears a couple of evenings back. Well, it was reassuring to know he hadn't been feeling uneasy for nothing. No angst creeping in as yet, no existential illnesses. Tears, yes. She wouldn't have the second baby now. She'd started using contraceptives again. She wouldn't have the second baby in case it turned out like Raymond. Well, that was new, where had that come from? He didn't like the way the family was encroaching like this. She wanted to see consultants and have tests done before she'd even consider a pregnancy. Well. If that was on the cards they should have thought of it the first time, right?

Fred hovered outside Kirsty's door. Being the one who tended to wake up at night it was understood to be his duty to go and check that Kirsty was still under the covers, hadn't got a foot through the rails. But he hesitated, the risk being that in trying to ensure she didn't wake later from the cold, he might well wake her now, in which case it was all hell getting her back to sleep again. He switched off the light in the bathroom and felt for the one in the kitchen which filtered a lower safer glow through to the second bedroom. The trick with the door was to push it quickly and stop it firmly, so that the squeak of the frame didn't drag out into a squeal. When was he going to do something about that? When was he ever going to do anything about anything with a year's worth of lectures to prepare?

Kirsty slept. Angelic.

Not that he didn't foresee the second baby as one enormous obstacle. There was no denying it – which was why it was so important to time it for winter, right? When the worst thing it could screw up was lessons, rather than the following summer when he should be making the big push (military one there, semi-concealed) on 'The Deconstructionist Myth,' if, that is, he managed to get the notes made this summer. Yes, it would be uphill (almost dead that one). There would be sleepless nights, gob, vomit, etc. But you had to get these things squared away (carpentry?) young in life. Push them through (oh enough!). And if they left it any longer, the kids would be too far apart to really play with each other, which was what the whole project was about, wasn't it, having healthy, well-balanced children who played together and didn't hang and whine around their parents all the time? Because you were hardly doing the world any favours having an only child, were you? With the kind of problems that could lead to. Though he'd got away fairly cheaply himself he thought. No, Lorna should get Crackle finished, and if possible another similar deal during the pregnancy; that would give her a sufficient track record to be able to get back into everything after the inevitable pause. Simply a question of planning. Let's see, as long as she got pregnant by about Easter (which was so close now of course), or shortly after, then . . . The advantage being that he would get the confirmation for the lecture course toward the end of May, on the strength of which they could buy a bigger apartment, settle that by mid-July and – except that if she was really serious about this . . .

On his back in the dry bedroom dark, Fred's mind churned on. There was something manic about it, he knew that. He knew he wouldn't sleep. There was something even rather ill and out of control (runaway train metaphor?). But there you were. Lorna laughed at the way he was so determined to organize their lives, to do the right things at the right times, to plan, to line up the day's chores so they wouldn't have to go out of the house more than once, to make steady progress careerwise, to pass all the big mile-posts on schedule. But if you didn't treat everything as the rat race it was, then the only place you'd find yourself was at the back, no? And wasn't it paying off? His success now, hers on the way, and the happy family very much on the blocks (as it were, as it were – you couldn't get away from it, could you?). No, if anyone were mad, it was her, saying she loved him one minute, she hated him the next, she was dying for another child one minute, she was going to abort if she was pregnant the next. She was going to Cleveleys tomorrow – but no she never wanted to see her parents again. She . . . Perhaps – it came to Fred – perhaps some of her family's madness had rubbed off on her ('Language: a Graveyard of Metaphor' – good first year course) in the form of this incessant capriciousness (buying a house with Lorna was a nightmare). Certainly her mother wasn't quite all there in more ways than . . . but no, now it was him getting alarmist. It was just a question of being female, the way all women handled their emotional lives, as if they were playing yo-yo (don't ever let the feminists hear you thinking). That's why women needed such a strong hand behind them, to have any coherence at all. (Bit sweeping that. Fruitless line of thought anyway.) Go over tomorrow's lesson. Okay. 'Metaphor: Sine Qua Non of . . .'

Or try to get to sleep?

Fred stared at the dark. Strange the way it seemed to be made up of small brown particles sometimes, floating in a liquid that perhaps was part of the eye itself, perhaps . . . so that it was the subject fused the . . . was this what darkness meant, when . . .

Try to get to sleep.

But now he needed to piss again. God damn. Why was he pissing so much? And why were English houses so cold, so damp, so dusty?

73

Raymond to Fadima

April 9th   Broughton Street
                                             Cleveleys

Dear Fadima,
    Allah has now made it clear to me that the last Holy War must at any moment envelop in a blinding pyre of flame your beloved country and your mattress of pleasure. American aircraft carriers flit like dark angels around your coasts and I am deeply distressed by the thought of the great dangers which may all too soon overtake your parents, your brothers and yourself.

<u>Cunnilingus</u>

So I am writing to instruct you that you must all come to England as soon as possible. My father extends his humble invitation to all Children of Allah to share what is ours and to partake of our simple family way of life. He is in possession of three flats and a large house, so you may rest assured that there is room for all and all are welcome. I shall be in touch as soon as possible with details of immigration requirements and visa procedures, but these will present few problems, since we shall be married soon after your arrival.

<u>Fellatio</u>

My dear mother sends warm greetings.

May Allah protect you all.

Your lover and well-wisher.

      RAYMOND ALI, avenger of all wrong.

Having scribbled this first in English, Raymond translated it some ten or fifteen times into French before typing it up and stretching sellotape across each line. He was extremely excited and sent the letter Swift Air, which cost his father one pound twenty. Returning from the post office though, he was careful to keep close to the walls, his back well covered, and would not look at the people talking about him. There seemed to be more than usual today. If they asked he would say he had been paying a bill for his father. And there was a smell too that was threatening now. Menacing. An acrid nauseous paint smell. They had so many weapons. Raymond broke into a shambling run over uneven paving. His breath came quickly. Mustn't, he absolutely mustn't come out without Father again; a big mistake. However loathsome the little pig was, he certainly knew how to keep them off.

Mr Baldwin to Lorna

April 9th   Broughton Street
                                            Cleveleys

Dear Lorna,

   You obviously don't understand the kind of pressure I am
obliged to conduct my life under. If I sent you some pleasant
mementoes rather than a letter it was because that was the
absolute maximum I had time for, and I can only say that I
am very, and I mean <u>very</u> surprised and hurt that you did
not appreciate this. I am also fed up to the back teeth, frankly,
with hearing about your and everybody else's unhappy childhood. So just let me tell you, dear daughter, that your
childhood was neither happier nor unhappier than that of
any average young girl anywhere. Do you think other families
never argue? Added to which you were given the enormous
advantage of growing up in various different countries and
thus being perfectly fluent in three languages by the time
you were 18, an advantage which I see you have not been
sufficiently astute or adventurous to capitalize on. This uni-
versal feeling of sour grapes towards one's parents, apparently
so in vogue at the moment, is nothing more than the product
of half-baked modern psychology and sociology which set
out to ingratiate themselves with the public by pandering to
the eternal desire to lay the blame elsewhere and to refuse to
accept one's responsibilities either towards others or oneself.
I am surprised frankly that you of all people with your
excellent education and supposedly intelligent mind haven't
seen through this. So let me say it now: you were a privileged

child; you were clothed and fed (something that can truly be said of only about one third of the human beings on this planet). You had the best that money could buy, or at least you did from the time you were about eleven on. And if you didn't go to a private school for more than a year or so, you must ask your mother the reason why, since it was she who was so eager to cart you around everywhere. It was certainly no fault of mine. Remember the motto: 'Unicuique fortunae suae faber est.' That is, don't blame your parents for your unhappiness, and if you think the work you are doing is stupid, then you are all the more stupid for doing it. I suppose it hasn't occurred to you, Lorna, that one of the reasons why I chose to work abroad, often in the most primitive and squalid conditions, was not simply to guarantee the welfare and education of four children, two of whom your mother planned without my acquiescence, but because it was only there that I could find work which satisfied my ambitions and exploited my talents more or less to the full. Self-realization requires guts and a spirit of independence. So, and I repeat, if you don't like what you're doing then do something else. I always felt you should have remained in America, since we as a family made considerable, and I do mean considerable, financial sacrifices to give you the opportunity to study there, and since, on your own admission, a university career was available to you. England on the contrary is a depressed place and will be more depressed still if the next election produces a Labour government or worse still a hung parliament (as our young politico idiot appears to hope). Do think about it, because, to be quite honest, it upsets me to think of my gifted daughter accepting second best after such a promising (and expensive) start. I am sure the university would be happy to take you back. For myself, I only returned to England because I have property to administrate and because over the years I have become more and more susceptible to your mother's eternal hectoring. Though I may very well not stay. I am a great believer in maintaining a constant sense of potential. Unlike your mother who is a dreadful fatalist and speaks of wanting to 'die in her own country amongst her own people', etc., etc. As far as I'm concerned, we are all citizens of the planet Earth, that is how we should think of ourselves and our home and family is where we decide to make it.

Another thing I am fed up with is hearing people insinuate that I am not doing enough about the Ayatollah here. Graham has been down every weekend to nag me about his 'future', your mother insists that he have his thyroid tested, re-tuned, removed, re-vamped, re- or de-activated, etc., and now you have the impertinence to enquire whether I have looked for a new doctor! The fact is, dear daughter, that I do nothing but look for new doctors and scour the newspapers for new ideas. Put yourselves in my shoes. Obviously I do. They are my only hope. Otherwise I'll be stuck with this albatross round my neck (his description not mine – apparently I shot him down and now he haunts me) for ever and a day. And of course you simply can't imagine what life with him is really like. That said, however, if Raymond refuses to do the requisite tests, there is very little I can accomplish on the thyroid side, is there? I can't force him to let them stick needles in him. He is six foot one and a half, weighs the best part of seventeen stone and is only too well aware of his civil rights, if not his duties. I have, however, at the advice of a local mental hospital consultant, persuaded Raymond to do joint therapy sessions with a psychoanalyst (that is, myself, Raymond and the analyst – he wouldn't do it on his own), although he uses these occasions, much as I expected, mainly as an opportunity to hurl abuse at me. The latest rubbish, as of yesterday, is that I did not give him enough 'social space' in the family. This turned out to mean that I had not allowed him to bring his playfriends home when we were in Sudan, and that I was generally 'hypercritical' of anyone he formed a relationship with. What he appears to have forgotten is that these 'friends' were worm-ridden street urchins. Of course I didn't let him bring them home. Of course I was hypercritical. What kind of father would I have been if I had behaved otherwise? In fact if I'd had my way your mother would never have let him out on the street to play with them in the first place. If I'd had my way he would have been in a boarding school in England. Another of yesterday's gems was that I was in the habit of beating him mercilessly and savagely, because jealous of his relationship with your mother who apparently has always loved him more than she does me (this wouldn't surprise me actually). At which point I felt obliged to defend myself and recounted an anecdote which you might do well to bear in mind yourself now that you are a parent. When I returned on leave once, before the twins were born, I got furious with Raymond whining to sleep in our bed, another of your mother's foibles, and did indeed give him a damn good hiding in the hope that he would finally appreciate where he belonged and stay there. It was the first time I had really hit him hard and I was worried about it. So seeing as I had to go to the doctor's in any case for some other problem (my health is not and never has been as good as you like to imagine), I mentioned the business to him. The doctor was a sensible man with children of his own. 'How old is the boy?' he asked. 'Almost four,' I said. 'I am only surprised you waited this long,' he said!

You see.

Anyway, as for Raymond's presenting some sort of physical threat to yourself or Fred or little Kirsty, this is absolute crass nonsense. He is always saying how happy he would be if the various members of the family would only get together again and I don't doubt that as soon as he has actually met Fred and seen that he is not a member of the US bomber squadrons, then he will accept him. I believe that in what remains of Raymond's normal personality he has a great yearning to re-establish family relationships, which is why it is so selfish of yourself and Garry never to come and see us. What's more, a visit would probably be the best way to stop the flow of letters you mention, because I certainly can't do anything about it, if that's what you were angling for. Unpleasant letters are the very least of my worries.

If you speak to Graham or Garry I hope you will share this letter with them and consider the good sense of what I have said.

Meanwhile I am growing old and still haven't had the pleasure of seeing my granddaughter. Do give her a kiss from me. I'm enclosing a photo of you as a two-year-old, so you can compare with Kirsty. As you will see, you were not deprived of either pretty dresses or ice-creams at the beach. Having said which, I must confess that had I had all daughters my family troubles would be at an end, and if I write to you like this it is because I know that you at least of my children are mature enough and intelligent enough to weigh up what your father says and appreciate that he is right.

I am also enclosing a postal order for £200 for Garry, as well as a newspaper article you may be interested in.

You have had your letter.

My love to all the family,
Your FATHER

By the way, re. the politico. I have no intention whatsoever of making an arrangement which will allow him to take my support for granted. I am not an impersonal source of social security. If I give him money it is out of sheer generosity, and generosity is of its nature both impulsive and irregular. As regards this latest gift, I expect a visit from him as soon as possible to account for himself. Otherwise there really will be no more this time. The damp-proofing on the main house is proving far more expensive than I imagined. As for his ideals, whatever they may or may not be, I don't see how they give him the right to wine and dine at everybody else's expense.

'He doesn't mention anything about your mother coming,' Fred said cautiously, studying the postmark. 'Or her breaking her arm.'

And he said: 'No, don't write back angrily. There's no point.'

Because Lorna was already up to eighty w.p.m., glaring at the screen.

'Really, what's the point?'

She went on writing, straight-backed in the new ergonomic chair they'd bought in the general hunt for tax write-offs.

'What's the point? Tell him about the weather. Tell him how cute Kirsty is. I don't know. Tell him maybe you did have a happy childhood after all. Who cares? It's all past and gone now.'

The keys pattered and squeaked as fluorescent letters appeared on a yellow screen in this two-bedroom suburban London flat.

'After all, you're always telling Garry not to blame everything on your parents.'

'But . . .'

The quite incredible, the utterly infuriating thing about her father was his imperviousness: his imperviousness to criticism, his imperviousness to anger, his imperviousness to love. You would speak, or for the last few years write, in one tone, and he would reply in quite another. He just didn't seem to have noticed what you had said nor even less the way you had said it. Being a father somehow made him less rather than more amenable than everybody else.

But having opened her mouth, Lorna found she didn't have the energy to explain any of this to Fred. And after a moment's huffing and puffing, she pressed the CANCEL command.

'He doesn't say anything about your mother coming,' Fred began again, but then thought it would be a mistake to gloat too openly when she was in this mood. So he asked: 'What about the article he said he put in?'

'I've thrown it away.'

'What did it say?'

'Oh, just stupid things.'

'What?'

'I thought you were so busy you didn't have time for my family, never mind provincial newspaper articles.'

For no reason they were arguing again.

'I'm making conversation. You're always complaining I never bother. Anyway, I always let you read all my post.'

She stood up. She was in her dressing gown he didn't like and there was still Kirsty to be got up and all the Saturday shopping to do. She started to walk out of the room.

'Lorna?'

'What the hell does it matter?'

'So why don't you just tell me?'

'It was about some pensioner in Fleetwood who got locked out of his house after an argument with his son and daughter-in-law about what to watch on TV. They told him to sleep in the tool-shed and the next morning he was frozen to death of course.'

'Nice.'

'I wouldn't even have let him have the tool-shed,' she shouted from where she was drawing the curtains in Kirsty's bedroom. 'Stupid old sod.'

'I just have these visions,' she carried on an hour later, bumping the buggy over a kerb. 'I have these visions of all of them in a pool of blood. I just can't get it out of my head.'

But Fred thought she shouldn't let it worry her. Seeing as what was the point of letting things worry you. No point. And if she kept on picking at her nails like that he would probably go insane himself before too long. He couldn't bear it when she picked round her nails.

Mariangela to Garry

April 9th   Milan

Caro Garry,

I am very happy for your decision. I have found already 4 language schools which say they need often teachers. My parents say that you can stay in my house first and then we find a small flat. Also there is much to do for the party which is very strong in Milan.

Do not ever lay apart your ambitions. I cannot love a man who does not have the ambitions. And you must not either abandon your family. Your family is the only people that love you only because you are yourself. My father is also very difficult, but we all tolerate ourselves. Remember it is the capitalism which has destroyed the family.

I come the Sunday May 24th. I arrive to Gatwick at the 14.00 local time, flight n⁰ VE7676.

> I expect your big kisses,
> MARIANGELA

PS. Why you use so many words that they are not in my dictionary (yobbos, cushy – are they bad words?).

Having given all but the £20 destined for Garry to Graham when they parted that morning, Mrs Baldwin was at rather a loss on stepping out at King's Cross. She hadn't been in London for anything more than a train or plane connection for upwards of fifteen years. She stood on the Marylebone Road under a thin drizzle wondering which direction might be which. Her right arm with the plaster was in a sling, the cat's basket in the crook of the elbow, her left held the battered holdall. And she asked a Negro, for old times' sake, the way to the Edgware Road. Directed to a bus-stop, she set off in what must then be the direction.

'And I just couldn't believe my own two eyes,' she was saying some hours later, drinking port.

'What?' Lorna asked, staring at her mother's hair.

Fred was still down at the station after Graham had called to tell them of Mother's arrival. So that Lorna had half her mind on an imminent irate phonecall.

Chiquita scrabbled at a curtain.

'Guess,' Mrs Baldwin said. She hadn't seen her daughter for five years, since they had eaten a hurried breakfast together in a Holiday Inn in Boston, to be precise, and Mr Baldwin had asked Fred how old he was and given him the business cards of various well-placed acquaintances in the local construction industry. But Mrs Baldwin didn't appreciate how much she herself had changed since then (starting with her hair), nor notice how much her daughter had. She just plunged straight in, having seen what she had.

'Guess.'

'I give up,' Lorna said. Quite simply it had been transformed from black to blonde. That was it. And with ringlets too.

The phone rang.

'I've waited five trains,' Fred began, dutifully, hopefully, 'and she wasn't on any of them.'

'Amanda!' Brenda Baldwin cried when her daughter hung up, it wasn't clear whether in disgust or elation. 'Can you just believe it. Amanda. As bold as brass. They didn't even seem ashamed of themselves.'

'In bed? Naughty!' Lorna added to the cat.

Apparently not. They had been drinking tea when Brenda arrived, as she always arrived, unannounced, feeling her son to be more in need of sorting out than her daughter. And this bony snob of a girl, as Mrs Baldwin thought of her, hadn't been embarrassed at all, despite all the business of the debts she'd insisted on being paid when they broke up and then marrying another man so shortly after the holiday in Algiers at Mr Silly Moneybags' expense. On the contrary, she'd sat quite composed and made polite conversation in her public-schoolgirl accent and showed no signs of moving to let a mother have a word with her son on her own, until Mrs Baldwin had lost her temper, gone down the stairs and spent the £20, or quite a lot of it, on a taxi.

'They wouldn't let me get the cat out of her box either. Allergic, she said. Poor thing. After all the train journey too.'

Brenda drained her port and because, she said, she hated to see nearly empty bottles cluttering the place, poured herself another glass, full. Which didn't quite, however, do the trick. Her finely wrinkled face glowed with animation, though it would have been difficult to guess what emotion was uppermost. At last she stood up and took off her coat, exposing a chunky winter sweater.

'Of course they're having sex,' she proceeded, as if answering a foolish question that hadn't actually been asked. 'Two ex-lovers don't sit around just drinking tea on their own in a flat all morning, do they? And then there'll be tears and pieces to pick up all over again, with him doing all the suffering of course. Like last time. What's a mother supposed to think.'

Lorna held Kirsty who followed her grandmother's extravagant gestures with undivided attention. Since the cat had disappeared in the kitchen now.

'The bed was unmade,' she added. And she said: 'He's a fool, like his father. A stupid fool.'

But Lorna was disturbed above all by the lack of any sense of occasion; as if Mother always visited Sunday afternoons; as if this ridiculous honey blonde didn't need some explanation; as if Garry and Amanda were a continuing saga of which they'd never missed an episode. Disconcertingly, she felt at once drawn to and repelled by this fierce source of energy that was her mother, as though under the influence of opposite poles of a magnet.

'Not a scrap of pride. Doesn't he realize he'll have her husband knocking on his door before he knows where he is? Why can't she leave him alone?'

Lorna put Kirsty on the floor. 'How did you break your wrist?' she asked.

Slipping on the stairs.

And after a moment's silence she suggested, 'Perhaps we should put some earth in a box, before it's too late.'

When Fred came back the mystery was how Graham had ever imagined that Mrs Baldwin must of necessity go to Liverpool Street, since it was well-known that most trains, and particularly the Intercitys, went to King's Cross. Everybody doubted Graham's intelligence, who had failed his first year exams at the university, and Mrs Baldwin shook her head and insisted that she had made him *promise* not to phone to say she was coming, since she didn't want anyone to put themselves out for her, not the tiniest bit; she didn't want them buying in special food or preparing special meals or making up new beds for her. She was just a mother visiting her children, she would sleep on the couch.

And she kissed Fred and embraced him and thanked him profusely (but she had made Graham *promise*) and congratulated him on all this success he was having and said he was her only son who wasn't a complete fool. But they really should take the handles off this cupboard, because children were little demons for hurting themselves on cupboard handles, and if only she'd brought the potty Frank had rediscovered in the back-room the other day that they'd used for the twins, with the giraffe's neck to hold on to, so much better than this Mothercare thing, nobody would ever want to widdle in that, but she hadn't imagined she'd be coming down to London, since . . .

'Four hours,' Fred hissed in Lorna's ear when they were alone together a moment in the kitchen. 'Four fucking hours. Wasted.'

Before nine the following morning, Brenda was at Garry's again, bringing the leftovers of Lorna's shepherd's pie of the evening before, plus the five pounds fifty-five that remained now after a surprisingly expensive bus trip.

With no duties at the Centre that morning, Garry had to be woken up: and watched her as she made tea and washed up and wiped across the various stained and crumb-studded surfaces. Then while he drank and ate the pastry she had bought for him in the ABC below, she rehearsed, once again, using the same gestures as the evening before, the whole ridiculous situation with his brother Graham, which required, she couldn't help feeling, the most immediate intervention. So much so that Mrs Baldwin had already, without realizing it, changed all her plans. And hopefully would change Garry's too.

'So first he tries to put me in a hotel. Really. But I wasn't having any of that. I'd far rather sleep on the floor I said and have him keep the money, since he'll need it if he's ever going to marry and buy a house, won't he? Heaven knows, he's always saying he needs money. And I am his mother.'

Garry would have liked to have turned on the radio for the now daily pre-by-election round-up. His future perhaps being at stake. He fidgeted with his plate.

'It's not as if I haven't slept on the floor before in my time. Anyway, it turned out he has two nice little rooms on the top floor of an Indian's house, except, he says, that the Indian has strictly forbidden him to have guests for the night for insurance reasons, or some such story, quite silly. And no animals. So I went down and spoke to the wife and she was perfectly charming, really quite a delightful person, the way Indians usually are in my experience, and of course she said there was no problem whatso-ever about my staying as many nights as I wanted; in fact they had a put-you-up her husband would take up for me, just as soon as he got in. And some scraps for the cat. Really, she couldn't have been kinder. I expect they only told him not to have people stay in case he had girls every night. Very wise of them with all the things there are around these days.'

Mrs Baldwin stopped and puckered her mouth. She caressed the teapot a moment before topping up his cup.

'Which settled that.' She bent down now to pluck a grape pip from the carpet, slipping it into her corduroy trouser pocket.

'And so?' Garry found himself asking, as Lorna had the evening before.

'And so?' she demanded, her face suddenly clouding dramatically, in what was at the same time, or almost, both real and parodied anger. For this was how Mrs Baldwin was, and experiences perhaps only took on any shape at all for her when later she plunged into the telling of them and found the mood they needed to catch a listener's attention. Just for the moment this mood was indignation. Her pressed lips and finely hooked nose spoke worlds of it. Only the careless vanity of those blonde ringlets seemed from another planet.

'And so at exactly six-thirty he gets in the car his own stupid parents gave him, didn't they, and goes off to have his dinner with Sophy.'

'And you didn't feel like going?'

'Feel like it? I wasn't bloody-well invited, was I? A mother goes to visit her son, a mother, after years abroad, and the first thing he does is disappear off to his girlfriend's. And it's not as if he'd met her last week, is it? He can't not go now, he says, because they're expecting him to bring some shopping, and he can't invite me because it wouldn't be fair on them at such short notice. I ask you, with all the meals I've prepared in my life at no notice whatsoever.'

'And when in fact,' Garry remarked, 'you arrived fairly early in the morning and he could perfectly well have called them then.'

'Exactly,' cried Brenda, to whom this now occurred for the first time. 'Exactly. He could have called them at ten o'clock if he already knew he was supposed to be going there in the evening. Couldn't he? You'd have thought if she's so marvellous he'd be dying to introduce me.'

'He does the same thing to me on the phone. He . . .'

But now Garry noticed a paper towel he had used to masturbate into the previous evening to get himself to sleep. Right there on

the bedside table. Did the room smell? He pushed his chair back
to get to the window.

'So I spent the evening with the Sumrays, these Indians. Very
nice people, really. Very good food, if you've got the stomach for
it. Anyway, they'd been in Sudan, so we had a good chat about
Africa. They'd actually been to the hospital your father put up in
Khartoum when their second baby was born. Fancy, I . . .'

Garry came back from the window, reflecting that it would be
too much of a give-away just to pick the thing up, and anyway it
might still be dreadfully sticky. There were plenty of other things
for the room to smell of.

And inevitably a man masturbated when his girlfriend lived in
Italy and then being around Amanda so much. What did you
expect?

' . . . until half past 11, if you please. He could have got away
earlier, don't you think, with his own mother visiting, but no
there was a spy serial or something he didn't want to miss on
television, because it was so complicated that if he missed an
episode he'd never be able to catch up with it again. And
then you know what's the first thing he does when we're back
upstairs?'

'Hogs the bathroom,' was all Garry could think of.

'He turns on Radio Two.'

'Oh.' This seemed only mildly unforgivable.

'And then his phone rings and guess who it is?'

'What?' Garry hadn't realized Graham actually possessed his
own phone in his own room. For a moment he was thrown.

'Guess.'

'But why didn't he tell us he had one? I mean . . .'

Mrs Baldwin made a gesture of impatience.

Was he afraid of being called reverse charges?

'Sophy!'

'Ah, he'd forgotten his umbrella.'

'She was phoning to check that he'd *got back safely*, I ask you,
all one and a half miles of it.'

At which point, again following the motions which had raised
Fred's only laugh the previous evening, Brenda Baldwin began
to act out the scene.

'So your brother grabs the phone quick as quick and immediately throws himself on the bed.' Which Brenda now did, raising an imaginary receiver from the bedside table with her plastered hand.

But Garry didn't find this funny at all. His handsome eyebrows rose in alarm.

'And begins to talk in a low voice, lovey dovey, lovey dovey, kissy kiss kiss, hedgy hog, rabsy rab, and all sorts of the most babyish rubbish I've ever heard. Poetry too. When he'd already spent the whole flaming evening with her.'

'No,' Garry gasped.

'Yes. So thinking I was doing him a favour, obviously, I hurried over to the radio and turned it off, didn't I? But, "No, no, what are you doing? You can't turn it off," and he rushes across the room, turns it on again and carries it back to the bed and plonks it down right by the telephone.'

Now apparently represented by the wank rag.

For Mrs Baldwin had scuttled across the room and back, fetching *Software Made Simple* as an imaginary radio. She made a great show now of making herself comfy with her plastercast in his dirty sheets, then leaned over the table to adjust the volume on the broken spine of the book. Obviously she was having a whale of a time.

'And so he goes on with his sweet nothings and that wet music in the background for half a hour. HALF AN HOUR! When he hadn't had so much as a word for me. I would never have believed it, I thought he was such a serious, practical boy. And then the same story, exactly the same, every single evening, all five evenings I was there! His mother who he hasn't seen for heaven knows how many years. I mean, I wouldn't mind so much if they were planning to get married, or if they'd just met, you could understand it, but this is ridiculous. She's just leading him up the garden path. It's been going on for ages. She's 35. Lovey dovey dovey, going nowhere. His whole life will have frittered away and he won't even have noticed it. He'll never have a family!'

Garry simply walked over, unstuck the crumpled piece of paper from the plastic surface and chucked it in the waste basket by the desk.

'The only time we went out together was to see the place she was born, if you please. Really. In some village somewhere. He took photographs. And it was raining. I couldn't believe it. Your father may be a fool, but he was never quite so much of a fool as that. He knew that love was supposed to lead somewhere, even if he did try his best to get out of it afterwards.'

Mrs Baldwin sighed, remembering now that she hadn't as yet put forward her plan.

'Speaking of which,' she said, 'I've been on to Mr Scrooge every day about you and he says he'll be sending something soon.'

Garry didn't enlighten her about what had already arrived in the letter to Lorna. Finding himself standing, he considered his face a moment in the mirror. Which was always reassuring. Someday surely he must arrive. And he went over to hug her. 'Poor Mum,' he crooned. 'The way we treat you.'

'Your fly needs sewing, love,' she said. And taking back two pounds of the five fifty-five, Mrs Baldwin went out to buy needle and thread. It was an African woman the other side of the counter, which reminded her again of Khartoum and waking in the night in the airport hotel when Frank had tripped over the suitcase he was trying to pack in the dark. While she sewed up the fly she would think how best to put it to Garry.

In a small hospital consulting room Fred was telling a bearded urologist how often he and his wife 'had intercourse'.

Anything from twice a day to twice a month.

The urologist had pushed a finger in his anus, inspected his gland and felt his testicles.

'It could just be stress,' he said. 'Are you under any particular strain?'

Fred replied truthfully that he always felt himself to be under strain. Who didn't in this day and age? And almost took the opportunity to tell the man about his job.

'Any particular strain?' The consultant consciously enjoyed turning down conversational gambits.

Fred wasn't entirely sure. He said no.

'Or then again, it could be something more serious.' And stroking his beard, the urologist began to scribble down a series of tests. Fred watched his white cuff jerk across the pad:

Sperm Test
Urine Test
Blood Test
Stamey's Test.

'And if none of those show up anything we'll try a urography, okay?'

With these new words and worries to help him through the day, Fred returned to 'Metaphor as Narrative Structure'. But before going home he popped into the library and looked up Stamey's Test in the *Britannica*. It could hardly have been more depressing.

Mr Baldwin to Graham

April 13th

Broughton Street
Cleveleys

PRIVATE AND CONFIDENTIAL

Dear son,

You will excuse my writing to you at your office, but Raymond appears to have stolen my address book with your box number so I had little alternative. Obviously with Mother there you won't be down at the weekend and I needed to get in touch at once.

To be brief, I am writing to ask if you could loan me a thousand pounds for a very short period. The fact is that much of my money is still tied up in bonds and will not be available for some months, while the pension is proving insufficient to cover the cost of much needed building materials for the house and of supporting two good-for-nothing sons (if only they were all like you!). I am sure that when you think of all the things parents do for children over the years, you won't be averse. I would ask Fred and Lorna, but I don't want to go outside the most immediate family.

Not a word of this to Mother obviously. Tell her that Raymond has calmed down again now and I think she could safely return, though there is no hurry and she certainly deserves a long break. I hope you are looking after her well, as one only has one mother in this world, and of course she has suffered a great deal with Raymond. Perhaps this is why she frequently seems more than a little mad herself.

I trust all is going smoothly at the office and promotion is at hand.

Best wishes,
FATHER

Postscript: I am grateful for all the interest you take in Raymond and in his future and should you have any constructive proposals to offer, nobody would be more delighted to take them up than your father. Example of my difficulties: yesterday I received a bill from Heffers in Cambridge for £170 worth of books on physics and linguistics which Raymond had already received and written all over so as to make them unreturnable. What am I supposed to do about that? Apparently he believes the world revolves around some mysterious code which he is determined to crack.

Other small problems for you to consider while we're about it:

1. He often doesn't wash and never flushes;
2. He threatens me physically if I don't give him money for a) chocolate, b) letters (invariably sent Swiftair or Recorded Delivery), c) five or six scientific/pornographic magazines a week, d) photographic equipment he never uses;
3. I have frequent difficulty moving from one room to the next because he insists on locking the doors and not letting me out until it is 'time';
4. He almost never leaves me alone for more than five minutes since he apparently fears that a group of Israeli/CIA agents are out to get him; in the meantime he harangues me with political arguments of the utmost futility;
5. The authorities have now confirmed that he can't be forced into 'care' and will continue to be treated on an outpatients' basis: that is, a young and rather dowdy Blackpool girl comes for an hour twice a week to talk to him. He explains his support for Gaddafi and being a socialist of the silliest kind, she agrees. On leaving last time she told me she thought he was becoming 'more

stable'. To make matters worse one continually has to pretend one doesn't want him in 'care', otherwise they think every story you tell is invented to that end. In short, I find myself in a stalemate position which I would be most grateful if you could resolve.

One of the advantages, Lorna had noticed, of having her mother stay was that Graham had stopped calling. Today, with Mrs Baldwin at Garry's again, and finding herself unable to get to grips with 'Crackling Hot', the third album, she decided, because she couldn't seem to get it out of her head somehow, to use the time so frequently wasted on the line to Leeds to write the definitive reply to her father.

No sooner had she started, however, than she found her eyes pricking with tears.

And she was aware, as always, of how many different ways there were of starting a letter, or indeed anything, so that she paused a few moments, reviewing alternatives, as if at a crossroads in a maze. Which opening would take her to where she wanted to arrive, and by way of the things she wanted to say? Why was it bothering her so much? She cancelled three lines and began again, though equally unsatisfactorily.

Dear Dad,

How can you write me such a long letter without even mentioning the key event, the only news: Mum's breaking her wrist? I don't understand you. Or do you compartmentalize the family and channel news about as it suits you? I remember speaking to Graham last year and being amazed to discover that despite having been on the phone to you he hadn't heard about Garry trying to kill himself, didn't even know he was in hospital.

And why do you have to write to me in that tone? I'm sorry if I offended you, but I really did mean well. Perhaps I just get impatient sometimes because it all seems so difficult and I'm so afraid for you and Mother with Raymond, so that there seems no place for silly sentimentalism of the old-cruise-menus-wrapped-up-in-tissues kind. And then because one tries and tries to think why it happened and continually comes up with a complete blank, tries and tries to see how the future will be, how the damage can be limited, where one's own responsibilities lie and so on, and again the blank is complete. What will become of Raymond? When he is 40, 50, 60? Who will take care of him? One of us children? Mum told me he absolutely refuses to pick up the dole because he considers it demeaning and feels it's your responsibility to pay for everything. And yet he isn't mad enough to be forced into a hospital. It seems the State wins both ways.

Of course I do have many happy memories of childhood. Mum and I have been laughing over them since she's been here. I remember all of us packed in a Morris Minor with fish and chips to see the Illuminations; I remember when you took us to the Arab bazaar in Beirut and Mum bargained and bargained with the man selling cloth till he got up and left in disgust, and then it turned out she hadn't understood the exchange rate and she wanted to run after him. I remember in Ecuador when you took me and Raymond on a tour of all the hospitals and the Landrover got stuck in the mud and we had to get some donkeys to pull it out. You let us drink from your whisky flask when it suddenly got cold.

These were happy times and we had fun, but somehow — and I don't say this to be ungrateful, Dad, I really don't — somehow my overall impression when I think back, is of gloom and anxiety. I have always imagined that this was because you were so often away and Mother so often on the verge of a nervous breakdown. But perhaps I am wrong. Perhaps I simply have a natural disposition for gloom and doom. Perhaps it's me should see an analyst. One thing though: I always felt that it was terribly terribly important to do well at school and so on, and I know Raymond did too, because you were always so proud and enthusiastic when we did well, and so scornful of everybody who did badly, particularly if they happened to be our friends. But then there were always such obstacles, changes of language, changes of curriculum and so on. I remember despairing of ever learning South American history with all their battles and revolutions that didn't seem to lead anywhere at all. And then I felt rather inferior to tell the truth, with Raymond being so bright at everything and you calling him the hope of the Baldwins and talking to all your friends about him. I remember how awed I was when he built that laser thing at the American school in Quito and they invented the special prize for him. And I was so determined to see good marks on my report and hear you say how much brighter we were than Trilling's children and who was the other man? the project manager, Billingsworth, or Billingsgate. I appreciate now that a lot of your enthusiasm for school and belief in end-of-term exams was part of the conditioning of your generation and to do with having worked your way up on your own from nothing like you did, but when I was in my teens I must admit it often seemed just a strategy for trying to get Mother to agree to send us away to some expensive private school where we wouldn't be in your way, so that I suppose I started to feel resentful as well as anxious; I wanted to show you we could do well without leaving home (I utterly loathed my year with the nuns in Birkenhead). So studying became my raison d'être, as if only by getting good results could I keep being part of the family, and my sense of gloom was of because of how impossible it would be to be top of the class in French as I had been in English, or again in Spanish as I had been in French.

I'll tell you a funny story. I actually stopped studying in America more than a year before I told you I had. I never started doing my PhD at all. I was just so afraid of telling you I didn't want to go on, especially since I was finally on scholarship and it wasn't costing you anything. I didn't know how to break it to you. That's how much influence your enthusiasm for schools and careers had on me. I had a crisis – something to do with finding Raymond like that, and something to do with meeting Fred – I suddenly couldn't see any point in it all, 15th century Spanish writers, I lost interest. And when I think of myself as an adult now, a grown-up person, I somehow date my grownupness from the moment when I stopped believing in what I was doing and pulled out of my 'academic career' without telling you. Because it was the first real decision I had taken on my own.

As for a career, I don't really know whether I want one any more. I understand what you said about why you worked abroad, but is career really the only channel for self-realization, the only way of achieving self-esteem? I do so hope not. Fred is on your side naturally; he lives his career, the only difference being that his wife has to have one too, otherwise he couldn't be quite sure whether he respected her or not. And so I do this job ghostwriting this silly book, more as a sop really to old ambitions, to Fred, and so as not to feel I've burnt my boats entirely, than because I like or want it. My heart's not in it at all. Which is dismal, isn't it?

Although it's not as if I had a passionate desire to build up a big family either. My heart sinks when I think how Mum still wanted more children even after the twins. You should count yourself lucky you had the mumps, frankly, or God knows how many postal orders you'd have to mail every week. I don't think I'm a good mother myself. I resent Kirsty a great deal of the time and spoil her the rest, so I completely forgive whatever your own attitude to us was. I constantly have the feeling she's pulling me away from somewhere else, yet can't bear to be without her for very long. I give her too many sweets and hit her too often. Yesterday I even hit her across the face and felt guilty about it for hours, which meant chocolates and tedious games in the garden. Is this an experience one wants to repeat? It made me laugh you quoting that 'Faber' thing, Father; it's such a wonderful, straightforward, pompous image: each of us like blacksmiths fashioning our own destinies, as if there were only a few basic obvious shapes to choose from, pokers, horseshoes, swords and shields. And I know it's totally banal, because one gets bored with people who moan about not knowing what to do, but I wouldn't know what shape to choose, nor how to go about the fashioning. I think our lives are much more the combined result of impulse and merest chance, which explains why I'm so anxious perhaps, anxious about what others might do, anxious about what I might do myself. In fact, look at you and Raymond; you can do all the fashioning you like, but if destiny lumps you with a problem like that . . . or what if I had a handicapped child? One of Fred's aunties had a mongoloid. The funny thing is how friends are always admiring me for being so busy and purposeful, when the truth is I spend half my time staring out of the window here, trying to decide if the trickles on the pane are drizzle or condensation (actually, if you ever come and visit that's a problem you might be able to solve for me).

So have you learnt your lesson, Dad? Don't write such critical letters to Lorna, otherwise you could find her baring her heart again, and then God knows what might come out . . . !!!

Still, I do think it's worth saying these things now, because we're obviously going to meet again fairly soon after all these years, and they have to be got out of the way. Otherwise what kind of relationship can we have, now I'm no longer your clever daughter at school you used to boast about?

Hugs

LORNA

PS. Perhaps all I'm trying to say is, you can't just get mad at me because I don't see the family as you'd like me to. For me, that's how it was.

In the psychoanalyst's study, Raymond was explaining his Oedipus complex in great and gloating detail. His mother, he said, was a big-breasted, handsome woman who often went about in a careless state of undress, so that as a boy he frequently saw her breasts and cunt. She did this on purpose to stimulate him, obviously. While his father was away, which was at least half of the time, he used to sleep in Mother's bed and she often rubbed up against him and sometimes masturbated herself with her hands when she thought he was asleep. When Father came back and he didn't want to change beds, Father would beat him violently. But this beating only stimulated him, and often, once Father had gone to sleep, his mother would come to his bed and wank him off.

'None of this is true,' Frank Baldwin interrupted. 'He gets it out of psychology books to fool you with. He has a stack of them.'

The analyst, who had a strong Scottish accent, sighed, as well he might in this squalid study. 'It is not documentary truth we are interested in, so far as it exists. It is the way things are remembered.'

'But it might be as well to establish what actually happened if you want to appreciate how distorted what he's saying is.'

'Unfortunately,' said the analyst, 'we have no way of knowing what actually happened.'

'Well not that, anyway, I can assure you. And it's not remembered,' Mr Baldwin went on. 'It's invented, on purpose to spite me. Which would seem to be an important distinction if you ask me.'

Raymond smiled. With an air of condescension. Having an infinitely superior knowledge in this particular field. And jingling keys in his pocket he began to explain how his father had begun to go to brothels and his mother became very upset and would cry and say things like, 'What about me? I've got a cunt too,' in front of all the children. So that one night Raymond had offered to make love to her, and she . . .

'Do we have to?' Mr Baldwin interrupted.

The analyst, who saw this threadbare carpet in Blackpool very much as a kind of purgatory before moving further south, asked: 'Perhaps you'd like to tell me how you see your son's relationships with women.'

In his armchair, the small, stout man had both hands behind his bald head. Not knowing in particular what to say, for he had long since given up seriously pondering his son's condition, he nevertheless spoke with confidence:

'Well, towards his mother he's extremely dictatorial. She's always slaved for him so he treats her like a slave. He complains if his food's not ready, or if there isn't enough and so on, and frequently threatens her over the most trivial details. Sometimes he is actually physically violent. A couple of weeks ago he twisted her arm so hard she broke her wrist, though I don't think he meant to go that far. Hard to tell. On the other hand, although she does slave for him, she's very intolerant over certain things, like him not getting his hair cut, or wiping his mouth on the table cloth, or wearing clean shirts. She insists on keeping up appearances, for his own sake, she says, though obviously it's partly a question of personal pride. Quite often they shout at each other.' He paused. 'They fight and then of course at the end of it I have to hear that it's all my fault for some reason or other.'

The analyst nodded at what was after all just the run of his particular mill: 'Other women?'

Mr Baldwin said that he didn't know that his son had, or had had any relationships with other women. Except maybe for the occasional prostitute when they were in Algeria. Come to think of it, he had proposed marriage to one and they had had quite a job explaining to the girl's family that he was disturbed, because of course so many of the girls out there wanted to marry Europeans to get out. Mr Baldwin thought for a moment. 'Then of course he went through a period in his early teens of reading a lot of romantic poetry, which I think gave him some rather silly ideas about women.'

'Ah.'

'Led him to expect too much perhaps.'

'But no formative first girlfriend. Nothing like that?'

Raymond sat crosslegged deep in a green armchair, his lower knee jerking steadily with the bounce of his toes. He did not appear to be especially agitated. If anything faintly amused. At his father's inadequacy. Or perhaps it was just an expression on his face.

'There was a woman in Quito.'

'A girlfriend?'

'No, it was a woman in his school, a teacher. She must have been at least 32, 33. Raymond was around 17. And then she was married with children I think, I can't remember the exact details. Anyway, she pestered him for a couple of months. He used to visit her every afternoon after school. Then he stopped going and she started telephoning all the time and writing and even visiting. Seeing as Raymond was shy and obviously upset about it, I had quite a row with her and told her to leave him alone. She was a rather unintelligent, hysterical kind of woman. But when Raymond set off for the States a couple of months later, to go to the university, she turned up at the airport and made a terrible fuss, weeping and screaming, you know the kind of thing, typical Latin exhibitionism.'

'And what did you make of all this?'

Mr Baldwin shrugged his shoulders, dropping his hands to his knees. Despite the fact that all tests were negative, there was very clearly something very wrong with his gut. Such a fierce cramp.

'I thought: the usual problems one has with women as a young man. I didn't delve into it too deeply, frankly, as I tend to believe that everybody has a right to their own private lives. Raymond was doing brilliantly at school and we were very happy with him. And then of course I had other things on my mind. I was in charge of building three hospitals. I thought perhaps he had had sex with her, which wasn't entirely a bad thing as an initiation, but then didn't want it any more. Which was also no bad thing.'

'And your version?' The analyst turned to Raymond, who was examining carefully manicured nails.

'It's all news to me. I've never heard of the woman.'

There was a short silence.

'I'll tell you one thing though,' Raymond said, leaning forward and with the air of giving the analyst some useful information at last, 'in Europe they fuck you right enough, but in America they really castrate you. Really.

'Because of the Jews,' he added. 'It's all part of the formula.'

Mr Baldwin checked his watch. Just five more minutes of this nonsense, then a cup of tea and perhaps a brisk walk on the pier to set his stomach to rights.

'To eradicate the manhood that lies at the heart of Islam,' Raymond was intoning. The waxy smile on his face had a sphinx-like serenity to it, as impenetrable now to the analyst as it had always been to this young man's father. For there seemed no question here of facial expression illuminating whatever lay within, according to the normal human semaphore, however imprecise that might sometimes be. Nor was it a matter of cunning disguise. But as if, bereft of proper instruction, the features, the very skin and muscle flesh that lay over heavy bone behind, were arranging and rearranging themselves in more or less conventional patterns, some only half remembered, as best they might.

'He's been pro-Arab,' Mr Baldwin explained, 'ever since his sister married an American. When we went to Algeria.'

'I see.' The analyst pondered, but was consciously filling in now. The only thing he honestly saw were the two black hands of an electric clock closing to mark the midday hour.

And indeed fifteen minutes later father and son were in an amusement arcade out along North Pier. At Raymond's insistence, they played a complicated form of Pacman together and actually enjoyed themselves for a few moments without noticing.

Graham to Mr Baldwin

April 20th

Dear Father,

I enclose a cheque for a thousand pounds as requested (I also feel the family should pull together). Given that I had to remove the money from a high-rate investment account, however, with the loss of three months' interest, I hope you will agree to repay me that (£27.25), plus an equivalent interest rate of 9%. As I said before, Sophy and I are trying to save up for a flat and every little bit counts. I'd be grateful if you could repay me inside the year; do tell me if you can't.

I'm also enclosing a couple of our company's publications which you might be interested in seeing.

Mother has moved on to Lorna and Fred's as she was eager to see them.

Best regards,
GRAHAM

Re: Raymond: the following steps seem essential:
1. Application for act of interdiction of civil rights, and in particular of the right to administer money;
2. Application for tax relief and disabled person's pension on the grounds of mental ill-health;
3. Sale of main house, with proceeds from which you:
   a) purchase a small and comfortable flat for your-selves;
   b) set up an investment fund to pay Raymond a small weekly allowance (to be administered by yourself);

4. Give Raymond the Broughton Street flat to live in.

I hope you'll find those ideas useful.

Yours again,
GRAHAM

encs. Cheque = £1000
'Insurance for the Over-Sixties'
'How to Make a Will'

Had Fred had more time at his disposal, or not felt he had so little, he might have enjoyed the opportunity of observing his mother-in-law in action. She was at once so modern and so old-fashioned, alternately so determined and so despondent, hot and cold, aggressive and passive. Returning from Garry's, she would say things that would have left his own Unitarian, rather conservative New England mother flabbergasted. 'That boy just lets himself get pulled along by his prick,' she complained. 'You'd think he had a ring through his foreskin, never mind his ear. You know what he came out with today? He says, "As soon as I think there's anything between us again, I'll stop seeing her." Would you believe it? When he's got a photograph of the girl half naked by the bed, hasn't he, and probably tosses off over it when she isn't there.'

This sort of talk disturbed and disorientated Fred, who was used to assuming a slightly unctious, rather puritan stance in the presence of a more or less staid older generation who couldn't be expected to share the same unconcern for taboos as his contemporaries. Even Mrs Baldwin's boisterous manner of playing with, indeed monopolizing Kirsty, had something rather racy and overly modern about it: 'Who's got a beautiful little bumsy wumsy?' she would shout, splashing water with her one good hand over the giggling child in the bath. 'Who's going to get the men going? Isn't she? Isn't she? With these little titsies!'

But then again, Mrs Baldwin would frequently express opinions that even his own mother had successfully grown out of in the general trend of sixties enlightenment. Why didn't Graham find a nice sensible young girl from a good sensible family and marry her and settle down before it was too late, instead of going on interminably with this effete upper-class fairy nobody had ever met who apparently studied poetry by post and seemed to be having her period all the time, if it wasn't already menopause. 'Your father wrote inviting her mum and dad to visit us in Cleveleys and they never even bothered to write back. Not so much as a word.' And why did Garry have to go scuttling after foreigners when London was full of wholesome English girls ready to drool over a handsome bloke like him, kids around 19 or 20 who would be glad to do what he told them and would never give him a hard time and were still young enough to have good children? No, instead he had to run after a wop, and a medical student at that, who would never settle down and have kids with the ambitions she probably had.

'Poor girl though,' Mrs Baldwin added of another person she had never met, 'with that Amanda sharking about.'

She sat beside a fresh bottle of port in corduroy trousers that had bright patches expertly introduced in the crotch to accommodate a behind that had grown heavier with passing years yet would still have been perfectly respectable were it not for those bright patches shouting attention – but the material was too good and warm to be thrown out. 'Do you know where I bought these, Lorna? Guess how long ago. Before Sudan!' No, she was determined, quite determined he wasn't going back to that snobby scrubber Amanda – 'over my dead and decomposing body' – she would separate them physically. Absolutely determined. And five minutes later she was despondent, she was utterly despondent, because all her boys were fools, the kind of women they went for, and there was nothing anyone could do about it, nothing; it was just a cross she had to bear. She fell silent for five minutes. But not surprising really, not surprising given the fool they had for a father. Which reminded her she must tell the old skinflint to send Graham £100 to renew his car tax. How could the boy be expected to pay taxes like that when they hadn't even taken him on properly yet? And with Mr Selfish just throwing away £15 a month on that monstrous television. It was the end it really was. Though he only used the car to go the mile and a half to see this bloodsucking girlfriend. Why couldn't he see sense when it was stuck in his face?

In the despondent moods her face would grow dark with

misery. The colour about the eyes really did change, until 'glower-ing' was the only adjective that might describe this cocktail of shadow and energy that brooded in her fine hawkish features. She alternated long sullen silences, perhaps a whole evening, with periods of unrestrained garrulity.

Yes, if only she had been around all the time they were at the university forming these disastrous friendships, if only she had been there to help instead of gallivanting round the world with Mr Itchy-Feet Globetrotter who could never get enough of places he despised. She had certainly failed as a parent there. She could and should have saved them.

Though he had retired too soon, that was for sure. Since he was so obviously incapable of doing anything in retirement apart from sitting on his backside getting fatter and sending up his blood pressure with all his coffee and cigarettes so he could then go and get it measured at the doctor's and come home and tell her he'd been told to take it easy. The main house would never be finished, they would die in squalor in the Broughton Street flat, the laughing-stock of all their neighbours.

It was all that travelling had sent Raymond mad of course, it was obvious.

And she said: 'Others that stayed back in Cleveleys are well enough off now. They've got their nice houses, their extensions. Your Uncle Harry's done marvellously for himself. He's put that pebble stuff on, you know; makes it look like a cottage. Only Mr Ambitious who went away to make his fortune comes back with his pockets hanging out. And whining about a pain in his belly into the bargain, doing nothing but put his feet up from morning till night.'

For the next half hour Mrs Baldwin roamed moodily about the flat, picking things up and putting them down, lifting curtains to stare out of windows through her own disgusted reflection. And if she noticed, seeing herself there, the odd contrast between the implied vanity of that permed and tinted hair and then these shabby clothes preserved beyond reason with only penny pinching in mind, she saw no cause to feel ashamed, nor to make any adjustments to the odd impression of raffishness the combination lent her. She bit her bottom lip, muttering fiercely under her breath, scratching at a drip of the wrong paint on the windowsill, turning up a ragged sweater cuff. Until finally she swivelled round and sat down abruptly in the middle of the living room carpet where Kirsty was playing with her toys. 'Give Granny a kiss, lovey.' Her voice was almost a croak. 'Go on, give us a kiss.' The little girl obliged. So that after a moment the two began to play a kind of pat-a-cake, exciting the cat who jumped up to scratch. The little girl shrieked. Granny tickled. And then, as always when it came, the change of mood was immediate and complete. Brenda Baldwin was bright again. Chuckling. Talking away as if she had never broken off.

'You have to laugh though, the old fraud. Every other morning at the doctor's. Tests, tests and more tests. His guts, his back, his heart. Piss in a pot. Shit in a dish. And then you should see it,' she said, shifting up a gear, 'when he *does* do something. I don't know which is worse. The other day, for instance, he decides to make a start on the garden. So out he goes after breakfast in his suit and tie. His suit and tie! I ask you. And hat! "I'm not going to stop dressing respectably just because I've retired, not me." You know how self-important he always is. Mr Stuffed-Shirt, boss the fuzzywuzzies around. "Not me," he says. "I'm not going to pieces now I've retired." You could hear the neighbours giggling. Mrs Ratcliffe parting the curtains. So there he is, standing in a complete wilderness, weeds up to his waist, a fork in his hands' – Mrs Baldwin kissed Kirsty putting her aside and began to act out the scene in their front room – 'looking like he should be on the way to the office. Mr Natty Snappy' – she twisted and stretched her neck as if easing a tight tie and then began a series of digging motions. 'Except that after ten minutes, of course, he's getting a bit hot, isn't he, and so off comes his hat and he fights his way over to the plum tree and hangs it on a twig.'

Mrs Baldwin wiped her brow with the back of the plastered wrist and pulled a grim face.

Fred looked at his watch, snapped shut a book, tried and failed to catch Lorna's eye.

'And all the way back to where he's digging, through weeds, bracken, brambles, rubbish, the place is a complete tip. Somebody even chucked an old toilet over by the fence in the corner. Ten minutes more work, and then, hot again, off comes his jacket. Back to the plum tree. He folds it up carefully and hangs it over a branch, all neat and tidy, you know how he is, like an old woman, "I'm not going to bring down me standards, not me." And back to work. Five minutes later it's his tie, isn't it? What is this? I shout from the house, an executive striptease, or what?'

She burst out laughing, delighting Kirsty. 'You're a little scally-wag,' she tweaked the child's nose, 'that's what you are.'

Perhaps he could do the dishes himself, Fred considered. Other-wise they would still be there in the morning. Late start to the day. That critical half hour.

And nobody had emptied the cat litter either.

'Until he goes and plunges down the fork, doesn't he, and "Ow, shit, my fucking foot!"' Mrs Baldwin shrieked, loud enough to have Fred worrying about their neighbours. ' "My fucking, buggering foot!" You can imagine how respectable people think you are after using language like that, I said, if you . . .'

Part of what disturbed Fred was not so much the time slipping away, not so much even the fact that after almost a month here (the Easter holiday come and gone, wasted) Mrs Baldwin had not as yet allowed herself to be drawn into giving an approximate date for her departure – no, what disturbed him was the way Lorna, while at first criticizing her mother in private with him, now seemed so happy to be close to her, and so perfectly at ease with this endless, futile and obviously exaggerated monologue, giggling like a teenager, occasionally throwing in an encouraging question, apparently content to let Kirsty hear the worst language and keeping the whole family up until past midnight despite a day's work to be done tomorrow – as if somehow hypnotized by this older woman's crazy energy. And quite apart from the language, he was surprised and confused to see how at home Lorna was with her mother's general coarseness (she seemed quite a different person). For whereas racy talk was fine between man and wife, or young people in general, it seemed out of place, or at least it did to Fred who had always observed a certain decorum at home, for a mother and daughter to discuss, for example, the father's sexual prowess in front of the daughter's husband. Himself.

'Every night.' Brenda Baldwin was laughing so hard she was holding her sides. 'He's a devil really. You have to love him.'

'No! Come on.'

'Yes, I swear to God. He gives me a walloping big nudge with his knee, and I say to him, there can't be anything wrong with your guts then, duckie, if that's what you want. And he . . .'

'She's full of bullshit,' Fred said later, when Lorna was still chuckling over this in bed. He would have liked to have asserted his authority in some way.

'You're just jealous,' she said.

'Leave off. I bet they do it once a year. You're always saying they're always arguing.'

'That doesn't stop him being a randy old bastard, does it? Or even mean that they don't love each other,' she went on. 'In their own way. I mean, they've stayed together all these years. And she's such a warm person, you must see that.'

'Staying together doesn't mean anything at all. It's just a question of economics and inertia. What would she be now if she didn't have her place in the family? Obviously she stays with him.'

'She was an excellent seamstress once.'

And Lorna said: 'I like to think of them making love still. It's more than we manage most of the time.'

There was the breathing silence of a couple on their backs in their bedroom. Projected through the curtains a crack of light stretched and flitted back and forth across the ceiling as somebody tried to get a car away from others parked too close.

'Mrs Innes,' Fred said when the car stalled, and he half laughed: 'That was a pretty funny story though about your dad trying to sneak out of the Khartoum hotel.'

'Typical Dad, tripping over his knickers.'

They listened to Mrs Innes making her nightly move from kerb to garage.

'Still,' Lorna said, 'he's had plenty of other opportunities and never took them. I mean, he could run for it now if he wanted, couldn't he?'

'Probably thinks it's too late now.'

'But layers of affection must build up, mustn't they? It's so cynical to think it must just be economics. They had such a romantic courtship, I read some of the letters once, real heart-throb love-letters, and then waiting those years when he was in Germany, it must leave something. Not to mention all the emotional investment in the children. Think of it, four of them! God!'

'And layers of resentment,' Fred said.

And Fred said: 'What pisses me though, is the way she goes on and on for hours and hours telling stories and planning how she's going to sort out Garry and Graham, completely obsessed, typical behaviour of the frustrated possessive older woman, and then never says so much as a word about the main family problem, which is Raymond. We don't know anything about how he's really behaving, what plans they've got for him, the financial situation and so on. The things we really should talk about, that need sorting out, because they could have a real practical bearing on our lives; like if they were to die tomorrow, what on earth would happen? Who would be responsible? No, she just tells ridiculous stories about Graham reading Shelley over the phone to his girlfriend and how many times a night your dad gets a hard-on. And most probably the lot of it ninety-nine per cent apocryphal to boot.'

'I mean,' Lorna said, 'I often feel I'd like to run away myself, sitting facing that ugly screen with the lights on all the time because of the condensation on the windows and never going on holiday because you can never spare the time. You can understand . . .'

'Oh Lorna, come on, you . . .'

'But then I think, where would I be without . . .'

'You're perfectly happy,' Fred insisted, for whom this was an eternal truth she must never deny.

' . . . without Freddy and Kirsty. I've invested everything I have in them.'

Forming as it did the cornerstone of all his well-laid plans.

'And even if it would be nice to have a bit of a break and not be woken up so early every morning, weekends included, and have to rush straight into nappy changing and spoonfeeding, you couldn't really want to be alone all your life, could you?'

'But *I* change the first nappy in the morning,' Fred protested.

'So that after a while you'd just start wanting the same things over again. You'd look for somebody else. So there'd have been no point in having left in the first place.'

'Decidedly not,' said Fred, who had built a stone wall of purpose here as only he knew how. 'Anyway, you've got everything you want, haven't you? House, baby . . .'

Otherwise he might have left himself. But if one didn't decide things and stick with them . . .

'Which doesn't mean you don't still get the urge sometimes.' She paused, 'And maybe even find yourself packing your suitcase in the middle of the night.'

'Lorna!' he propped himself up on an elbow and tried to kiss this heresy out of her.

'Before you trip over your knickers and creep back to your bed.' She started giggling again. 'Come on, you've got to admit she's a barrel of laughs, the way she tells those stories.'

For a while they embraced, before he said: 'I think I'll just grab a last piss if I can, then maybe I won't wake up.'

'The reason she doesn't talk about Raymond,' Lorna told him then when he came back disappointed, 'is that she can't bear to. And she feels ashamed. Sometimes she talks to me about him, if I insist, but it's mostly lies, I suspect. She's ashamed about it all. She can't bear it.'

And Lorna said: 'He was her favourite when we were little. She was all over him. You should have seen her. Her first boy. She had a kind of love-affair with him I suppose.'

Fred said: 'I wish I could take you along when I have to go and jerk in this jar. What if I can't get it up?'

Rather at random, in residual obedience to his mother's request, and then partly because he really had so much time on his hands it was difficult not to take initiatives occasionally, Garry wrote:

'Dear Bruv.'

He sucked.

'I've been thinking lately how much fun it would be if you came down to London and shared a flat with me. It could be like old times in Sion Road. What do you say?'

If he didn't go to Italy after all, which was always on the cards, then it was certainly a better alternative than going back to Cleveleys, if it kept funds flowing. If Mother could persuade Father.

So many 'ifs'. But Garry was used to them. For it must be said that this young man was very close to giving up on himself sometimes, or at least on that self-image he had had. There were days, too many, when he found himself a purely cynical agent, when he almost prided himself on it. Yet at the same time he would always be more than half aware of hanging on in some deep recess of that fine head of his to at least a thread, however slender, of what he had meant to be. He fingered his earring.

'Mum told me what a small place you'd got, and I thought if we pooled our resources, pitiful as mine admittedly are, though I do have a couple of irons in the fire, we could find something fairly decent. The papers are full of jobs in insurance and I'm sure with your experience you could get something in no time. The way I see it, you're trapped in a pretty boring provincial situation up there in Leeds – the place is okay when you're at the university, but not when you've left. And then when you start talking about your precious BT shares and interest rates and house prices and promotion and pension policies even, I wonder if you remember how exciting and positive we meant our lives to be when we used to talk so long into the night in old Lozinski's freezing bedroom. At least if you came down to London things would open up a bit, remember when we threw the striptease parties in the launderette?'

But Graham had been a half-hearted partier even then and Garry didn't really feel he had the energy or will to bother getting close to his twin again. Twins were supposed to be so alike of course, and so intimate, and to feel each other's moods at a distance. But the truth was that Graham was just a bore in the end, the kind of bloke you might expect to find at a Conservative Party Conference, with his new layer of buttered executive flesh and put-on humourless laugh. You wouldn't want to sense his mood even if you could. Because he wasn't even trying to do anything with himself, just slipping into a pre-prepared rut. And Garry reflected that really he had very little in common with any of his family: his father's selfish, self-taught pompousness, his mother's uneducated hysteria, Lorna's self-righteous, sissy prissiness. No, he had grown out of his family. He couldn't talk to any of them and there was no reason really for remaining in contact with any of them. Their plans for him, however well meaning, were all off the wall. No more than a distracting temptation. So that the decision to go to Italy might really be the right one if they didn't give him a job after the election. Obviously Mariangela would understand about waiting until after the election, now it was so obviously on the cards, just a question of Thatch the Snatch deciding the day.

He looked at his writing pad. There was no harm in keeping all bridges open though. Or rather, if a boat was there, why burn it? Though sometimes it seemed one had to work fairly hard just to keep the things from self-combusting.

'Mum is still around being the usual pain in the butt. She hasn't changed at all. She sleeps at Lorna's but comes over here every day, partly because she can't stand Fred (who

116

can?) and partly because she has to bother me about what I'm doing with my life, of course. She always brings about three newspapers with circles round the most inappropriate jobs – Junior Sales Rep and Systems Analysis Manager today's plums, as if I could sink to the one or aspire to the other. It's really annoying, because I should be putting in as much time as possible at the Centre now, since after the election they'll probably be expanding it and there should be something at least part-time for me in the Economic Observation Dept., so it's important to seem eager.

I tried to explain to Mother that it was precisely this mindlessly interfering attitude of hers and Dad's, based, of course, on an exclusively petty bourgeois vision of social status and human values – remember Dad's drawerful of business cards he was so proud to have – that had split the family up in the first place and helped to send Raymond round the bend. But she wouldn't have any of it. She's got this fixation on thyroids at the moment. If only he'd get his thyroid checked everything would be all right. The usual pie in the sky that keeps her going. Next it'll be his hormone balance or sugar levels or whatever else they turn up on some TV documentary. One feels rather cruel shooting it down, though somebody has to, otherwise she'll never face reality.

By the way, as far as Ray's future is concerned, I'm not so worried about the money, just as long as Dad sorts out a solution that really is a solution and that'll keep him off our doorstep in years to come. Can you imagine if he simply forced himself on us when the old folks peg out. I'd emigrate. In fact, maybe it would be just the push I need.

All best to Sophy and do think of coming down, on your own if the other half won't budge.

GARRY

PS. Mum tells me you have a phone. Presumably this is a new development. Perhaps you could send me the number, seeing as she apparently forgot to get it.'

'Graham dear,' Mrs Baldwin was writing at more or less the same moment, having learnt not to trust the slipperiness of phone conversations, not to mention the danger of being interrupted (and with Fred being such a miser).

'I talked to Garry about what I mentioned to you and he thinks it would be a good idea. He says you'd have a lot more commercial openings down in London and the two of you together could get a decent flat.

Seeing as it would be unfair to force him to come up to Cleveleys as your Father wants, I think it would be very good for Garry if you were to live with him in London. That girl Amanda is bothering him again and I think if he weren't so lonely he'd find it much easier to get rid of her and settle down. Being rich and a girl she can afford to muck about and she gives him all kinds of wild ideas whereas what he could do with is a sober practical influence like yours.

If you go down to Cleveleys at the weekend, can you remind Dad to send some more money, as I'm having to borrow everything from Lorna at the moment and I do hate to be dependent, especially as it obviously upsets Fred.

Remember what I told you. If Sophy really cares for you, she will follow you down here. If not, then good riddance to bad rubbish.

Love and God bless,
Mum'

To Raymond Mrs Baldwin wrote:

'Raymond love, I am so sorry I've been away for so long. I feel so guilty. Please don't think I've abandoned you. I shall be back just as soon as they take this plaster off in two weeks' time. We don't want the neighbours talking, do we now? You know what they're like. Do be reasonable with Father while I'm not there and remember he hasn't got the kind of nerves I have, poor man. Don't let him drink too much coffee as it upsets his stomach and puts his blood pressure up. Perhaps I'll go to a hospital here soon and see if they can take the plaster off early.

Everybody here is well and asks me to send their love. I think of you all the time.

Love and hugs. I miss you.
Mum'

Finally on a separate sheet of paper to go in a separate envelope, she scribbled:

'Frank, could you send money as soon as possible. I hope you are well. I decided not to insist on getting Garry to go up to Cleveleys right away as he's on the brink of getting a job. Do check you've finished off all the meals in the freezer before buying fish and chips and make sure Raymond changes at least his underwear. TTFN. BRENDA.

PS. I forgot to say, Lorna says she heard on the radio that conditions like Raymond's may be due to an enzyme deficiency in the brain and that they have made some sort of breakthrough in treating people. Could you look into this?'

Brenda found envelopes and stamps in the top drawer of Fred's desk and went out to the post.

DESERTIONS

DESERTIONS

In the event Lorna took the phone call which today at last confirmed her worst fears. It came from a public callbox.

'I wish to speak to a Mr Franklin Baldwin, please.'

'Raymond!'

'Could you put me through at once please, this is an urgent, long distance call.'

'But . . .'

'I wish to speak to Mr Franklin Baldwin. I presume you must be his secretary.'

'Dad's not here, Raymond . . .'

'Mr F. S. Baldwin please. This is an urgent matter.'

The pips went.

'I'll call you back if you give me the number.'

'I know Mr Baldwin is there, so it's no good pretending he's in a meeting. I have something very urgent to tell him.'

'If you phone back this evening you can speak to . . .'

The line had gone dead.

But a moment later was ringing again. Would she accept reverse charges from Blackpool?

'Mrs Shaker, I received and read with interest the slanderous letter written by yourself to Mr Baldwin senior, otherwise known as Mr Glans, due to the likeness between his bald scalp and the top of an erect, circumcised yankee prick, such as that of your venerable husband, for example. As . . .'

'Raymond, please . . .'

'As far as concerns the libellous references to one Raymond Baldwin, otherwise known as Raymond Ali, in the same, said, abovementioned letter, I wish to inform you that legal proceedings have been initiated and . . .'

'Raymond, for God's sake!'

'. . . a warrant for your and big dick yankee boy's arrest will be issued within the next few days.'

'Can't you understand you're ill?'

'Tell Mr Franklin Baldwin to come to the phone at once.'

'I told you, he's not here. And if you keep saying insulting things I'm going to hang up.'

'You've really done it this time, spermsuckle, get that, get that, get that! This time you've really done it. Tell fuckface I'm coming. Tell him I'll have his balls and . . .'

Lorna hung up.

After a few minutes the phone rang again. She picked up, but there was only the buzz of an old-type payphone waiting for coins. The line went dead.

When it rang again, it was only for two rings. By the time she was up from her seat it had stopped.

And the same again at six o'clock.

And at seven.

Oddly, Brenda Baldwin's first response was: 'Oh God, if he's done something to Frank . . .'

At which, rather irritated, with all he still had to prepare for tomorrow, Fred pointed out that if he'd done something, as she put it, to Mr Baldwin, he wouldn't be asking for him on the phone, would he? The most likely explanation was that Mr Baldwin had cleared off. Or might even be on his way here.

'But Raymond is ill,' Brenda told him, in a way that precluded all argument.

And she went straight to the sewing box, took out Lorna's best scissors and set about ruining them on her plaster cast.

Fred insisted and insisted there was no point. Raymond wasn't about to die just because he'd been left on his own, was he? So why should his mother feel obliged to rush back? 'Persuade her not to.'

Lorna had already moved heaven and earth to persuade her not to. The fact was when her mother had made up her mind she had made up her mind. She wouldn't hear reason.

'The truth is your whole fucking family are mad,' Fred said, unwisely.

'Including me, I suppose.'

'It is indeed d-difficult to avoid that c-conclusion on occasion.'

'Pompous ass,' she told him, though his mimicked Oxbridge stutter was always a sign of intended humour.

'Then let her go on her own, if she has to go.'

Which was the nub, of course. Let them go, all of them. The whole stupid family. Forget them. Whose life was it in the end?

'When he just went and broke her arm?'

'But she says . . .'

'Oh come on, you don't believe what she says any more than I do. Of course he did it. You know what she told me?' She told me they have to lock themselves in in their bedroom at night because he's always trying to bother them. They even had to block the keyhole. He's weird. I'm telling you.'

Fred took a deep breath: 'Look, she's been living with him for years and years, and often with your father away, or at least out at work all day. The authorities haven't forced him into care because they don't think he's dangerous. So there's no reason to believe that quite suddenly he . . .'

'I have a premonition,' Lorna said flatly.

'Oh dear, stop the world, everybody stop working, Lorna Shaker, née Baldwin has had a premonition.' Fred cupped his hands to a megaphone round his lips.

And a moment later continued in a lower voice: 'Lorna, remember, we always said we'd never let the other's family come between us. We've been over this. The fact is there's simply no need for you to suddenly . . .'

'Meaning you're just too bloody selfish to deal with Kirsty on your own for a couple of days and miss a bit of work.'

'Have I complained *once*, just *once* about her being here all these weeks. Not to mention the health risk of the fucking cat and her stinking shitbox. Christ, I've lost hours of work, hours, and never said a thing. Have I? Not once.' And Fred said: 'Okay, okay, let's forget all our plans. Forget them. Finished. Done with. Sorry. That's the end of it. No second baby. No. Out of the question. Sorry. It could be a monster. No career for Lorna Shaker; her family presents her with too many obligations to accept any contractual responsibilities. No career for Fred Shaker, because while his wife is away saving parents and brothers from finishing up in a pool of blood, Doctor Fred will have to spend every evening from four onwards, not to mention weekends and bank holidays looking after his daughter. Am I right or am I right?'

Lorna, with her back to him, had entered her mute routine. She picked at the skin round her nails with an irritating nervous action. Perfectly aware that he was digging his grave, Fred continued in lucid anger, though low-voiced now, remembering Brenda Baldwin on the other side of the wall.

'You do appreciate that this is really a form of escapism indicating a gross lack of self-confidence? You suddenly see your brother as the perfect excuse for not having another baby, good, so you clutch at that because you feel you might not be up to another pregnancy. You don't want to be bothered. Too difficult. Am I right? Which is precisely what Graham's doing of course, who you criticize so much, excluding himself from family and fatherhood officially on Raymond's account, but in reality most probably because wimp Sophy still at home at 30-whatever is scared of life. When everybody knows that schizophrenia is not, I repeat *not*, hereditary, and when we've already had a perfectly good normal baby. And now this having to go away with your stupid mother gives you just the let-out you wanted from finishing the book, because you're afraid they won't accept it and you'll feel stupid, or you're afraid they will accept it and give you more work which you don't really like doing. So now you'll break the contract and they'll never give you a job again. Plus you won't have any track record when it comes to asking for work elsewhere. And you know the first job is the most difficult. God knows, it took long enough to get this one. Didn't it?'

He talked at her long thin back in the dark light of a bedroom life never gave them quite enough time to tidy.

'Just because your father decides to pull out of all his responsibilities, if he has, if he hadn't just gone down the road for a beer, doesn't mean you have to take them on, does it? You're under no obligation. Father walks out on children, Lorna Shaker steps in. Queen abdicates, Lorna Shaker accepts queenly responsibilities.

Problems? Call Lorna Shaker at Atlas, the agency that holds up the world. When the truth is that your responsibilities are here.'

He waited.

'The best thing would be just to let him go mad on his own so that the authorities are finally forced to step in and put him in a home. Don't you agree? You know you do. Because if nobody's been able to help him for the last ten years they're not going to be able to help him now, are they? And if your mother won't hear reason and just leave be, I don't see that you have to feel responsible for . . .'

'I hate you,' Lorna told him.

'Or at least you could get one of the twins to go. If your mother won't give us Graham's number, we could get him Monday at the office.'

'Graham has a job.'

'And so do you, for Christ's sake! What's the book if it's not a job?'

'I'll take my work with me.'

'Without a typewriter. Great. You're going to lug the whole fucking processor with you?'

And Fred said: 'It's obvious anyway that she's only interested in the boys. First she goes to Graham's and now she spends all day everyday down at Garry's and insists on travelling in the rush hour at our expense. So why doesn't she go to Cleveleys with him. That would be the most logical thing. Then he's a man, he could offer some real help, not to mention all these ideals he's supposed . . .'

'His girlfriend's arriving this weekend.'

Fred hardly paused for breath: 'Oh, his girlfriend's arriving tomorrow! Do excuse me, *one* of his girlfriends. That settles it then, doesn't it? You've only got a contract and a child to look after. You . . .'

'You fucking slave-driver,' she shouted. 'What an arsehole you are! Don't you realize I want to help them? They're my family.'

'Keep your voice down, your mother's . . .'

'I don't care if she hears. We're having an argument, aren't we? Why shouldn't she hear?'

'But . . .'

'You really are an arsehole. You should listen to yourself. And don't be surprised,' Lorna said, 'if I don't come back. Right? Because I don't want another baby, mainly in case it turns out like you, and I don't want a bigger flat if I'm expected to clean it, and most of all I don't want to write crap about crappy pop groups just so that you don't have to feel guilty of robbing me of a career when we started a family. So fuck off, okay. Just fuck off.

'And remember Raymond's my brother, okay. *My brother*. But not having any, you wouldn't know what that means.

'And speaking of normal children, Raymond was *perfectly normal* till he was 22, okay, quite perfectly normal. Which is more than I can say for you, shithead.'

Some time later, both fully aware how ridiculous all this was, these two young people went to sleep back to back, furious with each other.

If Brenda Baldwin was on the tube rattling towards Euston before the others were even out of bed, it was not primarily because she didn't want them to put themselves out for her – she hadn't, after all, been especially furtive about her departure and was surprised nobody had heard (the cat had squawked terribly on being forced into its basket) – but rather because her impulsiveness simply could not wait for decent hours. Once she had decided to go, and unable to sleep as she was, what was the point of hanging around? She dressed quickly and carelessly in the only clothes she'd brought, the trousers with the patch, the shabby sweater, pulled on her old green coat, found the necessary money in Lorna's purse, went back to the bathroom to take a half bottle of perfume and a lipstick (since her daughter seemed to have so many and she personally would rather give what little money came her way to the twins who needed it), and let herself out.

People, she knew, accused her of being impulsive, and in a certain mood she might have admitted they were probably right. It was just that Brenda Baldwin was incapable of imagining any other way she might go about this business of living and loving. All her life it seemed she had been reacting to one kind of emergency or another: the war, her brother's death, her mother's collapse, coming, as it did, simultaneous with the arrival of the twins; then Frank's desertions, the children's illnesses, the non-arrival of cheques, illegitimate babies dumped on their doorstep in third world countries, not to mention the stray cats and dogs to care for, Raymond's crises, Garry's attempted suicide – and on each occasion Mrs Baldwin had reacted by hurling herself into things in the way her instinct led her; as she would have sorted out Garry and Amanda given a bit more time, for there was another emergency if ever there was one, he'd be filling himself with pills again before long, and Graham and Sophy too – if only her children weren't so stubborn.

Deprived of a job since she had married Frank, who had refused, as was right perhaps in those days, or at least the norm, to have a working wife, Mrs Baldwin had become a sort of reserve force, a rapid deployment unit, ready to head for any situation where she might make herself useful. And through the long years in Quito, then worst of all Algeria – when all the other children had left and poor Raymond was working on site with his father, supposedly operating the telex – through all those years, incapable of understanding the local language spoken around her, frustrated, shut off from the outside world, her dressmaking talents reduced to sticking together or repairing the crudest clothes for needy children she would meet in the street and could converse with only through smiles and gestures (which perhaps explained the extravagance of her play-acting now) – through all those years she had longed for nothing more than these emergencies which could still transform a mother into a protagonist and thrust her suddenly into life's front line (for she was afraid of nothing), even if her children had become unrecognizable. Hadn't she, for example, flown in the face of all Frank's arguments and set out directly from Quito for New Haven when Lorna cabled about Raymond. And again for England when Amanda's father phoned to say Garry was in hospital. This was what life meant to her, loving Garry, loving Graham, above all loving Raymond, against all the odds, in the teeth of all circumstance, without any prospects for his recovery. So that to say that she was unhappy now, buying her ticket for Blackpool North, or worried, squeezing into a seat in the smokers' section, apologizing for the cat, defending a frail arm from a man wrestling with a case, would be to mistake her mood entirely. She was agitated, yes. She was embattled. She was grim. And had she told her story to a fellow passenger, which, at least apocryphally, she might well do (for Brenda was still far from over the returning emigrant's sense of luxury at being able to talk her own language to any and everybody), she would perhaps have burst into tears at the thought of how cursed, and so unfairly, her family was. She might have cried. But such eventualities aside, she was in the main just terribly excited to be on the move again, with so much to do and so much to put to rights, and all the last few days' feverish planning on Garry and Graham's behalfs momentarily forgotten.

Exactly how she would put exactly what to rights, Brenda wasn't sure. But nor was she considering it. For if there was one conscious idea that went hand in hand with the instinct for swift intervention whenever alarm bells rang, it was not so much a sense of what to do to resolve the situation, in this case to calm Raymond or to find Frank (and anyway he would be back), but of how to cover up, how to hide from Harry and Mary and the neighbours, despite everything, any signs of collapse in the family front – for it was to strangers one told one's story, not to friends, and least of all to relatives. Which was why, of course, she'd left home in the first place when they put the incriminating plaster on her arm (it was unthinkable that people should know how bad their life was), and why, before returning, she had hacked it prematurely off. And why, again, she was so shocked when the first voice she heard, walking down Broughton Street, was that of Mrs Howarth from the sea flats asking how her poorly arm was. Because Frank, like a fool, had told everybody. Seeing as Frank didn't care about anything but gathering sympathy. That was what the family was for Frank, a story he could tell for gathering sympathy.

'Poorly? There must be some kind of misunderstanding.'

And her bitterness knew no bounds. Poor Raymond in his sickness did a thing like that to her which didn't matter at all, and Frank, crass, selfish Frank, had to turn it into a cry of poor me, telling everybody about it so they would think how difficult his life was; when of course the crowning irony was that Frank himself never got into serious fights with Raymond because Frank didn't care what depths their son sank to, how long he didn't wash for, how badly he ate, what language he used, what it was that had made him mad. Frank didn't care about his son, the boy's self-respect, his inner person, his soul. All Frank cared about was that he personally was left to do as he damn well pleased, or rather to do nothing as he pleased. Frank wasn't willing to give real time and effort to helping the boy come through. On the contrary, all Frank wanted was for Raymond to do something so awful, commit some crime so terrible that he would be put away for ever; rape someone, kill someone; and again he didn't care about the someone, only about his own peace and quiet.

But Brenda was never going to let that happen. Never, never, never. She swore it. She'd make sure that anything the boy did was done in her exclusive presence. If he had to abuse someone he could abuse her. So that only she would ever have reason to complain, and she never would. Because you couldn't have a baby and feed him at your breast and cuddle him in your bed as a delightful little boy, to then let them lock him away in a National Health mental institution where there would never be any hope for him again. You just couldn't do that.

And she was in such a hurry now to get back home and set him to rights (she had been away far too long, whatever had come over her?) that she didn't deign the sympathetic Mrs Howarth a single word more.

At Fairfield Close that Saturday morning in May, the post brought only a birthday card addressed to Kirsty Shaker. It bore the printed message: 'Now you are TWO / How clever of YOU!' and underneath, 'Your affectionate GRANDAD'. A twenty-pound note was also enclosed. The card was two months too early.

Did he think he was posting from some desert watering hole? Or had he simply forgotten the date?

Still holding cotton wool to his lip, still worked up, Fred was looking at this card and its attractive design of a little bear holding two balloons, when the phone rang.

'Like to speak to Mr Baldwin please?'

Apparently Fred's father-in-law had given this number to Uncle Harry in case anybody should want to contact him. Which was odd.

'Woman in flat above theirs, Mrs Ratcliffe that they sold to, says there's all 'avoc down below. All 'ell let loose.'

Painfully, through his swollen mouth, Fred explained that Mrs Baldwin was already on her way up, and likewise her daughter, though an hour or two behind.

'You'll be this American then,' Uncle Harry opined, somehow conveying a Lancashire bovinity across two hundred miles of wet cable.

'In the meantime, if there's real trouble, it might be as well to call the police,' Fred thought.

'Oo, I wouldn't know about that.'

'But what does she mean exactly, all havoc?'

'I wouldn't like t' take it 'pon meself to call police without 'aving spoke to Frank or Brenda.'

Fred reflected that the immense frustration he suffered when dealing with the Baldwin family was the sense of not knowing what exactly one was up against, nor therefore what to expect. And worst of all was the now new feeling of uncertainty as to how far Lorna was, or was prepared to become, involved, how far she really was a part of her family, and thus how far his own interests were at stake. When he had met her six years ago she had spoken so scornfully of her parents, married without even telling them. So that he had never had any feeling of marrying into a family, had given no thought to his in-laws. But now it seemed, with their return, her personality had undergone some subtle change and she was no longer quite all his and all his plans'; she seemed weaker, in the sense of not being concentrated here in one place, with this life together, the opinions they had mostly shared (even her accent had begun to slither and slide with hints of Lancashire); and then again so much stronger, in the way she had just rounded on him and lashed out like that.

Perhaps, he thought, instead of taking Kirsty to the playground he could treat her to a bus ride down the Finchley Road, find Garry and try to persuade him to go up north and help out.

Garry, however, two hours later, was not at home.

Amanda to Garry

May 23rd

Curlip Ave
Haddenham
Bucks

Dear Garry,

I won't be around for the next couple of weeks, election run-up or no election run-up, so I thought I'd ask you if you could give Roger the subscriptions-in-arrears list from my locker and arrange for somebody to cover my two afternoons at the Centre. Okay?

I'm not going to be around, I should tell you, for the perfectly simple reason that I can't bear seeing you about with that mouse of a girl. Partly for purely aesthetic reasons, and then because she makes me feel so sorry for her I'm afraid I might go and tell her the truth, which is that you are leading her, and probably yourself, up the garden path. I might tell her that you have a photo of me you always take down just before she arrives and keep under your football photos in the bottom left drawer. How insufferably feeble and silly you are! Either you like that picture or you don't. You can't keep putting it up and taking it down.

But I'm not going to Manchester either. Surprise, surprise. And this is what my letter's about, really, and why I decided to write instead of popping round and having a good laugh over your preparations, sheet changing, condom purchasing, etc. I've decided to leave Antony. It's become clear recently that marrying him was a big mistake. We don't get on. He tries to monopolize me and is always jealous. It's very tiresome. And then he does nothing but talk about money markets and bank rates and zinc futures. Which I was quite excited about at first – he seemed to be one of the only men I knew who was actually involved in the real world – but now it's getting rather irritating. Not to mention the political arguments. So I've decided to call it a day before it becomes a lifetime. Anyway I hold you responsible for my having married him in the first place.

And so while mousey wet Mariangela is here, I shall be staying at my father's, getting in a bit of riding and sleeping soundly on my own. Thank God. I hope that makes you happy and wipes some of the beaten-dog look off your face.

The big question being, Garry dear, are we two going to get back together again? The old team, Arkwright & Baldwin Ltd. Or has too much water flowed under that bridge?

I've been weighing up the pros and cons and frankly I think we should both give it some considerable thought. I mean, I don't want to jump right back in unless you are willing to agree to certain binding conditions.

I left you, as I've explained a thousand times, because I suddenly got fed up with the way you were always talking about how important it was to really do something with your life and help people and change the political climate of the country, etc. etc., and then the next moment whining about not getting anywhere and having no money and being cut out and turned down, and always blaming it on somebody else, the government, the capitalist ethos, your family back-ground and so on – actually, when we went to Algeria, I thought your parents were extremely friendly, if just a trifle gauche, and Raymond was always painfully polite to me.

You kept on groaning about your parents, but you still took money off them. Not much, admittedly, they aren't splendidly generous – and in university days they should certainly have sent more – but enough to make you look ridiculous when you complained. And enough, I realized later, to keep you more or less independent from me. Seven years we had been together, right, since the very first lecture of the first year, and we still weren't actually living together.

When I had plenty of money to pay for a nice big flat, and was perfectly ready to do so. But no, it had to be a place cheap enough for you to afford to pay half, and of course there simply aren't decent places cheap enough for you to pay half, are there Garry love? And I refused to live in some squalid Hammersmith bedsit with a communal loo and the bed folding up against the wall so as to have space to sit in front of a rented TV. Why should I when I've got the money? What on earth were you thinking of? Then even when we went on holiday together, you had to consider half the price as a debt to me, keeping track in your silly notebook and forcing your poor father to pay back when he could probably have done with the money himself.

Why this pathetic, petty, provincial insistence on paying your way with the money of somebody you do nothing but bitch about? When the person you love is throwing it at you and certainly has no intention of asking for it back. Or put it another way, why stall and stall over marrying me and then try and kill yourself when in the end I inevitably go off with someone else? I just don't understand. I never have.

Yet I have to confess that you're still a magnet for me Garry, your bright black hair and big smooth shoulders, your jokes, your silly seriousness. And that's why I kept my pied-à-merde in London, that's why I came back so regularly with the excuse of working at the Centre. Of course I do care about the party, and I'm as excited as anybody else that we seem to be doing well at last. But I could have worked for the party just as well up in Manchester, in fact they need people more there. So the only reason I came back to London was you.

And I don't even know if it's so much you and your darling face and delicious way of walking and talking, your delicious body, let's face it, which goes so nicely with my delicious body (a better-looking couple than us when we're walking down the street you won't find anywhere) – or if it's more the past, the way you're so much bound up with my being 20 and 21, with the wonderful partying life we had in Leeds, the silly debates and the Foreground Theatre Club and binges in the launderette when we used to wash everything all at once and sit there in our swimming costumes – and all the discos you cut such a figure at, even if you do move like a Japanese cartoon. I'm trying to decide whether I'm in love with you now, or whether I'm in love with the way we were in the past.

And I can't decide, frankly. The two seem so frightfully inextricable, but at the same time I don't seem to see how that past could be projected into the future, and more particularly, I can't quite see you in a nice gentrified Crouch End house going out everyday to a medium-exciting responsible job and never complaining about your parents or wishing you weren't some idealistic hero or putting up and taking down pictures as expediency demands. I can't see you growing up.

But I would love to be able to see it, Garry, I really would. It would be the solution to all my problems, and I really am pretty bloody miserable at the moment – you've never realized, have you, how impossibly miserable I often am. You think I'm a tough person! You think just because you took an overdose once – or rather a carefully calculated underdose – you're the only one who suffers. But look at me. I went and married somebody else to get you out of my system and instead here I am, back at square one.

Anyway, if there's one thing I am 10,000% sure of, as Roger always says, it's that every time I see you I get the hots for you, and I know you get the hots for me, because I can simply feel the tension oozing out of you. We've got inside each other's skin somehow, isn't that true? We watch each other so hard, and my feeling is we really ought to make the best of it. Seeing you the last few months I've felt I was going to explode if we didn't jump into bed. And yet we never have. Just because I was married. What moral creatures we are!

So here are my conditions for getting back together; think about them: first, we immediately go to live in a flat chosen and paid for by me; second, you allow me to use my father to wangle you a decent job somewhere – I know that on principle we both despise the jobs-for-the-boys situation, not to mention my father's politics, but when you can't beat them . . . you beat them at it. There's really no alternative; third, as soon as I'm divorced we get married.

How about it?

And do have the best of times with Mariangela. Don't show her about too much though, as it might make you feel silly when you come back to me.

I'm sending a packet separately with a nice shirt Antony never found time to open.

Ciao,
AMANDA

'I'll go down next weekend,' Graham was saying. And he hurried on: 'She shouldn't have gone though. I told her not to. Raymond is dangerous. I don't know if you've ever met him, but he's definitely dangerous. He hit me over the head with a frying pan once. I know it sounds funny, but it wasn't. They had to keep me in hospital for a couple of weeks and give me a brainscan and everything. And of course nothing happened to him. Because that's the way things are getting in this country. You pay your taxes – I paid more than £250 last month, not to mention the tax on investment returns – and do you get a service? Do you hell! They come all this crap about community therapy and it being better for him to be in the family, but it's all economics in the end. The only person in the country who doesn't want him in a home is the Chancellor of the bloody Exchequer. Until he goes and kills somebody and then they'll all pretend how shocked they are before letting him out again in a couple of years' time so he can do it all over again. I'd vote Labour over this health issue, really, if it weren't for all their other policies. You're miles better off in America where at least you don't pay for what you don't get, if you see what I mean. In fact I think if the Conservatives would only out with it and say they plan to introduce a proper private system here, I think that would be a vast improvement. It'd . . .'

'Couldn't you,' Fred asked, who had had reason to be favourably impressed with the NHS of late, 'take a couple of days off work to go and check the situation out. I'd go myself, except that there's nobody to look after Kirsty. I don't want to dump her with someone she doesn't know at all.'

'I would, but I can't.' And Graham added cagily, 'I'm still in my probation period, it'd be too risky. They don't like people always claiming they have personal problems. I already had enough trouble with Mother barging into the office looking like an overweight scarecrow and haranguing everybody for hours, not to mention the cat running all over the place.

'I'll go at the weekend,' he said again.

The wires waited a moment. Rather expensively at 9:30 on this second morning of Lorna's absence.

'Isn't there any way I can get in touch with her from here?'

'Get her to call you,' Graham said unhelpfully. For if she was going to call, she would have already. And Fred had no intention of explaining about their argument to his brother-in-law.

'Or you could call Uncle Harry and get him to tell her to call you. Except he's notoriously unreliable, and he never realizes anything's urgent because Mother always de-dramatizes everything. Which is another absurd aspect of my parents' behaviour. Instead of being open about it and dealing with it in a practical way, they treat it as if it were some obscure venereal disease they can't really talk to anybody about.'

For some reason this made Fred feel uncomfortable. 'Well you can understand it must be unpleasant for them to . . .'

'Oh come on,' Graham was almost scoffing, in a voice that was growing to have an unmistakably executive edge to it. 'I don't have any trouble talking to Sophy and her family about it, and I have a lot more at stake seeing as they're obviously worried about the hereditary aspect. Whereas for the parents it's just a simple practical problem, an illness, that should be solved like any other illness by the Health Service. And the only real difficulty is getting the State to accept its responsibilities. Though I think we'll be able to wangle a decent mentally disabled pension out of them if we play our cards right. The trick is . . .'

For brevity's sake, Fred said yes to all this.

'Or you could send a letter asking her to phone. She's probably just trying to save money. They've scrapped telegrams of course, but a letter still arrives the day after in a fair percentage of cases. Though I'll give you Cleveleys is a bit out of the way.'

'Yes,' Fred said, 'I'll do that,' and with the excuse of somebody at the door, he rang off.

But then only a moment later Graham phoned back, Fred

realizing at once that he'd made the mistake of picking up far too quickly for somebody who had another somebody at the door.

Graham, however, was in no state now to register details like this.

'But Dad can't just disappear! I lent him a thousand pounds only a couple of weeks ago. A thousand pounds! Someone must know where he is. I mean, if he's just walked out with a thousand pounds, it's a complete disaster. It's typical of my parents. You never know where they are or what they're doing. I'm trying to save up for a house, for Christ's sake, and they pay me shit here, it takes forever to save anything.'

'If it's any help,' Fred told his brother-in-law, 'he left our address in case anybody wants to get in touch with him.'

Needing to piss again, Fred went to the lavatory and stood looking into the bowl for a few minutes.

Incapacity to urinate, he thought, when you felt you needed to, would be an excellent metaphor for catharsis withheld (or vice versa, as was the case with all good metaphors).

And catharsis was so often withheld; marriage was a case in point, more and more tense with every passing day, or take the Raymond business, where anxiety just went on mounting and mounting. In fact death was the only catharsis one could reasonably feel sure of.

Tritely pessimistic today.

Or perhaps he was just trying to tell himself that this was merely another minor problem along the general line of so many others. Nothing to really rock the boat. The old career forging (!) ahead.

There were exactly six hours before he had to be back at the nursery again to pick up Kirsty, and then another evening trailing ducks round the carpet and trying to stop her turning the television on and off. So get moving, Fred.

Why didn't Fred feel like getting moving?

Mariangela was too horrified by the price of luxury to really enjoy it. Quite apart from the subject of their conversation. She picked mechanically through mussel shells and her pasty face under imitation candlelight was a mask of worry clouding even her only glory, those bright green eyes, usually wide as saucers.

Whereas generous Garry appeared to be relishing it all.

'So Lorna was convinced he was holding Mother hostage and goes off to get the police. And of course as soon as the police arrive, along come the local telly people too and the papers; only then after they'd been there a half an hour or so talking through megaphones and things, Mother comes out perfectly okay and says she just locked herself in the loo because they'd been having an argument and he'd been shouting at her, but that in fact he hadn't touched or threatened her at all. Seems she was furious with Lorna for . . .'

The waiter brought along the main course and took away Mariangela's half-finished mussels. The girl pouted fretfully, twisting hair round a finger as she would. Garry poured more wine.

'One thing though, I mean, on the one hand he's obviously raving mad, but on the other he's smart enough to unplug the fridge before hacking it to bits. You see what I mean? You wonder where madness ends and sheer bloody-mindedness begins. Sometimes it's as if he just had it in for everybody.'

Garry paused, uncertain as ever whether Mariangela was really capable of following all this. And she *was* rather dowdy in jeans and a black blouse, such a stark sad contrast to his own orange cotton 'United Colours of Benetton' spring sweater draped round broad shoulders with the thin gold chain Amanda had given so long ago winking over the tendons in his neck. For a moment then, Garry enjoyed the exquisite consciousness of all his fine body with all those fine clothes covering it in this fine and expensive Soho restaurant. Because he wouldn't be done out of what was good in life, not by anybody, nor in any circumstances.

He felt fleetingly resentful.

'Anyway, in the end they took him away and questioned him for a couple of hours and had a doctor examine him and by some miracle or other they managed to persuade him to go into a clinic for a while to cool down.'

'That is terrible,' Mariangela said, quite suddenly and with her mouth full. ' 'e will never get better in the clinic. Your poor family.'

'Yes, but at least he won't be bothering anybody else.'

'That is an egoist attitude,' she said, pouting again. 'You should be ashamed yourself.'

Garry smiled, being used to playing little boy to another's bossy motherliness.

'And we must not think 'e is doing it on purpose. Is the very typical reaction to the patient with mental problems, and very contraproductive. You 'ave to courage 'im, not to blame, like so you make worse his persecutory complex.'

'Oh, I'm not saying he does do it on purpose, just that it feels like it. Anyway, part of his madness is a natural reaction against my parents for the way they've always treated him. So obviously there's an element of vindictiveness about it. In fact, come to think of it, vindictiveness is always a kind of madness really.'

Mariangela frowned, but her small mouth, from the mechanical way she ate, was really too full now to say what she knew about this aspect. And perhaps anyway it was only an indirect continuation of their earlier argument about money.

'Still,' Garry said, 'quite apart from whose fault it is, who'd ever have a fucking family when you think of all the things that could go wrong? Really. Syndromes, handicaps, drugs, AIDS. Quite apart from raving bloody lunacy.'

Mariangela swallowed. 'I want the children,' she got out quickly, as if not to let him get away with this. 'Yes. Anyway, the schizophrenia is not 'ereditary. So we 'ave no problem. I 'ave controlled in all the books.'

'You have?'

Was he flattered?

'Sì, caro.'

And the conversation suddenly brought about one of those transformations from bossiness to kittenish girlishness which, in any woman, could so charm Garry. She cocked her head to one side, impish and all at once very Italian.

'Big bacio,' she said, showing teeth.

The waiter hovered.

'Big bacio,' he replied, loving her accent. And with the breasts she had, 'mousey' was definitely not a fair description. Though how were one's friends to know with the deliberately sloppy clothes she wore? And the way she wouldn't do anything about her hair. That was the problem.

Tackling her food again, she said: 'But if your father is not sending the money any more, at least make me pay the half.'

'Christ, I said no. We're celebrating.'

'You are so maschilist. Is a form of possession, you know, paying for my food. I 'ave money.'

'But I just spent a week working my bum off in a pub specially. Washing dishes too.'

Which was the way Garry tended to lie, on the spur of the moment, so that he was consciously filing this away now for any necessary future cross reference.

'But you shouldn't. You must be thinking of your career. I tell my parents: I don't make any work which is not for my career. You must be thinking of your ambitions.'

She finally lifted her serviette to cover her mouth.

'Hardly worth it if I'm coming to Italy, is it?'

'But you 'ave said they give you this job after the election.'

'If they do, they do; if they don't, they don't; but I mean, there's no point in worrying about it now. The job, or Italy, I just wait and see. Difficult to make plans in these circumstances,' he added.

She pulled a face.

'And anyway' – all at once Garry seemed to be in rather glum earnest – 'if I take the job here, that means we won't be able to be together, doesn't it? So I'm not really terribly enthusiastic about it, frankly; I mean, it wasn't exactly what I've always planned to do with my life, working in a research department. I'd rather be with you.'

She didn't hesitate for one moment. 'No. If they give you the job, I come over here. We live here.'

This was a development that had simply never occurred.

'But your studies . . .'

Oh, she was only in her second year, Mariangela explained, and it took at least eight in Italy before they gave you paid work as a doctor. Probably it would be better to come here and do something else. She didn't mind. So they could be together. 'Don't you think?' She was quite bright now, licking her fingers clean of butter and fish. Her round eyes twinkled.

'But you just said about not doing anything that wasn't to do with your career . . .'

'Oh, but maybe my career is you,' she laughed.

Was she joking?

'Anyway, it is looking always more like your family is needing you to be near to them. Not in Italy. You just cannot abandon them.'

'No,' and he looked down at his own plate. 'Would you like some dessert?'

'You sure you 'ave the money?' She was laughing still, rather irritatingly actually.

'I told you I . . .'

'Che caro che sei,' she said. And she announced: 'profiteroles.' And a moment later: 'But if you 'ave spent less money on clothes, you 'ave more to live and you do not 'ave to wash the plates.'

'Oh, I was given most of these clothes. Richer friends in the party,' he added quickly. But perhaps again she had only been joking. Why did he take everybody so seriously?

'They should give them to the poor. In Milan the Radical Party collect twenty tons of clothes and sell them for helping the poor in the Third World.'

How would the committee react to a suggestion like that, Garry wondered. At the very least it might stand him in good stead having made it, even if it never got taken up. And of course he did believe in such things.

Shortly afterwards and rather too loudly for the kind of restaurant they were in, Mariangela said: 'In any way, the only thing I like about your clothes is when I take them off.' And her smile, swallowing a last profiterole was radiant.

If only, Garry thought, the others knew how hot she was in bed, there'd be no question of sniggering.

And as usual he relaxed, he didn't reason it out, he let himself be carried along on the stream, smiling a smile which was a slow complacent widening of an already wide mouth. Making sure a bottle was empty, he chuckled: 'Why do Italian men always have moustaches?' She shook her head. 'To look more like their mothers.' And he burst out laughing, his eyes watching hers watching him with love. For there were dimples to be seen, he knew, just above the shaving line, and strong sharp white teeth. People sometimes said he looked like Robert De Niro. The young Robert De Niro, that is.

It was hard to imagine in a mood like this how he had ever agonized over Amanda.

Raymond to Colonel Gascoigne

Dear Colonel Wanker Gascoigne,

I know you are in contact with revisionist forces.

What is more, I and my family are extremely disappointed in you. It has become patently clear that your intentions toward my honourable brother, Graham Ali, are far from above board. You are humiliating him. We are well informed about this. You have him drive you to hospital every time you need your bleeding haemorrhoids looked at, you have him do all the shopping for you and the washing up and the gardening, but you won't give him your precious little daughter in marriage as is now his just desert.

In short, you treat him as a slave. And this is not permissible with one who is blood brother to Raymond Ali. Especially because your chief purpose is evidently to undermine my image through him. I am not unaware of subterfuges of this nature. It is not the first.

What is wrong with your daughter? Doesn't she have a cunt? Isn't she capable of having children, which is woman's true purpose? Or are you fucking her yourself, a typical perversion of capitalist militarism, to which you, with your colonialist executioner past, are no stranger?

Listen. This is a WARNING.

Either you give your little CUNT to my brother so he can

have a FAMILY as is every man's right under Allah. Or you will come to HARM.

Understood?

Have I made myself clear?

RAYMOND ALI THE AVENGER

Raymond To The Bolton Meet-A-Mate Agency

Dear Sirs,

I am writing in the hope that your agency will be able to put me in contact with my future wife.

I myself am six-foot one, well-built and thirty-two years old. I have short black hair and hazel eyes. I studied mathematics at Yale in the USA and have travelled widely, doing a variety of jobs in South America and in the Middle East (I am fluent in French and Spanish with a smattering of Arabic). It was due to this travelling, I am afraid, that I did not have the opportunity to get married earlier on; but now I have returned to England and am settled here permanently.

I should explain that I myself had a very unhappy childhood and was abandoned by my parents at an early age. So I am now looking for the kind of girl who will be willing to make a large happy family in the traditional manner so that we can share the pleasures of bringing up healthy contented children. I should also add that while I was in Algeria, I converted to the Islamic faith, and although I am in no way prejudiced against other religions it is important that any prospective partner should understand my position. I would not, by the way, be at all averse to a mixed marriage with an immigrant of Asian, Arab or African extraction who also upholds the Islamic faith.

In gratitude for your prompt attention,
RAYMOND BALDWIN

Please reply c/o: Green Trees, Kingscote Drive, St Anne's, Lancashire.

Raymond to the Head of the English Faculty
University of London

Dear Professor,

I have thought a great deal before sending this letter, but now I feel bound to do so if for no other reason than to defend my fellow students. I am a first year student attending Dr Shaker's lecture course on language and metaphor. I want to report that on two occasions, Dr Shaker encouraged me to have sexual intercourse with him in return for which he promised he would make sure I passed my exams and received a travel scholarship. I am writing anonymously because I do not want Professor Shaker to be prosecuted. But I think you should warn him that he cannot go on trying to push his big circumcised American cock into all his little students.

      Yours,
      A VICTIM OF SEXUAL IMPERIALISM

Lorna to Fred

Dearest Fred,

It was good of you to arrange the phone call, and I am so
glad we've spoken. But not everything gets said on the phone,
however long you speak. And particularly not with all that's
going on this end. In fact, having picked up my pen I don't
know where to start really. Except to say that it's gone
midnight here, that I can't sleep, partly because of talking to
you and partly because I haven't slept anyway ever since I
came here. I've been pacing about the room for hours until
finally I decided I may as well sit down and arrange a few
thoughts on paper, as much for myself as for you, and then
to see if anything comes out in the way of decisions.

I seem to have told you everything and nothing on the
phone. No, Raymond didn't actually hurt either Mother or
myself, though it's not quite so simple as that. Yes, he is in
a home, though again, things aren't so simple. Obviously it's
impossible to be sure of anything Mother says, but what
appears to have happened is that when she found the place
in such a chaos on arrival (and he smashed literally everything,
even the mantelpiece, even the kitchen sink), she started
screaming at him and hitting him. He went for her – with
or without the axe I just don't know, she swore not, but he'd
certainly been using it on the furniture – and she locked
herself in the bathroom. When I turned up a couple of hours
later (and thank God I did), he wouldn't let me in; he said
he wanted to be alone with Mother because all the rest of

the family had it in for him, but I could hear her crying and calling from the bathroom. She was saying: 'Just be good, Raymond. Please be good. Be my Raymond.' Pretty heavy stuff. So when he still wouldn't let me in, I went to the police, who already knew the whole family saga from Dad and came pretty promptly.

They put him in this home on a treatment which basically seems to involve heavy sedatives, but I'm not at all sure how long he'll be there, since Mother did her best to play everything down and kept saying it was as much her fault as his and she'd abused him and hit him first. She seemed in something of a daze frankly, I was surprised they didn't get her examined for shock. Raymond was very clever. He claimed he'd smashed the flat up partly out of spite for my father's walking out, 'on Mother', he said, and partly because they were planning to re-do the place completely anyway, so he knew it would be no great loss. And while we were all sitting there drinking tea in the police station, he pulled a photograph out of his wallet showing Father and another man, both naked, being fondled by two naked black women (very graphic); he said that was the kind of pig Father was and he'd got emotionally worked up when he found it in a pile of things in the spare room. It was after that that he started smashing the place up. So he said. Mother backed him up on everything. She was very strange in her manner, she kept swaying her head from side to side, but then I suppose if you didn't know her you wouldn't realize. She identified Father in the photograph and said she wasn't at all surprised – there seems no limit to the lengths she'll go to protect Raymond. She cried. The doctors, as always, were puzzled, since it's clear to anyone that Raymond's not quite the same as everybody else, but so difficult to pin down exactly what's going on, especially since he really can be so reasonable when he wants. He never comes out with any of his fantasies outside the family. The police said he hadn't actually committed a crime, unless one of the family asked for charges to be pressed for damage to their own personal property, and Mother wouldn't of course. So in the end it was only at my insistence that he was dangerous and that I was terrified for Mother and myself that they agreed to arrange for him to go in a home and keep him under observation 'for a short period'. I can't tell you how difficult that part was, testifying against him as it were. I felt such a traitor, to the family I mean, and so bad. He said: 'If it is absolutely necessary.' He sounded far more reasonable than I did.

Since when, Mother hasn't spoken to me at all. Nor to anyone else for that matter. Not a single word. For four days. And you know how talkative she usually is. It wouldn't be so bad if her own mother hadn't stopped speaking five years before she died (but I must have told you about that) and the doctors could never find any physiological reason for it. She just lay in her room completely silent apart from the occasional sigh or groan. It happened after Mother's elder brother was killed in Malaysia around the time the twins were born. So I'm terrified the same thing may be happening again now. I keep telling myself it's just the shock, and then her being furious with me for finally getting someone to put Raymond in a home, because she sees it as such a terrible stigma, as if he'd never really been crazy until it was all 'official'. Or maybe she's just overwhelmed with Father clearing off and so on and then the whole business getting in the newspapers. You can understand. She's always seen the family as her struggle against everybody. To hold it together. What I fear now is that she may be giving up.

As for the house, I can't describe what an appalling mess it's in, and with Mother mute and refusing to see anyone or to help, it's been hard to know what to do. When I arrived the floor was literally inches deep in smashed furniture, torn books, old letters, shredded photo albums, mouldy food, great chunks of plaster from where he'd hacked at the walls, you name it. Anyway, after immense effort I managed to clear all that up, taking twenty! wheelbarrow loads to various skips in the vicinity, and then this morning I went to Blackpool to order a new sink and loo and fridge; when Graham comes down at the weekend he can help with the heavy jobs. Unfortunately I haven't been able to discover whether Mother even possesses such a thing as a cheque book. I fear my father keeps all that side of things to himself and just gives her housekeeping money. So I imagine I'll end up paying for all this myself, at least for the moment, until Dad reappears, as like the bad penny he is no doubt he will. By the way, before I forget, can you go and see Garry and tell him to come up here at once; maybe with three of us we'll be able to talk some sense into Mother.

Which brings me to the most difficult part of this letter, Fred. Given everything that's happened, I've decided to stay here for a few weeks, or at least until Raymond comes out, perhaps longer even, if they've managed to calm him down and we can get on together. I think Mother needs somebody here, otherwise she may just close up in herself entirely. So yesterday I phoned Rock Pub. and told them I couldn't go on with the book.

Shirley was very nice about it; she said she'd pay me for what I'd done and get somebody else to finish the thing. It's not as though it's a great work of literature or anything to say the least.

I can already hear you blowing your top, Fred, and screaming blue murder and stamping your feet and generally throwing a tantrum worthy of our Kirstyship herself, and I'm glad frankly that there's no phone here so I won't have to dread it's you on the other end every time it rings, ready to tell me what a stupid little girl I'm being and how I've ruined all your plans and my own life into the bargain. Perhaps I should tell you something here I haven't mentioned before. Recently, writing to my father, I started explaining for some reason how I'd lied to him years ago about exactly when I left university, because I was afraid of what he would say, afraid that I had upset his plans and calculations, removed his last cause to boast over his children after Raymond went mad and ceased to be the family darling and genius. Then immediately after writing that letter, you and I had an argument (and it wouldn't have been the first, would it?) about how many hours I was working a day, and whether I'd finish this book on schedule, and so on. And all at once during that argument, I think because it came so soon after writing the letter, it finally came to me that you had simply replaced my father as the slavedriver in my life. It's amazing how the obvious can elude one for so long. Or perhaps slavedriver is a bit unfair. I mean the person for whom I have to perform or they will be upset, the person who imposes their pattern and vision and lifestyle and determination and wishes for me on me, in the absence of any such pattern or determination or wishes coming from myself. And I've been asking myself the last couple of weeks, but why don't I have such a pattern? Why don't I regularly insist that you do things you don't want to do? Why is it never me trying to shape our lives and careers, making plans? Because the simple truth is, I don't like that flat we're living in now, I don't like North Finchley, I don't like working at home on my own behind windows drenched in condensation; I find my work utterly futile and don't give a damn for any vague kudos that may or may not accrue from being able to tell people I'm a freelance writer (who cares!). And while we're about it, I don't want to have a bigger family. I love Kirsty with all my heart and soul and skin. But I am terrified of having another child. Somehow I know things would go wrong. I am terrified the baby would not be normal, or that I wouldn't love it for some reason, because I feel daily more unsure of myself and my behaviour and how I will react and what I will do in one situation or another. I could never have imagined, for example, two weeks ago, that I would be writing such a letter to you, that I would be saying, basically, let's have a trial separation, let's see if we really want each other, or each other's plans, because quite suddenly I'm not sure.

I'll come down one morning next week and pick up Kirsty at the nursery and bring her back here. I don't want her to be in a nursery all day while I do jobs I don't want to do and that we don't even really need the money from; why, for heaven's sake, are we, and everybody else for that matter, always pretending we're poor, that we 'need' this or that extra money, as if we'd die of hunger without it? Your salary is quite sufficient to get by on, and seeing as you're so eager to earn it, so be it. I don't want my daughter to grow up surrounded by people who are concentrating all their attention elsewhere, as if her presence were entirely incidental. Sometimes I wonder if either of us has really taken in that she is a person, and not just the baby we had.

My head is a jumble of things to say next. I've been sitting here picking at the skin round my nails. So what's new? But at least there's nobody around for it to bother. Big Fred, I don't want to write a nasty letter. I really don't. I don't want to hurt you. Or not just to hurt you. I want to tell you all the things I've been thinking here, plunging back into my family after all these years, finding all the old photographs (or scraps of photographs actually), even school exercise books, walking round the empty rooms of the big house and along the seafront where I used to walk with Raymond on the way to school. I hadn't been back here since I was fifteen, and coming now, with all the old smells and nooks and crannies, and then with this new turmoil that in more than one way has grown out of that time, it has suddenly made me feel unsure of our own lives and family and where it will end. How will our Kirsty grow up with the kind of tensions there are between us? Why are we doing it, Fred? What will our relationship with her be when she is 30 and we are 60? What can we expect it to be if she goes on seeing what she saw last week? Raymond was such a good boy when he walked me along the seafront to school, when we played games of running from one sandpit to another before the next wave flooded up and wetted your shoes. And I don't want to end up at 65 like my grandmother and now my mother, locked up in myself, refusing to talk to anybody. I am losing faith. I keep feeling I may be caught in some kind of hereditary trap, becoming so like the people I imagined I'd escaped from and planned never to be like. The last time I lost faith I remember I grabbed at you, because you were so positive and optimistic and knowing and generally bright and bushy-tailed, and of course I loved you. But now I am losing faith in all that as well, in us and our family. For fear

157

that it may just lead back to this smashed up flat with years of bric-a-brac and odds and ends we must have hung on to in the hope they would turn into happy memories, only they haven't. I still have the remains of a very large bruise on my arm, Fred, plus a considerable bump on the temple. If you knew how much I'd cried in the train, and now too.

Thinking about that episode, I suppose another way you are like my father is that whenever I'm against your plans and we argue, you always manage to suggest that I'm irrational and hysterical and not quite right in the head, just as Father always accused Mother of being mad and said Raymond got it from her and from her mother and it must be hereditary; there was a period for weeks and weeks when he kept insisting she should see a psychoanalyst, only of course there wasn't one in Bougaa and she never would have gone anyway.

That's why I hit you when you said I was getting hysterical and should see a doctor with all these premonitions and fears, when you said it was demonstrable insanity to go after my mother, especially since she'd chosen to sneak off on her own. I know I shouldn't have hit you; I know that probably it was just something men do say to women in arguments. But it had such an echo for me. And then, I never imagined you could hit back so violently. With Kirsty watching too.

You see how easily plans can go to pieces, Freddy love? I've watched you building things up in your careful insistent way these last years. You have your whole life mapped out, don't you, so that in a way it's as if it were already finished. Or rather our whole life: the second child, the houses, each one bigger than the next, the lectureships, each one better than the next, until at sixty you're a famous, respected, but still dynamic professor doing your 'research' for half the year and your well-attended lecture courses for the other half, supported, of course, by your bright, still attractive, but most of all intelligent and independent wife with her own 'projects' – an excellent, well-managed team. You see us at sixty, don't you? You think of our lives as something other people are already talking about and you get obsessed with the kind of image you think they'll admire and fight to achieve it. But will it work out, Fred? My father also had his plans: twenty years abroad so that he could return to England to live like a king. And instead . . . The fact is you both see life as a rising curve on some newspaper graph with the years along the bottom and the achievements up the side – and any bump or dip in the line is an aberration and intolerable.

Perhaps I should never have started this letter (how long is it since we wrote to each other – and they were such love letters, weren't they, so sparkling, and we called each other such delightfully edible names). But the fact is that on my own in the night here, without the embarrassment of the sound of my voice actually saying these things out loud, and of having to watch your face reacting as I say them, without those obstacles I've begun to say things I'd really perhaps only half been aware of till now, but always felt deep down. Big Fred, I don't know what I want for us, I really don't. I'm going to live a different life here for a few weeks and think about it. For the moment you'll just have to accept – and I know this will be the most difficult thing for you – that everything is up in the air.

Your

LORNA

PS. I suppose I was relieved really that it was only prostatitis. I had feared something worse. Still, Doggy mine, at least it's one milepost you can say you've passed – or pissed on – way, way ahead of schedule.

Speaking of peeing, I'm now going to have to go out into the garden for a quick one, since the loo's still out of order here and I can hardly go upstairs to bother the old lady at this hour.

REMEMBER: 1. to tell Garry to come up; 2. that I'll come and pick Kirsty up early next week – just think how much work you'll be able to do without either of us!

Lorna squatted in the dark garden. It was damp spring weather and her feet trod into the mess of earth and roots her father had recently dug over. The sky was low and luminous over low rooftops and the smells were those she knew to expect, but which nevertheless surprised her: a wide open freshness, a tang of salt air. Across the soil, the cool breezy darkness induced a mood of serenity, which was also, she felt, unreal somehow, disembodied, or suspended even, but anyway detached from the day that had gone before and the day that was to follow.

The last thing she should have been feeling, surely, was serene? Unless it was just relief at having no more book to write.

With no desire to sleep, she pushed out of the gate into familiar streets, following low orange-brick garden walls, endearingly toytown here the way they put the big curved blocks on top. She remembered how Raymond once had learnt to open this same lamp-post and tamper with the timing device, while she hopped from one foot to the other terrified he would electrocute himself or be carried off to prison. Now, between the hours of one and two, the lamp cast a flaring, struck-match glare onto the roofs of parked and polished cars.

There was something about suburban streets at night, the sureness of all they represented, that made Lorna feel quite calm in her helplessness.

And she reached the main house in Fleetwood Street with its rather pretentious bay windows, now curtainless, its dinky chimney pots, the garden they had played in, the outhouse where she and Raymond had peed in jam jars once for some reason she couldn't remember (a dare perhaps, or just to watch each other doing it?), where once, coming out to get coal for the fire in the early morning, she had found a tramp asleep and screamed.

This was where it had all begun presumably: Grandmother ill and mute beyond the window now hidden behind the leaves of the sycamore; Father away, earning the money that would 'guarantee their future'; Raymond aping him in his absence, bossing and scolding her, bossing and scolding the twins; Mother run off her feet, alternately festive and resentful, showing a morbid favouritism for Raymond in Father's absence, having him sleep in her bed, asking his opinions, treating him as a grown man almost. So that it would be all the worse when Father came back and thrashed the cockiness out of him.

Obviously it had started here. Nothing could be clearer. And yet it wasn't explained by what had happened between these four walls. The Freudian and other formulas weren't enough. Mother's favouritism, Father's aggression, both understandable, still weren't enough; and then it was so difficult to remember exactly what *had* happened, how exactly they *had* been with each other – so much of life washed off one's back. At fifteen, sixteen, seventeen, in Lebanon and Ecuador, Raymond had been as normal as anyone, quite unscathed, had had a period of excessive kindness in fact, and generosity, always helping about the house, helping the twins with their maths, an attractively shy and brainy elder brother her own few friends had all had crushes on. Until some years later again, in Boston, she had received a telegram from her father, because Father had always always sent telegrams, so long as they existed, since in a telegram you could command without explaining, give information without apologizing ('letter following', they always finished, but it never came): he had received a letter from the rector; she must go and visit Raymond. And she had taken the train down to New Haven and found her brother in his room, unwashed, stinking and covered with tiny razor cuts; the walls, ceiling, carpet, furniture, all smothered in a deep dark brown paint, reeking and sticky; even the bedclothes were painted, the pillow, the mattress. Quite simply he had metamorphosed, in that ugly cocoon of a room; and whereas at the beginning everybody had been determined to know the reason why and embarked quite energetically on the psychiatric detective hunt that so much modern newspaper talk prepared you for (which infant trauma had it been?), now it was merely a question of deciding how to live with it, willy-nilly. Because no reason had been forthcoming. Or rather, there had been thousands of reasons; when you started to look and count there were no end of reasons for anybody's going mad, but none in this case which had led to treatment and cure.

So that if she was staring at this bare house now, though some of the brickwork had been freshly pointed, it was not for any mystery or explanation, nor least of all for any key that it might hold for her. It was just that for a moment she was fascinated by the absence of either mystery, or affection, or interest. For that bare house meant nothing now but whether Mother could be persuaded to sell it, and what in the event should be done with the money (how much?). Or whether Father would come back and they would live in it.

Lorna didn't turn the corner to look at the sea. She knew what it would be like. Instead she walked back briskly to the flat. And of course, she could send the letter to Fred, or not send it. What she had written there was true. She was sure of that. The only thing that disturbed was how every time she felt she had put everything down on paper, to her father first, and now, more momentously, to her husband, she discovered afterwards, in just a few minutes of being herself and looking about her after finishing, that the half had not been said. There was more, so much more in the air around any piece of paper. So that, on its own perhaps, that letter was not what she had meant to say at all.

Stretched on the couch, but still not ready for sleep, she settled down with an old book of do-it-yourself medicine from the thirties, *Dr Hibbert's Home Diagnoses and Remedies*, another relic from the back-room and one of the few that had survived Raymond's ravages, albeit with its cover torn. Scanning through the index she looked up 'prostatitis' and read: 'Are you in your early sixties and still perhaps rather too attached to certain voluptuous little vices? Do you find yourself dragging your weary bones out of bed in the early hours to stumble downstairs and cross the yard to the lavatory, once, twice, three times, four? Or have you already started using a chamber pot? If you haven't, it is an idea you would do well not to discard too lightly. And do you feel a certain wearisome tension in the space between the legs, as if sometimes you felt you were brooding over an egg? Do you feel that you're never quite comfortable whatever position your limbs assume? Dear reader, I very much regret to inform you that you have prostatitis . . .'

The old fart seemed so sickeningly sure of himself and pleased about it all!

Softway Systems to Garry Baldwin

May 29th   SOFTWAY SYSTEMS LTD

Dear Mr Baldwin,

Following your interview of May 20th, I am now pleased
to inform you that we are able to offer you the position of
SOFTWARE MARKETING EXECUTIVE. Your starting salary will
be £10,500 p.a. plus benefits. Hours are flexible, but we
expect all staff to be in 5 days a week and always between the
hours 10 – 12 and 2.30 – 4.30. Within those limits you may
organize your 40 hours as you choose. I enclose a separate
page outlining your responsibilities. Please get in touch with
us immediately to let us know when you can start.

I very much look forward to working with you.

My warmest congratulations.

Yours faithfully,

DONALD BENBOW
Personnel Manager

163

If Mr Baldwin had occasionally acted strangely, he had always had his alibis, which was more than could be said for Brenda. The time he announced he was off to the beach, for example, and then stopped away for two days – a story she endlessly retailed as an example of his unreliability – he had genuinely remembered something that urgently needed telexing from the office in Manchester. And there was no point in relying on someone else to mess it up. Likewise, the time in Khartoum when she'd 'caught' him packing his suitcase, he really had promised to meet Trilling early in the morning at an outlying site a couple of hundred miles away so as to spend a day checking over foundations. And if he hadn't explained to Brenda the evening before, it must have been because with all the noise the kids were making, trapped in a couple of grubby hotel rooms, quite inappropriate for children, not to mention everything else a site-coordinator inevitably had on his mind, it had slipped his memory. Of course he hadn't been 'doing a flit'.

Whether these alibis were more for himself than for others, or whether, more subtly, Mr Baldwin needed stories he could believe in himself, not only while addressing them to others, but even more crucially at the moment of doing what very much seemed like something else, wasn't clear. Suffice it to say that he always had an alibi and was always genuinely indignant when his wife inevitably jumped to dishonourable conclusions and made unpleasant accusations – even if, or perhaps especially because, the crimes in question were things he frequently dreamed of. But dreaming was not doing, and their occasional apparent overlap in Mr Baldwin's case was indeed only occasional and only apparent. He had not 'run away', nor abandoned his 'responsibilities' (if he had not particularly wanted a family, he nevertheless had a strong and sentimental sense of himself as patriarch). Just as he most certainly had not been 'running away' when he first chose to go and work abroad. On the contrary, he had been doing his best to improve family fortunes as rapidly as possible, to get the financial problems out of the way so that they could really live. And if he hadn't, over the last week or so, informed anybody as to his exact whereabouts, it was: a) because the psychoanalyst had specifically told him not to tell Raymond where he was; and b) because it was so unutterably tiresome keeping people informed and feeling they were on your backs all the time and that every minute of your life had to be accounted for, when they should have been more trusting after thirty and more years battling through together. Nobody needed him just at the moment, so why should they know where he was? He was tired frankly, exhausted even, physically, mentally and spiritually exhausted with being with Raymond, with dealing with his interminable obtuseness. And Mr Baldwin was a great subscriber to the belief that tired, exhausted people had a right to a break and a breath of fresh air.

So detail by detail his alibi built up, grew of its own accord really, into the density of unassailable truth, and this precisely as Mr Baldwin went on not quite doing what he had always, always, since even before the knot was tied, planned and dreamed and fantasized doing: taking off. On his own.

Yes, first and foremost the analyst had told him it wasn't worth continuing the treatment; there was too much open hostility between the various members of the family which they seemed to thrive on rather than want to reduce (for Mr Baldwin this merely confirmed his belief in the fundamental charlatanism of psychoanalysis, since anybody who thought he was thriving obviously had no business in the medical profession); the only possibility therefore that he, the analyst, could suggest was that Mr Baldwin and his wife both live apart from Raymond for some time, thus depriving him of the day-to-day antagonism which simply fed his persecution complex. Despite its source this seemed like an excellent idea.

Then second, Mr Baldwin really did need to come down to London to sort out his finances, see about getting money out of tied accounts and bonds, if possible negotiate a loan against his pension with Sun Alliance (though he was quite definitely damned if he was writing a will). Since otherwise he'd soon be out of money again for getting on with the house. And if his travels happened to take him within walking distance of the Brazilian Embassy, what harm was there in popping in and finding out what procedures had to be followed to get a visa? It was something one did on impulse, on the vaguest offchance that the information picked up might some day be useful. So why not?

On his second day of freedom, Frank Baldwin picked up the receiver of a payphone in Debenhams and let Lorna's number ring twice, then hung up. He looked at a stack of phonebooks a moment, wondering if there was any way they could be used to track down a good private gut specialist. Because it was such a lottery with the NHS. God knew if a Blackpool doctor was capable of understanding his gut (there was so much of it). Certainly Raymond had run rings round the local analyst. You almost felt proud of the boy. But of course, socialism didn't allow doctors to advertise in the yellow pages. What a country! You were almost better off in Brazil on that score. He must, by the way, make sure he was around for election day when it came, if only to cancel out Raymond's vote.

And in Soho they had taken all the posters down. He had to pay £5.50 just to get a glimpse of tit, nor found it particularly exciting in the event.

If Brenda could take a holiday, more than a month now, why shouldn't he? But he was damned if he was sending her money when she was staying with family. For God's sake. When she was staying with family, family looked after her. Something he must mention to Lorna some time. And when you'd given them so much in the past.

He consulted his watch. What about looking in at his old company's office, see if there was anyone around to have a drink with. Why not? He deserved a drink and a chat with old friends. See what they were up to now, keep up with developments. Really, one quite missed the site now it was over.

Each evening, after his travels, towards 6, Frank Baldwin returned to the bed and breakfast he had found off the Goldhawk

Road and watched television in the communal lounge, smoking, away from Brenda's surveillance, extremely heavily. The bliss, the sheer bliss of being away from Raymond, and Brenda's way with Raymond, induced a state of dazed indulgence. If only the family would allow him a week's holiday every now and then, it was all he asked. He talked politics, he talked football; he talked of the Middle East to Arabs, of Africa to Africans, of Ecuador to South Americans. He mended the owner's daughter's bike and read the *Telegraph* and various magazines in his bedroom. A week's complete holiday. Or perhaps a little more . . .

DOLDRUMS

'Call for you, Mr Baldwin.'

'Thanks, Rachel. Hello, Graham Baldwin speaking, can I help?'

'Graham, Graham, there's been a terrible mistake. Graham . . .'

'Raymond . . .'

'Look, they've put me in a looney bin. Everybody's completely mad here. I mean, it must be some kind of mistake. There are people banging their heads against the walls, people incontinent. I . . .'

'You can't call me at the office, Raymond, I'm busy. Listen . . .'

'Graham, I'm the only normal person here. You've got to help me get out. There's been some kind of awful mistake.'

'Who told you I worked here anyway?'

'Who? Dad did. He said he was going to be in London for a few days and I could contact him at Lorna's or you at this number. Then the next thing I know I wake up in this place with all these raving lunatics and . . .'

'You do realize you totally smashed up the flat?'

'What flat? Graham . . .'

'You totally smashed up the flat and held Mother hostage in the bathroom and . . .'

'Oh don't be so ridiculous. I couldn't have done that.'

There was a short pause here until Graham said coldly: 'No, it's you being ridiculous, Raymond. We all know you've read books on schizophrenia, you know about partial amnesia, so you choose to have it. But it won't wash. And if you really do have it then that makes you even more dangerous, doesn't it? Either way you . . .'

'But I didn't smash up the flat, Graham, you've got to believe me. I don't know, it must have been somebody else. Look, Graham, really, I need help. I'm so scared here. If . . .'

'You're getting help. You're in a home because you belong there with the rest of them and the sooner you realize that the better.'

In a perfectly sane voice, Raymond was pleading, 'But I'm your brother, Gray, your brother,' when Graham hung up. He got in touch with switchboard and told her he didn't want any more calls unless the callers were willing to identify themselves and their problems. Then he phoned 'Green Trees'.

'Frankly I'm amazed that you let them have access to a phone. It's irresponsible.'

'Patients,' said a camp but aggressive voice, 'who take all their drugs and whose behaviour is civilized and promising are allowed to use the payphone in the canteen. Your brother has not been officially sectioned you know. We have no right to . . .'

'But I could lose my job if he keeps phoning me like that.'

And the following day he called back to tell them about the letter, which was still polluting the atmosphere at the Gascoignes'. He'd forgotten about that. Was that what they called civilized behaviour?

Graham gave them a very thorough piece of his very sane mind, just in case they had forgotten what such things were like.

Fred was a creature of routine, and this made growth difficult for him. Kirsty's growth in particular. Time was when one could simply dump her in her cot in the dark, let her cry for five minutes and she would go to sleep. But now she had learnt to climb over the rails and, being anxious inevitably over her mother's prolonged absence, did so, crashing twice the four or so feet to the floor. Other more time-consuming methods of inducing sleep would have to be applied.

Fred sat in the curtained dark on Lorna's ergonomic chair and stroked the nervous little girl's hair. On three occasions, imagining her asleep, he tried to creep out of the room, cursing himself for that creaking doorframe he had never seen his way to repairing. On each occasion, her yowls arrived a split second or so after that wave of relief he always experienced when he sat himself at his desk and felt the outside world begin to darken about him like shadow about a point of light.

The child wailed and screamed and rattled the cot rails.

At a loss, he tried to tell a story: he told one about a grasshopper who had to be very careful not to jump too high because of the crows always circling around looking for insects to eat. But one day the grasshopper fell in love and then he jumped so high, partly for joy and partly to show off, that a crow came swooping down to get him. Grassy Grasshopper saw Mr Black Crow and immediately took evasive action (as they say), but not in time to save one of his big back legs. The crow tugged it off and flew away with it and Grassy Grasshopper was lame. But fortunately (!) the little girl grasshopper, who was called Hula Hoo, was so sorry for him she looked after him for the rest of his life. Hula Hoo and Grassy Grasshopper had lots of children and Grassy Grasshopper always told them, 'Don't try to jump too high. Stick close to the ground and no harm will come to you!'

Narrative as metaphor indeed!

Pretty disturbing stuff this; and a good job the child was too young to understand the half.

Then he told another about a computer screen who fell in love with its operator and corrected her mistakes and tried to . . .

But Fred wasn't especially good at stories. A note of diffidence, of hesitancy, of self-irony in the voice, as, observing himself telling – and how could he not? – he consciously tried to be clever, seemed to make the child even more nervous than before. She whimpered, pushing her nappied behind into the air, her face into the mattress, wriggling.

And now it was ten-thirty, two hours behind schedule, when he should have been solving all kinds of problems. Not to mention the bomb-struck chaos of the kitchen, dishes to wash, garbage to take down.

'Go bye-byes now,' he said.

Kirsty sat up and wailed, 'Mummy! Want Mummy.' She stood up and threw a foot over the rail.

Fred would have liked to have taken the hard line, to avoid spoiling the child, because there was nothing worse than spoilt children, but didn't see how this could be done now there was the danger of her banging her head on the floor.

He took her warm body with her favourite blanket in his arms and tried to sing. Tomorrow he would have to: a) do the next Stamey's Test, which was agony frankly, quite apart from the humiliation; b) do the shopping – including a bulb for the spot gone over the desk; c) drop in at admin to find out why he'd been taxed so much last month; d) . . .

It was perfectly incredible, but he couldn't think what to sing, nor remember how to hardly. He began, despite the season, with 'Away in a Manger', and was astonished by the warbly thinness of his voice in the dark, the difficulty breathing. How long was it since he'd sung? Perhaps he wouldn't know how to ride a bike if he got on one. Forgetting the words he switched to 'The Star-Spangled Banner', with a crashing sense of irony at first, but then gradually relaxing into it, remembering, across the bridge music can be sometimes, a feeling of trust, perhaps even of pride he had had – or anyway unselfconsciousness – when singing this pompous crap as a child. And somehow that elusive feeling, which he found himself having to pretend not to notice, so as to keep it (for it would surely dissolve the moment he got his forceps out), that elusive memory of infancy, as he went on and on repeating the first verse, which was all he knew, redeemed the pompous song, and Fred, and eventually sent the child on his shoulder to sleep.

How gratifying! And rather fun even.

And how amazing that such tender feelings were still available.

Except that now, quite suddenly, he desperately needed to piss. The suddenness and pressure of the discomfort were frightening. And for the first time a sharp pain shot from the crotch down the back of his left leg.

For a moment Fred went rigid. Then gently, gently, gently, he tried to lay the child down in her bed; but the little hands began to cling, the puckered mouth worked, the eyes tightened. He took her up again, swaying from side to side till the small snuggling body relaxed (he did love his daughter), then stepped carefully through to the bathroom, picking his way between chairs and cupboards in the dark, staring for toys and other boobytraps on the floor (what a life for a man with his thesis published). And Fred might even have managed the delicate business of holding up the girl on his shoulder with one hand while the other fiddled his pecker in what he hoped was the right direction, had not the telephone begun to ring just as the thin stream finally trickled through.

Lorna could it be? He fumbled and made a dash.

'Father not been in touch at all, has he?' a plummy voice enquired. 'I just wondered, seeing as he probably thinks Mother's still there.'

'No, Graham.'

'Tysicle,' a voice said as he put the phone down. 'Tysicle, Daddy. Play tysicle.'

In addition to the anti-inflammation pills, the antibiotics and the vitamins, Fred had also been prescribed a mild tranquillizer as part of his cure. This he had so far ignored, since he felt that to a great extent he owed his academic success to a constant state of inner tension, and then to the way he had wired his brain, as it were, to sound alarms whenever the mill of his thoughts (there you go) turned up a metaphor, however carefully disguised. Tonight, however, forgetting the kitchen chores, he found the bottle, shook it, and took the maximum permissible dose; and seeing that there were indications for children too, he shook out a couple of drops for Kirsty to take with a spoonful of milk.

'You know you like medicine, honey.'

And she did!

At tomorrow's lecture, the last with this year's students, he would have to do a little improvising for the first time in his life: *Metaphor and Simile, a Substitute for Reality?* He would stress perhaps the unpleasantness and intractability of reality (not mentioning Stamey's Test directly though) and what a relief it could be on occasion to gloss it, or ennoble it, or even laugh at it ('like having a pogo stick up your ass'), with a . . . 'Okay then, just tonight, you can come into Daddy's bed, just tonight sweetie, come and sleep with Daddy now' . . . although one must maintain a distinction between that and mere euphemism which simply . . .

Fred's task was to be made no easier by the three or four items of post he would receive at eight thirty-five the following morning with Kirsty twenty minutes behind schedule still spooning Weetabix down her front.

The fat one from Lorna he slipped nervously into his pocket for when he was alone on the tube. Two bits of admin, nothing interesting. He opened the one from Raymond:

'I know you're behind all this, Professor Fuckface Spermshake, but just wait and see what happens to you when I get out of here.'

The black and white pornography enclosed with this brief message was surprisingly similar to that left behind in what Fred now thought of as the Jerk Room in the hospital; it was less sophisticated, however, than the expensive, airbrushed gloss of the *Penthouse* Mr Baldwin was leafing through in his B&B off the

Goldhawk Road; less personalized than the stack of photos Garry kept for the purpose under the Leeds University Second Team football photo and various other memorabilia, including one unsent letter, in the bottom drawer of his desk.

'So?'

'So we have our date, the campaign's on its way, all systems . . .'

'That wasn't what I meant. Well? Yes or no?'

'God, I can't talk about it over the phone from here. The place is leaping. The switchboard's been jammed half the morning. I've still got about twenty people to call. We're giving out canvassing duties. Speaking of which . . .'

'You only have to say yes or no.'

'Look . . .'

'Because I'm not going to come down to canvass myself unless the answer's yes.'

'Oh, I don't think we should let our private lives get mixed up with our political commitment at an exciting moment like . . .'

'Don't make me laugh. You just mean you haven't made up your mind.'

'I'm pretty sure there'll be a job on the cards at the end of it.'

'Garry, I didn't . . .'

'No, listen, I've been thinking, you know, and it is, well, it's a difficult decision to take. Especially with Mariangela being here.'

'Wasn't she supposed to be gone by now?'

'She stayed on.'

'At your invitation?'

'She's helping at the Centre.'

'Oh, she's helping at the Centre; and when exactly is she going?'

'I'm not sure. We . . .'

'Meaning you've decided to stay with her, right? Why can't you just say it? What in Christ's name's wrong with you? I didn't leave Tony *just* to be with you, you know, so it's not as if it's that important. I'm not going to start making extravagant gestures like someone we know once did. I just want to know so I can get on with organizing my life.'

'I didn't say I'd decided to be with her at all. All I said was . . .'

'Then why *are* you with her?'

'Look . . .'

'What did you think of my letter?'

'Well, I . . .'

'You could have replied, couldn't you? What did you think about what I said about you?'

'Maybe in a way, I suppose, you could be right, even . . .'

'Then what are you going to do about it?'

'Look, this is hardly the . . .'

'I believe I told you I loved you, damn you.'

'Keep it down, Amanda. The place is packed. I mean, so do I, but . . .'

'So do you what?'

'What you said.'

'Then say it!'

'Look, Amanda, love isn't . . .'

'Don't whisper.'

' . . . everything, is it? My parents loved each . . .'

'For Christ's sake, why do you have to drag in your stupid parents?'

'It's a statistical fact that most people's emotional lives tend to mirror those of . . .'

'But you're always saying they didn't love each other. Anyway, you can't allow yourself to be conditioned by the fear of having been conditioned. You've got to believe you have a mind to make up, otherwise . . .'

'All I was trying to say was, it's not the kind of thing you can decide overnight on the basis of a feeling that might or might not be going to last.'

'Not with a wop in your bed, I don't doubt.'

And Amanda said: 'Okay, then how do you decide it? We've only known each other about two hundred years.'

There was a pause.

She said softly: 'Anyway, I seem to remember not so very long

179

ago someone looking very lovelorn across a table in a restaurant. Am I right? So here's your chance.'

'Look,' he hesitated, 'you come down and we'll talk it over and . . .'

Amanda had hung up.

Garry ignored the various incoming calls and dialled a number in Oxfordshire.

'Oh, it's you,' she said, and hung up again.

And the next time the phone was off the hook.

Every time, it seemed, that life offered Garry a chance to be courageous, it always turned out to be not quite the occasion he had been looking for.

'Would you like me to do your hair?' Lorna asked. 'The colour's coming out.'

'Mum?'

She said: 'Shift feet a mo'. You know we should really get rid of this lino. How long's it been here? Thirty years? I remember the twins pushing cars across it. You know, those Corgi things Dad was always buying them off with on holidays. And the cigarette stains. Actually, it's pretty funny really, having four properties and nowhere decent to live. Nobody would believe it. They'd imagine we were stinking rich.'

She straightened her back and looked at her mother: 'Don't you think?'

She tipped the dustpan into the mouth of the bin. The cat patted her shoe.

'Was that Kirsty? I thought I heard Kirsty.'

But the distant wail was now clearly somebody else's child in some other house, or out on the street.

'She doesn't usually sleep this long. It must be the sea air.'

Lorna waited.

She said: 'Be great if they do change the rates system though. Save us a bomb.'

She waited.

'I must say, it was nice of Fred, hiring a car and driving her up here. I was dreading the train journey. Though he probably just wanted her off his hands as soon as poss. You know how he is.

'One thing I was thinking though. How on earth did you manage with four? And then Grandma in bed as well. I'm only just beginning to realize what a herculean task it must have been.

'Mum?

'I think I'm going to make another pot of tea. Want a cup?'

Rain blew against the kitchen pane, adding the last touch to drabness. And somehow raising the pressure. The cheap old bakelite of the socket she'd pushed the kettle in smelled strongly of rotting fish. Lorna listened for her daughter.

Then burst out laughing: 'Pretty bloody hilarious he went and wrote one of his letters to the Colonel though. Specially if the guy's really as much of an old fart as I imagine he is. I wonder where he got the address from. And the way Graham was so scandalized. He's so comic. As if we hadn't all been getting letters. Anyway, if she goes and leaves him over that then obviously she never cared for him in the first place. And if she stops seeing him because her parents tell her to then she must be a real wimp.'

Lorna was vaguely conscious here that she was using a word Fred used.

'But in any case it's no good his blaming the family. It's not our fault.

'Odd though, isn't it, the way Raymond sometimes goes and says what all the rest of us are thinking but don't have the courage to say. Like when he sent the telex to Dad's boss. Why doesn't she marry him, after all, or live with him or something? You can see he's dying to, running round to her place every night. Or at least let herself be seen sometimes. And why's she still living at home at 30 whatever she is? You expect people to break out at some point. Start a family of their own. I'd love to have a chance to see what she's like. The only thing I know is that Graham told Garry she has the best nipples in the world, which hardly gives you a complete picture of the person, does it? And Garry actually had the gall to tell me it would take a lot to beat this Mariangela's. They're all the same, aren't they? Men. It's always a competition. Cars, jobs, nipples. They all have to be better than everybody else's.

'Mum?

'Another weird thing – have you noticed? – is how Raymond always seems so obsessed with all our other halves. I know he wrote some pretty wild letters to Amanda once. Quite graphic. Garry used to show them to everybody as if they were some kind of joke. Maybe it's because he's jealous of our normal lives. Well, not entirely normal, but you know what I mean. Or maybe he can only imagine relationships between people as a kind of pornography. There's obviously some sexual hang-up at the bottom of it all somewhere. Along with other things. But how does it help knowing that if all they can do is give him sedatives?'

She pulled out the kettle plug.

'God knows what's at the bottom of this crack, Mum. Look at this. We should really have the wall replastered altogether.

'Even the Islam stuff fits when you think about it. I mean with his having a sex hang-up. They have such an authoritarian attitude to women it saves the men from approaching them in a normal way. Makes it easier for him, if you follow me.

'Have you ever thought he might be a repressed homosexual?

'I suppose we'll never know,' she answered her own question, 'but it could have been some experience like that that set him off. No?

'I'd hate to be inside his head though you know. Really. He looked so tense that evening, in his eyes, as if he were having to make such a massive effort to repress everything. And so frightened too. It's awful when you realize how frightened he must be all the time. How unhappy.'

She said: 'By the way, I was thinking, if Dad doesn't turn up, maybe Fred and I could help Graham out with his thousand pounds, seeing as he's so terminally upset about it. Or perhaps, as he says, we should just sell up the main house. If you can do that without Dad's consent. How much do you think we'd get for it?'

She looked into the pot: 'Do you really think he was broke though? It seems incredible. For twenty years he goes on about how much he's earning working abroad, always playing big spender, lashing money right and left on taxis and telegrams and expensive lunches and things – remember when we went on the cruise, the SS *Adriatic*, and he had to buy a gold souvenir from every port? – and then we're supposed to believe he's flat broke all of a sudden after just a few months' retirement.'

She said: 'It could be why he left, though, if he just felt too ashamed . . .'

Her voice trailed off. And now, when she heard herself say, 'Here's your tea, Mother,' she at last felt herself crushed by these tragedies she was holding at bay with only the thin whine of her voice, crushed by the aimlessness and emptiness and monotony of all her talk. When you spoke and the other spoke back it was so much easier somehow, however banal what was said, however far apart, as with herself and Fred sometimes, the wavelengths were. When you both spoke, and at least half listened, there was some interlocking device that held the words together across the space a morning, an afternoon, a day could be, across the gulf each single moment could present you with sometimes; there was a sense of routine, you speak/I speak, which got you through, of engagement, as if normal dialogue were really a kind of embrace in which each supported the other, even if you were both looking over each other's shoulders, or just arguing, or talking bus delays in queues under inadequate shelters. What mattered was that somebody spoke back. And she saw now why Fred complained so much about her own habit of staying silent in certain moods; because it was intolerable, this constant launching yourself into space; hearing the echo of your own voice, feeling its fragility, its inadequacy; you became provocative, desperate; you were locked out and beating on an obstinate door. Like Father's pensioner who had died of cold in the outhouse. Locked out by his own family.

'Mother.' Lorna sat down opposite her. In her dressing gown, Mrs Baldwin held her face between her hands. Her hair was woollier and whiter than it had been a month ago, though whether due to ageing or merely because she hadn't been to the hairdresser's wasn't clear. The ringlets fallen out, it straggled loosely about a head that could now be seen to have a disturbingly skull-like shape. Her eyes were blank. 'Mother, talk to me. Look at me. I'm drivelling on and on and on and you never say anything. I'm saying things I know will make you mad, like about selling the house and Raymond being homosexual, and you never answer back. For God's sake! I'm trying to help. I'm trying to be a daughter. I'm not a social worker or a maid or anything. I've given up a job, I've left my husband to come up here and help. I'm sorry, but I was afraid Raymond was going to kill you or something. Don't just ignore me or blame me. Mother. Please. Listen. He'll be out soon. He always responds to sedatives. Then

Graham came last weekend. Garry will probably come next. All your children care for you. And in the end Father's only been away two weeks. It isn't as if we hadn't heard of him for years. He could turn up tomorrow with a perfectly decent explanation. So cheer up.'

She stared across the two or three cluttered feet of table-top at where her mother was refusing (unless perhaps there was some other explanation) to look at her. Some kind of allergy, or nervous reaction had brought out tiny red spots around the older woman's mouth.

'Or perhaps you live too much for the children, Mum. Really. Have you ever thought of that? Perhaps you should just stop thinking about them, and about Dad and the family, find other interests. Your main responsibility's to yourself in the end. Everybody's main responsibility is to be happy themselves.'

But of course she wouldn't have been sitting here talking to her mother if she believed that crap. She was just churning clichés now to fill the space.

'Mother, listen, there's so much to be done. We've really got to get out and get our act together. Like Graham says, why don't we go and see Mrs Howarth and Miss Laughton and get them to pay rent direct to us. Otherwise where's the money going to come from, even for the housekeeping? Then as soon as you get moving, you'll feel better. Honestly. We could even go into Blackpool if you want, see a film or go for a walk on the pier. Remember when you took us walks on Central Pier?'

And Lorna took her mother's hand and began to rub it, as if afraid the older woman might already be a corpse. 'Otherwise I'll have to call a specialist or something if you just won't speak. We can't go on like this. I'll have to go and get . . .'

For the first time today there was some kind of exchange between their eyes, as if this threat had peeled a protective layer from the older woman's pupils, only to reveal a wound beneath. For Brenda's gaze was at once alarmed, and hurt, and defiant; and above all animal in its suddenness and cornered pride.

Her daughter was as if stung by this sudden revelation of vibrant otherness behind her mother's torpor. 'Well, at least you're not deaf,' she said, backtracking, and managed a smile. Then more softly she tried: 'Mum, you're usually so talkative, so full of fun. Remember when you were down at our place describing Graham on the phone to Sophy? Or playing with the cat. You're so great when you're bouncy. And when you were telling fairy tales to Kirsty. "What a long nose you've got, Grandma!" You're so good at it. I should have recorded you. What I'm thinking, Mum, is, what hope is there for me and my own daughter if we two can't just relax and enjoy each other's company now we've got some time together? What am I going to be like with her when I'm sixty? Don't you see, you must give me some reason to feel confident. Please.'

She waited. Her mother was pressing the wrinkles in her lips together. What an immense effort of will it must take not to speak. Or loss of it.

'Didn't you always say you were going to write a book on dressmaking someday? Why don't we do that? Together I mean. You explain how to do things and I'll put it into writing. We could make each piece as we went along, just to check the instructions work. You're so good at that kind of thing. I remember when you used to teach me, in Beirut, my first party dress. Remember? It must still be in the back-room somewhere. We could even make a lot of money. Why not? I can't see any reason why we shouldn't get it published when you think . . .'

Or was she beginning to sound like Fred now? Why did we all want each other to be so busy all the time? Why were we scared of people's inertia, reassured by activity, however futile? Forever making plans for each other.

She stood and went over to the window, looking out at the smudgy grit of the back yard where wind fidgeted pegs on the line and shook off raindrops. To tell the truth, nothing encouraged action of any kind. There was food enough in fridge and cupboard, the flat had been tidied up so far as was possible without incurring large expenses, and anyway, Raymond might yet have occasion to smash it up again. Then despite the season the world outside was inhospitable and deadening as only the North-West can be sometimes, as if the grey light were only there really to show the rain slanting on mean brickwork. She lifted and lowered herself on the balls of her feet and raided her imagination for openings;

but apart from Mother's book, which mightn't actually be a bad idea (a return to home tailoring of every kind – including fancy underwear? – as a leisure occupation) it came up blank.

It was nice of Fred, though, to have hired a car and brought Kirsty, nice that he'd been so practical and straightforward and unhysterical too. She hadn't expected that wisdom of him.

'Don't you ever think we might have done better to have stayed in Quito, Mum? I mean that hazy blue the sky always was and the temperature always the same, not too warm, not too cold. Nothing temperamental or extreme. The way even the poorer Indios always seemed so happy. When you think how shitty the weather is here . . .'

Unless it was just that he already had someone else lined up and was in a hurry to get on with it, might even now be . . . No sooner were you away from someone than you felt you'd lost all control, you didn't know who they were at all; which was why you formed families in the first place perhaps; to stay close to people, keep tabs on them. But then he wouldn't be sending her all these postcards, would he? Love you, love you, love you, day in day out. Or would he?

'I always felt the family was happiest there. You remember what a laugh the twins were when they were 13 and 14. The volleyball net in the garden. And Raymond was so sweet and shy.'

Should she feel angry with her mother, or sympathetic. Should she leave her to get on with it?

Was her silence a dignified way to suffer? To give up. And Lorna remembered now, with a powerful physical sensation, herself as a child, sitting in Grandmother's silent room, writing to her father to come home.

Would her own daughter sit with this grandmother, write to her father to . . . to what? What did the future hold?

She turned: 'You know, sometimes I feel so much like you, Mother. In all sorts of ways. Even if we've never been terribly close. You know that? It's funny, isn't it? I feel myself becoming like you. Physically and mentally. The way you have of being very busy one minute and then all listless the next. I've noticed myself getting like that. You just lose any sense of purpose. I even refuse to speak when I'm angry with Fred sometimes. He calls it my mute routine. He always says, "Be in touch, sweetheart, I'll leave a forwarding address." It drives him crazy.'

She looked about the kitchen for help. An animal calendar showed a marsupial, perfectly content to cling upside-down from her branch with her offspring in her pouch.

'I suppose given that we have these similarities we might do worse than to talk about them.'

But she could hear the falseness in her voice now, too obviously and too hopelessly prodding at this enigma. Which might also have been herself. And for just a second she wondered, rather extraordinarily, if perhaps people didn't die like stars, gradually sending out a feebler and feebler light, until it was all black substance drawing everything into itself.

'Have you ever thought that we might all be a bit mad, Mum? I was . . .'

Mrs Baldwin stood up abruptly, scraping back her chair; she rinsed out her cup and went into the sitting room. After a few moments Lorna followed. Her mother was sitting in an armchair Graham had unearthed from the back-room. On her lap she held the cat, stroking it limply, mechanically.

'Another thing is the way you used to argue with Father.'

Then trying for maximum effect, and at the same time on the point again of breaking down, she said: 'I'm leaving Fred, Mother. 'I've decided to leave him.

'Like you should have left Dad if you'd had any sense, dragging you around from one country to the next, going to brothels, getting the clap and leaving you to go to the clinic, going to the office Sunday mornings to read the papers, rather than helping with the children. Never letting you make friends with anybody else. Remember Sonya you always wanted to visit outside Quito and he never let you because she was an Indio. Why did you put up with it? Why do any of us put up with any of them? Fred, Garry, Graham, Raymond, they're all impossible, they . . .'

But Lorna had never been a convinced feminist, and she sensed at once how this sort of anger was just an easy side-track, not what she was after at all. In fact, she felt rather sorry for Fred with his chronic prostatitis at only 35, sorry for her fat, disillusioned father, however exquisitely exasperating he could be. Confused, she said: 'You should talk about it, Mother, talking is always a release.'

Though she was hardly an excellent advertisement for this particular cliché just at the moment.

'Mum?'

Mrs Baldwin's face, the finely carved nose, the sunken eyes, the unsightly rash around pressed lips, remained blank, not with the serene blankness of sleep, but as if in some fretful state of not-quite-suspended animation. A gust pressured loose panes. The silence in the room steepened suddenly, as if sloping into an abyss. From which Lorna felt a wave of hysteria rising like nausea. She would kill the woman if she didn't speak. She would wring her neck. What right did she have to deprive anyone of her company like this? Least of all her daughter.

And Lorna was determined to feel herself this woman's daughter. If there was such a feeling to be had. Determined that family should be family. If there was such a thing.

'Mother, this is so childish, so childish.' Her voice suddenly rose. 'The truth is you always cared more about the boys in the end, didn't you? You never had time for me. You always . . .'

Until at last, and mercifully, a little girl howled. Lorna turned and dashed to the back-room.

'Mummy, Mummy, Mummy,' her own daughter wailed.

'Kirsty, Kirsty lovey. My little jewel. What a long sleepy-byes.'

And standing up, folding the child in her arms, Lorna lifted her eyes as if by instinct to where Raymond's bloated grin was half obscured behind a window still uncleaned these twenty years and more. He squashed his nose against the grime and smiled broadly.

Graham to Garry

Dear Garry,

Thanks for yours, undated, received mid May, and for your invitation. Let me tackle the points you cover one by one.

First, Leeds is not a provincial dead end, either culturally or commercially. It is the home of Yorkshire Television, the most progressive of the commercial channels in the country, and it has various concert and theatre venues which Sophy and I attend quite frequently as it happens: one of the great advantages of going out with Sophy is that she does keep me up to date with all kinds of artistic developments which I obviously wouldn't have time for in the normal run of things. At Eastertime we went to see a cycle of medieval plays which were most interesting. Actually, I think it's quite important to combine one's business activities with a stimulating cultural life, and of course that kind of entertainment costs much less up here than in London, quite apart from the transport factor. To turn to the business side: the town is fast emerging from the doldrums caused by the collapse of the wool industry together with the drastically high levels of immigration, and a vigorous and highly profitable service sector, of which the Leeds Access is a part, is now developing. It seems to me that the next government, be it Labour or Conservative, or even a coalition with your lot, is bound to pour a lot of money into the inner cities of the north, and I intend to be around to make the most of it.

Second: it would be very silly of me to leave the Leeds Access before even completing my probation period, as it might then be imagined that I hadn't been given a permanent contract through some fault of my own. As a general rule of thumb, I believe one should wait an absolute minimum of 2 – 4 years in a company (depending on duties and seniority) before changing, if one is to get the most out of the present job experience-wise and also be in the best possible bargaining position for negotiating the terms of the next. It doesn't do to be a fly-by-night.

Third: it seems perfectly reasonable to me that I should no longer have the dreams and plans we had six or seven years ago and which you seem so nostalgic about. This merely indicates that I at least have grown up; I have appreciated that house prices and insurance and pensions are of paramount importance. In what kind of world could they not be? What is well-nigh incredible to me, on the contrary, is that you are still working voluntarily for an organization which has no hope of achieving real power, nor of giving you a serious job. I might be able to understand this if what you were doing was truly idealistic (to their credit, Sophy and her mother both do all kinds of things for local charitable bodies), but in the end I suspect you only stay on there so as to hang around Amanda. If you want, as you say, to really do something, then go out to Ethiopia or somewhere to dole out soup, at which point you will be assured of my cheques and respect, though frankly I think you would do better to swallow your pride and go for those junior salesmen jobs you so despise. One has to start somewhere, whatever one's education. I also, now we're on the subject, find it incredible that you quite merrily continue to ask the parents for money, obliging them to ask for it from me; and incredible again that you have such a blasé attitude to the very real problem of Raymond, and that you haven't even seen fit to visit yet, not even now Father's done his not unexpected bunk, with my thousand pounds, and Mother is going looney herself. We only have one mother, so you might at least find some of your unemployed time to go and see her. If you knew the hours, and I have very little spare time, I've spent in Social Security Offices and Citizens' Advice Bureaux trying to throw some light on the Raymond affair perhaps you'd understand why I feel quite upset about the extent of your non-assistance.

Fourth: I also resent what I am well aware is a plan between yourself and Mother to get me and Sophy either to split up or to marry at once. This is extremely ironic given your own complaints about family interference in your life. There was even an utterly obscene letter from Raymond to Colonel Gascoigne which basically expressed ideas picked up from Mother and which naturally did nothing for my rating as a future in-law, though I now seem to have ridden out that particular storm.

Anyway, quite apart from the fact that my personal relationships are nobody's business but my own, I can tell you that either of these courses of action (i.e. marriage/breaking up) would be folly just at present. Sophy is a fantastic and cultured girl, as you would admit yourself if only you knew her – not to mention certain other attributes we once talked about! She enjoys an excellent relationship with her parents and seeing as she is at home studying for her OU degree at the moment she is glad of their company and they of hers. I go over to eat at her place every evening – her mother is a fantastic cook – which saves me time and money, in return for which I do the daily shopping for them seeing as they are quite far from the nearest supermarket. Sometimes, if there's nothing good on the box we all sit round for a game of Scrabble or bridge. It's really rather a better family situation than ours ever was and frankly there would be no point in altering the arrangement just at present for any reason I can think of. Neither of us wants children, so the time factor is of no particular relevance and there can be no question of me 'wasting my life', as Mother insists on putting it. We will wait until I can afford a decent house. I hope this will satisfy everybody as to the soundness of my personal relationships and intentions.

Now for the other major topic on the agenda: the family, of course. I went down last weekend to clear up the mess left by Raymond's spree, which, as you can imagine, is proving extremely expensive – purchases included: a new fridge, a new cooker, and a new sink, quite apart from paying the rental company for the smashed television. To make matters worse, Mother was sulking, rather than making the best of a bad job; I didn't get a word out of her the whole weekend, which, considering the sacrifice on my part in time and petrol costs, was particularly galling. Likewise Lorna was too busy with Kirsty to offer much real help. The poor little girl (I was sad to see that she isn't really very attractive and will obviously have to have her droopy eyelids operated) had some stomach upset probably due to the change of water. I told Lorna, and I suggest this is the line you take too, that she had made a serious mistake coming up to Cleveleys and that the best thing would be for her to take Mother back down to London to live with her. At that point there would be no obvious parental household obliged to take Raymond in, which, on the basis of all the research I've carried out in the various relevant public offices, seems to be the only situation which will force the state to assume its responsibilities and take him into care.

Anyway, I made it very clear that I couldn't see my way to going over there to help again until Mother takes a responsible decision about the property of such a kind as to put her in a position to repay me my £1000 (I am sure the main house is in her name as she inherited it directly from her mother, so she's perfectly at liberty to sell it). So far all my attempts to get any real action have been entirely ignored, mainly because Father would never deign to do anything that we suggested, but if this new policy of mine prompts her to sell up, then I will have done her and everybody else a gigantic favour.

In conclusion, however, I can't say often enough that I really do feel that it's time you made some kind of effort and threw in your weight along with mine to make something radical happen. Otherwise we'll find that Raymond is out and Father is back and the moment when we could have done something to settle the family situation once and for all is past.

I'm enclosing £30 in case you don't have the wherewithal for a train-ticket. Don't spend it on anything else. If you don't go up I want it back. I just lost a thousand.

Best,

GRAHAM

Re. my phone. I'm not giving the number to anybody for fear it might end up in the maniac's hands.

Garry wished the election campaign would go on for ever. It was so nice to see everything in terms of predictions and opinion polls which could alter from one day to the next, one paper to the next, and which anyway their leaders frequently referred to as inaccurate and misleading. Of course it was nerve-racking to see the Alliance's share dwindling steadily after those exhilarating by-election highs, but the actual vote hadn't happened yet, had it? That was the point. It hadn't happened yet. It was to come. There was always time for everything to change. And so much busying about to be done in the meanwhile.

How could he possibly be expected to go anywhere or really decide anything during an election campaign?

Garry manned the switchboard for three hours a day. He put leaflets into envelopes and envelopes into letterboxes. He talked to people on doorsteps, defended the two Davids, coalitions and consensus politics, resisted accusations of nuclear wishy-washiness, and was bitten by a Doberman in Golder's Green. Taken to Casualty at the Royal Free, he distantly caught sight – what was this? – of Lorna's Fred across the foyer. Could he be seeing a nurse? Garry felt no desire to run after him, however, since he had already borrowed money off him the week before, and anyway he didn't want this to come out in front of Mariangela who was still complaining about all the washing up he'd done with her in mind.

But at least the bandage on his hand got him out of envelope stuffing. He sat around being matey with the others as they laboured on in the best campaign spirits. Mariangela, with a sliver of pink tongue held between her teeth, was the fastest envelope-stuffer of them all. He watched how she scratched the back of one calf with the toe of the other foot; in the evening it was he they usually sent out with money to pick up a round of beers.

And of course if the party didn't make the great quantum leap forward that would enable them to offer him a job, he could always fall back on the place at Softway, sell them some bullshit about having been up in Cleveleys for a month where Mother was dying and their letter, letters now, not having been forwarded. They would swallow that. Why shouldn't they? He could almost believe it himself. All over the country there must be people who went to see their parents dying and missed out on important letters. Or who said they did.

Yes, the time passed very pleasantly in the bustle and purpose of the Centre; and if only Mariangela had worn better clothes and had her hair done and stopped kissing him every five minutes and explaining to everybody how much smarter the Italian Radical Party were with their publicity stunts and their leader's cappuccino hunger strikes, if only she had been less voracious, less loud in her scruffiness, it would have passed even more pleasantly still.

But as the great day approached, the campaign almost over, so depression descended, a blend of angst and poignancy not unlike the feeling that will sometimes clutch at the heart-strings as a long and particularly happy holiday draws to its close. And as they all sat, on the night of June 11th, in the operations room as they called it, around a TV Roger had brought in, Garry was ever so faintly aware that the pricked balloon sensation he was experiencing as result after result was announced, was not so much a response to the rout of the Alliance (though this would make him look rather silly in certain quarters), but followed quite naturally from his growing awareness that tomorrow, or at least very soon, he really ought to decide what to do. And he wasn't sure he was capable of this. Nor of facing up to his incapacity.

He needed to defend himself, his personal integrity, that was the point, to feel he hadn't been bullied out of his ideals, his intentions, into settling for a life which wasn't what he had imagined. And none of the paths he had to choose from would appear to let him do this.

''ow totally absurd,' Mariangela spluttered. 'Other 28,000 votes are just wasted. We win nothing.'

The Liberals had come second in another Dorset constituency.

'This is stupid,' she cried. 'Here you want the PR. In Italy the Radical Party has only the 3 per cent of the votes and they have more seats in parliament.'

Quite suddenly it occurred to Garry, or rather he had just the most passing inkling, a flicker of insight, as if faint lightning had photographed a landscape different from the one he thought he knew, but nevertheless perfectly familiar – it occurred to Garry that he had chosen the Liberal Party, way back, *because* they were the losers and would always be so; because without PR they would never wake up in the morning with the responsibility of winners. As perhaps he had chosen his bedsit because he knew it would never become home, and Mariangela because he knew he wouldn't marry her.

This was his method of self-defence. This was how he was preserving himself for the opportunity when it came. Keeping the future where it belonged.

Whereas Amanda had chosen him, from the start. Which was why she was so precious. And so difficult.

But the insight, if it was that, was already fading. The chemicals of his mind wouldn't hold this unflattering image. There was his consolation beer to drink, he tugged at a ring-pull, and anyway the Italian girl now sat down hard in his lap, giving him something else to think about.

'I would like that we go to see your mother before to go back to Italy.'

They were beating a retreat with Roger down the Edgware Road at three in the morning, on foot.

Surprised on two fronts, Italy, Mother (and he was already aware of a new feeling of siege), Garry said, 'We'll see.' And hurried on: 'Not the remotest trace of tactical voting though, God, I ask you, after all that was said, and when you think . . .'

But Roger had had more than enough of politics for one night. 'How is the old family?' he asked, since everyone in the Centre knew the story. 'Amanda was saying on the phone the other night she'd driven over to see your mother when she was up in Manchester or something. A pretty heavy scene apparently.'

'She'd driven over to see my mother?'

For one unpleasant second, walking under the Martian green neon of the Kenyon's funeral parlour ad, surprise became alarm. Though unnecessarily; for Mariangela immediately said: 'Oh, that was very good from 'er part; especially now that she is not an interested.'

Whatever this was meant to mean it seemed innocuous enough. He said: 'Oh, the situation is really pretty stable, except that Mother's refusing to talk to anyone. Raymond appears to be taking his stuff though.'

'Let's go this weekend. Is absurd I don't see 'er never.'

'Yeah, they say it's a kind of self-induced block. With Mother. People do it when they can't accept the world as it is, a way of pretending that it doesn't exist apparently. Washing your hands of everything. Very convenient. I was thinking of trying it myself. Anyway, Graham was saying absolutely not to go since she gets very worked up if . . .'

'But 'e says to come.'

'What?'

'I 'ave read 'is letter and 'e says to come. 'e sent the money.'

'No, no,' Garry lied on automatic pilot now, 'there was another letter this morning. Since Raymond came out. The other one was before.'

But this was appalling if she'd been through his drawers!

Roger yawned. An overweight dilettante in his early forties, his accent was Oxbridge, his glasses National Health. 'That's the level of public service these days, letting loonies out all over the place. And they still all go and vote for her.' He laughed wrily. 'The loonies, probably. Ever thought of writing a book about him?'

'Sorry?' His mind had been searching in cupboards and drawers, through files and folders. What had she found? How would she react? This was awful. A police-car whooped by. Tory to a man after their pay rises and new riot toys.

'About your older brother. It might make a good novel. Or film. "How my brother went psycho." No, seriously though' – because Roger had published a good beer guide himself, he knew the business – 'you're well-placed to do an excellent case study.

And then the fiction market can't get enough of stuff about weirdos. Might even draw some attention to the problem. Quite apart from shovelling a bit of shit at Thatcher.'

'Is a very good idea,' somebody thought.

Actually Garry had once suggested this very project himself, so that now he could repeat what Amanda had rather disparagingly said on that occasion: that the problem with novels about loonies was that it just seemed like a gimmick to get everybody biting their nails waiting for some awful act of *Sunday People* violence to happen. It was corny. Like when you said there was a gun in a drawer or something and everybody knew that by page 150 at the latest somebody was going to use it.

But this only reminded Garry of all the time bombs in his own bottom drawer. Christ!

Though hadn't he been wishing her away only an hour ago as he listened to her explaining the Italian electoral system for about the one thousand five hundredth time?

'But 'e did kidnap your mother with the axe. Is a true story. Is not fiction.'

'Well actually there appears to be some doubt about that now . . .'

Her English seemed to be deteriorating rather than the opposite.

'She's got a valid point there. I think if you could just get over that the madness is real, factual, and not just a narrative contrivance, you could write an excellent documentary novel, like *In Cold Blood*, look into his motives, find out what really makes him tick. After all, you're close to the situation. Could be a more profitable way of spending your time,' Roger added with resignation, 'than coming down the Centre. In fact I think you can be a thousand per cent sure of that now.'

'Yes,' Garry said, who hadn't seen Raymond since the fateful last holiday in Algiers over a year ago and was damned if he was going up there to see him now. What for? What could he possibly offer? Or gain from such an experience? And Father simply couldn't have run out of money. What a story!

'Or you could focus on one key moment in the past that started the whole thing, like in *The Sound and the Fury*.'

Which Garry hadn't actually read.

'That's true,' he said. What he thoroughly resented was Roger's avuncular, have-a-go-at-this-laddy attitude, with no appreciation at all of what the evening must have meant for him in terms of lost job prospects. Quite apart from bringing out Amanda's name like that in front of Mariangela as if she were no more than the most passing of mutual acquaintances. Clearly she'd gone up to Manchester to make her peace with Antony, had dropped in at home in Cleveleys precisely so that he would realize it was all over between them, probably on a seaside day-out with hub. In any case, she hadn't accepted the freeze till election day he had proposed. He had lost her. Lost Amanda.

And now he found himself repeating something else his first love had said on that occasion: 'The only difference between the gun and the looney, as a device, is that the latter can go off on its own, which makes it all the more convenient, and all the more corny.'

Yes, she was always so confident when she came out with these things, Amanda, and at least twice as intelligent as little Miss Radical, though it did rather seem he'd have to hang in there with Italian politics now. He had no choice in the matter. And for a split second Garry was quite perfectly aware of the crashing irony that although he had never been able to choose to live with a woman, the idea of living without one was unimaginable. What a weakling he was! And how little it helped realizing. When he had set out in life with such good intentions.

Perhaps he would try to kill himself again.

'But just tell the true story, dammit. Don't worry about whether . . .'

A group of well-dressed men and women wearing rosettes climbed out of a taxi across the street and began cheering.

'Imbeciles,' Roger interrupted himself. 'How can they vote for her? I can't understand it. Just look at this street. Filthy, depressed. Eight years of Tory misrule, drunks in the doorways, decaying housing stock selling at outlandish prices, half the Irish in Kilburn unemployed, and these other drunks have to pile out of a taxi and cheer the old witch for it.'

Mariangela, who actually hadn't said anything for quite a long time, now chirped: 'We are going to go away without to pay the rent, aren't we, Garry? That will give the landlord a lesson. I bet he vote Conservative.'

'Are you moving?' Roger asked surprised. 'Not out of the area, I hope. You're one of the pillars of the party.'

'Landlord only declares half the rent, so I can only ask for half of it on the dole. I thought I should find . . .'

'Oh everybody does that. With the taxes you have to pay it's understandable. Move and it'll just be out of the frying pan into . . .'

But mercifully they had reached the parting of their ways.

'Goodnight, Rog.'

'Goodnight, Garry, Mariangela.'

Walking the last hundred yards, he kissed her hair in the dark. She turned her mouth to him. She kissed furiously. A street-sweeping truck clanked by.

'So?'

They were at the top of the stairs. He was fiddling with keys.

'So what?'

'So you are not going to ask what I 'ave found in your drawers?'

Having pushed open the door, Garry immediately went to lie down where there were two mattresses together on the floor. He closed his eyes, but then after a moment opened them again and propped himself up on an elbow. As so often he enjoyed a moment's consolatory consciousness of his own physical beauty – the jet dark head horizontal on the bronzed forearm.

'Whatever it is, don't let's talk about it. You know I love you.'

'I know. If not, they are not at the *bottom* of your drawer, the things I 'ave found."

Her smile was teasing as she began the evening's slow strip-show, unbuttoning, unzipping, unhooking. She didn't seem in the least perturbed.

'Eh? Is right?' She stood on one leg to push off a shoe.

But he had absolutely no desire to talk about the details of his emotional life. Quite the contrary. In fact, if she forced him to do so, he would scream. He didn't want to know about any of the things in his drawer (or his mind), to discuss any of his duplicities, to argue about any of their consequences. He really would scream.

He liked to watch, though, every evening, how the complications of her bra came away and the breasts plumped out into the simple curves of nudity. His prick stirred, reminding him he had still to undress.

She gave him a look, laughing. Then swooped down to cuddle by him.

'Don't waarry,' she said. 'I have thrown away everything for you. You can start from the beginning again.'

And after making love, she said: 'Is very good luck though if you don't want to come to Italy you can begin the computer work. I don't mind it which you decide.'

Fred to Lorna

June 11th
LORNA,
  *I'M SENDING THIS UNFINISHED SO AS TO ENCLOSE
THE ENVELOPE (FROM ALGERIA) ADDRESSED TO YOUR
MOTHER, WHICH APPEARS TO BE FROM YOUR
FATHER. HOPE SO AND THAT THIS THROWS SOME
LIGHT ON THINGS.*
  BEST, FRED.
*(IT'S DATED A WEEK AGO SO I'M GETTING IT OFF AS
FAST AS POSS.)*

June 2nd   Fairfield

Dearest Lorna,
  When I arrived home Sunday night – after two hours of
tailbacks on the M1 – I thought, I'll send you a postcard
every day, and then at the same time I'll write you a kind of
diary and letter put together. I'll give it exactly one full hour
a day for a week. An hour of meditation, or reflection – all
that time in the library yet one reflects on one's own life so
rarely. And every day I'll find a reason for making you come
back.
  So that was Sunday. Now it's Tuesday. I tried to start
yesterday, but spent the entire hour fidgeting and going and
turning the TV on and off and looking through one of the
photo albums. I mention that just by way of indicating what's

happened to Fred's famous self-discipline in your absence. It's as if all the scaffolding had been taken out of my life. The apartment is empty. Time is empty. No Kirsty to take to the nursery and back, to change and bath. You miss the interruptions when they're gone. No structure, no hurry. Sometimes I feel so disoriented I just mooch about pouring coke, stuffing myself with crackers and watching cricket, of which I understand very little, but it's the only thing that seems to be on all day.

Come back, Lorna baby.

Wednesday: regression to the four trips a night routine (oh, my old friend john – modern pharmaceuticals not proving very efficient I'm afraid), and on one of those trips I thought that having someone leave you is like having a limb amputated. You keep believing they're still there. So here I am still getting out of bed on 'my' side and walking all the way round, even being careful about the creaky board, rather than just rolling over to yours. Poor Fred, do have pity.

Otherwise it's been a completely banal day: library, piss, summer school committee, desperate piss, library, piss, tutorials, piss, piss, home, piss, work, piss, work, piss, fish fingers, piss, work, piss, glass of coke (unwise), pisssss, various pills, 'Newsnight' with candy bar (unwise), piss, work, piss – till now.

I won't indicate pauses for pissing in this letter (I wouldn't like to cause a paper shortage), but if it doesn't seem to follow on smoothly here and there . . .

Yeah, right there . . .

Kirsty. You said in your letter you wondered if either of us had taken in that she was a real person. Excluding any wrangling over your use of the word 'real', this is one of the areas where I am disposed to cry mea culpa. One gets so busy arranging life to make it workable – and I gravitate toward the clockworkable I know – that it does sort of slip your mind sometimes that this is a 'person' growing up, and not just a schedule problem. Having her gone, however, is curing me of that. Because I miss her. I would never have imagined this intense physical feeling of missing in her regard. I mean that I don't just have a wife I'm in love with but a child too. It seems you only see the bottom, the base and bass rhythm to your life when it's dropped out and there's only the crazy treble tinkling on on its own – lectures, papers, seminars. I miss all her cheeky looks, her bright squint, the way she skedaddles off on her tricycle trying not to be picked up, the way she lies blind when you try to find out if she's shat. I guess I miss the difficulties, strange as it sounds. And if someone asked me now what kind of person my daughter is, I'd say: a little person, a sneaky person, a smart person, a stubborn person, a jumpy person, a complicated person, and maybe most of all a fun person. With very white teeth. And dimples. In short, a fair old hotch potch of her Mom and Pop.

Which brings us to the next reason why you've got to come back. Because you can't let her grow up without me. That would be committing your father's crime in reverse.

Still, despite the inevitable, but commendable, don't you think?, sentimentalism of these last few difficult days, you've got to admit that Kirsty is <u>also</u> a schedule problem (what isn't?), and will remain so. To date we've solved this problem by sending her to a nursery so you can work. But if you want to change that arrangement now, I am willing, reluctantly, to back down. I think it's a mistake, I think you'd be better to hang on to a job, but you can have your own way. As long as I can work a reasonable number (8 – 10) of hours a day, I don't mind if you take on the herculean task of bringing up baby.

Enough for this evening. I know I may sound a bit pompous and silly here and there, I don't know what tone to write in, but the truth is, Lorna, I'm fighting for my life. I want you back, I really do. And half of me can hardly believe I'm having to write these things, at my age, after six years together. I thought all these relationship problems were behind me forever.

Oh, maybe a last comment on Kirsty. You say you're so

worried about how she will turn out when she's 30 and what kind of relationship we will have with her, etc. I think this kind of long range anxiety is a mistake. We're two pretty okay people 90% of the time, we play and have fun. Obviously we have our hang-ups and neuroses and obviously she sees them, like she saw that argument and that moment of violence – you may have had a bruised arm, but I had to talk about John Berryman through a badly cut lip. And obviously seeing that violence will affect her, will probably remain impressed on her memory. So it will become part of her education, then, that slap in the face, that punch in the arm, that ridiculous grappling and toppling on the carpet, shouting, tearing a skirt. And it's negative, I know, but still, it's no good being so overawed by the effect your actions could have that you just freeze, or start doing everything in relation to how she will react. Probably you were right to hit me for being my asshole insensitive worst, and unfortunately, in the heat of the moment, people who are hit often hit back. But the fact that Kirsty's discovered that two people who love each other (don't we?) can also hit each other isn't the end of the world, is it? It's not going to be that that makes her a drug addict, or a prostitute, or a schizophrenic. As long as we don't make a habit of it. Come the day, she'll turn out how she turns out. She will surprise us by becoming someone, because you can never imagine a person before they've developed – just as you can never imagine – you remember how freaked out you were – a baby's face before it's born. She'll surprise us by being different from us, though with splashes of sameness maybe: a lighter pigment here, a rounder curve above the eyes there, a sharper mind maybe, maybe a bigger bust, you just can't know. But however she turns out, that will be only partly our responsibility, so there's no point in being overwhelmed by it, like Raymond's condition is only in a very small part your parents' responsibility. Every time we've talked about it we've always agreed on that. We never sided with the two G's blame-everything-on-the-parents line. So I can't see why you're getting so upset about us and Kirsty now.

Though I do admit we should spend more time with her. But now she's learning to talk and you can get some change from her, that shouldn't be too difficult. All too soon, I don't doubt, it'll be she won't be wanting to spend any time with us, and that will be her responsibility and her decision, just as it will be her decision, not ours, whether to cock up, or perhaps even throw away her own private life to come and help us out when we're in all kinds of difficulties in our early sixties. And would you really want her to do that?

Friday: I suppose, actually, on a quick re-reading of the above, the answer to what I wrote at the end of Wednesday night's stuff is, yes. Of course we would want her to come and help us out. And why should it mess up her private life so much? I seem to have caught myself out here. In fact, I'm willing to concede you were right to go, and if I hadn't made such an almighty steaming fuss about it (but don't you at least understand my point of view? We were on such a winning streak, and it seemed such a shame to interrupt it) – yes, if I hadn't made such a fuss I wouldn't have to be trying to knock down this barrier between us now. With this qualification: 'For a while'. We'd only expect her to come and help us for a while. Wouldn't we?

So when the while's up, Lorna, come back. If only you'd say, I will, I'd feel reassured, I could settle down and get some work done instead of just worrying. Whyever shouldn't you come back? I'm capitulating on everything.

Obviously I didn't write anything yesterday because you phoned. It seemed futile scratching away at paper when I had the sound of your voice in my ears to take to bed with me. And of course it was great to speak to you, but why forbid me to come up at the weekend? I can't believe you're being so hard about this. Are you hiding something? It makes me feel quite desperate.

Sunday evening. Do you recall how I once bored you to death by insisting on explaining my theory that similes really function to identify things and establish their uniqueness, not their similarity to other things at all: the more you said two things were alike, the more you simply drew people's attention to the effort and ingenuity involved in overcoming the obvious differences – like when I compared having a partner leave you to having a limb amputated. Well, what I want to say is that I think the same thing's true of those 'similarities' you pointed out in your letter. I am not really like your father <u>at all</u>, you are <u>not</u> like your mother, our relationship is not like theirs, and most of all my relationship with you is <u>nothing</u> like your father's relationship with you, while Kirsty, as I said, will be like none of us, even if she takes after all. I think it's dangerous the way you're getting these determinism-type things into your head and then acting on them as if they were accepted fact.

Instead why don't you look at the facts. Your parents, or so you've told me, met during the war; they were then separated for 3 years (?). When he came back they waited another 4 years (?) before marrying while he got himself set up in the local construction business, then went to live in her mother's house. As soon as they'd married, he forbade her to go on working because he didn't think it dignified. He wanted one child, she wanted ten. He wanted to work abroad, she didn't, but was determined to follow him, whereas he didn't really want her to. Inside a year of the wedding she found he had been to prostitutes; she had never had other lovers. When her mother died, she spent upwards of fifteen years following him to the most god-forsaken places, producing children he didn't really want, trying to adopt more, and wishing she could open a seamstresses' school for the local inhabitants, except they moved too often and he just thought she was starry-eyed.

Have I got the Baldwin saga about right?

Instead the Shaker story reads as follows: we met at an Ivy League University; we had both had a number of previous lovers; two weeks (not seven years) after meeting we were living together and have done ever since and faithfully; we wrote each other love letters even though we were living together in a single room; you chose to give up your studies, even though I tried to persuade you not to; I saw you were very miserable in America (for reasons you were unable to explain) and so I agreed to go to England with you even before I got the job at UCL, and despite the fact that I had far better prospects in the States. At the time in fact I feared I was saying goodbye to my career, for a while at least, but I did it because I thought, if you can't take a risk at 30, when can you? Because I thought I'd lose you if I didn't go. Because I thought that back in your home country you'd find what you wanted to do and all the wonderful bubbling potential I've always seen in you would come out and be realized. But I wasn't pushing you in any direction. Not just then. I was following you. To a semi-basement bedsit in Islington for starters, furnished entirely from the local flea-market and with a lodger upstairs with a wooden leg and more or less the same nocturnal pissing habits I now have. A bit of a come-down from Beacon Hill, no? Though I loved discovering London with you, Lorna. Our Sunday morning bus rides those first few months were some of the happiest moments of my life.

So you decided that what you really wanted was to be a paediatrician. You would start your education all over again. You became terribly enthusiastic for a while, devouring mountains of books, preparing 'A' levels. But it was never feasible. School turned you down. At which point you spent a <u>week</u> in bed being utterly miserable about it, you had studied the wrong things, chosen the wrong path, etc., etc. I suggested a child of our own; you said not to try to brick you up in a domestic dead end.

You do remember all this, Lorna? Four or five years ago. I hope our stories tally on at least the principal points, though I know how easy it is to forget (I found I'd forgotten how to sing the other night when I was trying to get Kirsty to sleep), and particularly how easy it is to forget other periods of your life, what it was really like being oneself then, what loving meant, what quality it had. One tends to live in a continuous present, I suppose, oblivious to the skins one sheds. That's why I'm writing all this down, to say, don't just throw patterns over our lives and jump to conclusions, don't say I'm like your dad just because I said you needed a shrink one day and you hit me and I hit you back. Remember how it really was. I came to England because you asked me to, I put up with you moping for a solid week over what I'd always known was impractical from the start, but I hadn't wanted to discourage you. I brought you meals in bed and was very tender and uncritical as I recall.

But let's grasp the nettle now I've got to it. I have always been unnerved by the vacuum where your will should be, your ambition, your plans. You're full of bouncy vitality, sometimes you're fireworks, but you have no plans. Last week, when I was reading and re-reading your letter, I counted ten 'I don't want's and 'I don't like's, to one 'I want'. Okay, criticize me for pushing you in directions you don't want to go. Okay, the Crackle book may have been a mistake. But if there were some kind of direction coming from you, nobody would be more delighted and ready to let be than myself.

Or at least if you were <u>happy</u> to do nothing, play lady wife – but you're not. A week after that university rejection there you were reading all the job sections of the papers, applying for office jobs and counting on your language skills. Over a year you were offered three jobs, turned down two and hung in at the one you did take for about four months. You didn't want to be just a secretary, however many languages they made you speak; you didn't want to ride the tube every day in the rush hour. And you were right. But couldn't you find anything that suited you?

So then it was motherhood by default, right? And all the hassle of finding and buying the flat.

I'm sorry, I'm getting aggressive, but like I said, I'm just trying to remember what they've been like, these past years, so as to help you understand my growing frustration: why isn't she ever satisfied? Such a brilliant and attractive woman, why isn't she geared into something?

Especially because, unlike brother Garry, you are not lazy, nor lacking in courage or energy – speaking of which, or whom, he came round last week with his Italian number, to all intents and purposes on a very rare social visit, but then when she was in the john he asked for money and against my best principles I wrote a cheque for a hundred pounds, as I know you've done in the past – they were the only stubs you didn't write the explanation on, no? – the figures were too round to escape attention. I gave it him because I didn't want him to tell you how mean I was when I wasn't in a position to persuade you on the contrary how silly it is to keep giving him money. Still, he seemed very happy with Mariangela, all goo and kisses, which was cute.

Anyhow, you can see that your not wanting and dissatisfaction became a burden to me. And so I started pushing things in your mouth, trying to have will enough for both of us (the way ahead, honestly, does seem so clear to me, why shouldn't I plan for it, I can't understand why you should lose faith in it), forgetting that even if you didn't know what you did want you have always had more than enough spirit to reject what you didn't.

So there's this big difficult problem. But it can never alter the fact that I want you, Lorna, whatever you want. I'm not interested in other solutions or other women; you blinkered me that way many years ago. And all my plans can change to adapt to you. They really can. Even my career plans, with a massive effort, now you've woken me up, they can change. Just tell me how.

Monday. Something I forgot to tell you last night. Friday I asked Dr Khan, who has a rather gentler index finger than Johnson, and less bony, whether a prostate infection could damage my fertility over the long term; he said, of course. He said, unless I am one of the lucky few for whom the antibiotics actually work, I should think of 'having any more children you want in the next couple of years or so'.

How about it, Lorna? It's not my schedule I'm imposing now. It's life's. Or rather, perhaps, death's.

Then he said another thing Johnson didn't say. 'Keep the seminal fluid on the move.' I asked him what he meant by that exactly and he said rather shyly: 'Ejaculate regularly, at least two or three times a week. Don't let it stagnate.' I didn't tell him my wife was away for the moment, perhaps definitively. Another little dilemma. Would he have made the old wrist gesture?

Also, in the line at the International, I thought (don't huff and puff too much, it's half in fun) – I thought about a simile that could be drawn between my prostate and Raymond. (If you were here, of course, I wouldn't be sitting up past midnight with nothing to do but scribble such nonsense.) Raymond and my prostate are alike because: both are embarrassing; neither appears to be curable with drugs; both are part of our lives, close to us, and yet frustratingly inaccessible and mysterious; both tend to emblematize all that is intractable and beyond Big Fred's planning; both, or rather a combination of the two, seem likely to prevent us from having a second child, which I had set my heart on.

I leave you to decide the ways in which they are not similar.

Tuesday. Now I'm going to set down what I've been thinking and elaborating all day about you and why you must come back to me. And this time I really think I've got to the core of it. So, your diffidence, this loss of faith, is related to, though not entirely caused by (does it bother you that I set about analysing you like this, Lorna? Do you think it's crass and American of me? But what am I supposed to do? I do believe in solving things, though not in accepting responsibility for the unsolvable, i.e. Raymond, which sounds like a recipe for tragedy if ever there was one) – your diffidence is related to, if not exactly caused by your family past, some fundamental insecurity. You react to this in two ways: the way you were reacting to it when you met me, which was pretending your family didn't exist, that you'd descended from outer space already adult ('my father, who's he?' you said); and then the way you've reacted since they came back to England, which is trying to take them on, trying to get close to them, trying to have a new relationship with them, and so in a certain sense to recover, or at least be able to handle the past, which also in this case means to recover and handle Raymond, to make all well so that you will be well. I saw when your mother was here the way you were content to be a girl with her again, as though you were snuggling up to some security you'd never had enough of.

But this a trap, Lorna. You can get as close as you like to your mother, but your mother is tied to the boys, and above all to Raymond. Anyone can sense that. She will lead you back to him, because that's where her heart is. And there's nothing you can do about Raymond. Raymond is beyond cure. Raymond is the living dead. Like the past, the real past, or like your body (my body), he can't be changed, only accepted and tolerated for what he irrecoverably is. Deep down you know that. And that's why you're so diffident about family and domesticity. Because you see Raymond as one of the possible results, the possible casualties, the possible curses. You think, 'if we live like my parents lived we will be cursed like that.' And that's why your return to your old home was also a flight from the new and all it might hold – I've felt you escaping me ever since they came back and those letters started arriving, I've been so frustrated. But you can't let the disaster behind you throw you off completely, Lorna. Because domesticity, family – this was today's revelation – is still the great adventure, the great achievement, it really is, to stay together and build up something despite all the centrifugal forces ranged against it. Don't ditch your new family with trying to save the old.

But this time I'm not being callous. I'm not saying, dump them. I'm saying, if you think you can help your mother, <u>get her to come and live with us</u>, I'm willing to do it, though I swore I never would. I'm willing to do it exclusively because I want you back, I want you to have no excuse for not coming back, because I love you, I do, and I believe in us and I do see us together at 40 and 50 and 60 (and 70!), I'm determined to see us, with a family round us, whether happy or sad, or at our throats. That's how I feel.

And if your mother won't come back, then that is her business and her destiny – if she wants to cling to the wreckage, she can, it's hers to cling to after all, but you must come back here.

Lorna, this letter from Algeria's arrived, I'm signing off. If you don't phone beforehand, I shall come down next weekend, like it or not.

Kisses,
FRED

They walked along the seafront and she had her arm tucked in his; her other hand held Kirsty's. The wind pressed their clothes against their backs and hurried clouds across the sky. In mortarboard and black college gown an elderly man stood by a primitive zodiac chart lashed to an ornamented lamp post and offered to tell tourists' futures. His gown flapped at hesitant onlookers, but nobody seemed to want to take the risk. Unless it was the 50p.

Ninety-nine per cent of the time, Raymond was a lamb. He took his medicine as promised, slept twelve to fourteen hours a day as a consequence and followed his Mary around for the other twelve or ten. He showered when told to, wore what was laid out for him, carried shopping bags, washed dishes, ate in a civilized manner and apart from the occasional outburst against the Americans and the forces of Judaeo-Christian expansionism, was more or less reasonable and friendly. The psychiatric social worker was pleased and eager to take credit.

So that Lorna felt quite guilty. However could she have imagined such horrors? He was perfectly well-behaved with Kirsty, or rather didn't seem to notice her at all. And perhaps he *had* only smashed up the flat because he had been abandoned by her father, because he had been upset by finding the photograph of him with the Sudanese prostitutes and because he knew that anyway the place was due to be refurbished. Perhaps it wasn't the axe that had scared Mother into the bathroom, but just a general sort of fear of his dishevelled, wild state. She had shouted at him for being filthy and having smashed up the place, he had rounded and shouted at her and she had run and locked herself in the bathroom. Nothing more to it. When the police came after all she hadn't even realized it was for her house.

So feeling guilty, Lorna put up with his slack grin and

shambling walk (more side effects of the tranquillizers, they said) and with this irksome way he had of never leaving her alone for more than a minute all his waking hours. She put up with it, in the hope that she was helping. And kept trying to talk calmly and pleasantly as the social worker had suggested.

'From Aziza Hassad,' he said now in reply to her question.

He had received a letter this morning and squirrelled it away.

'Come again?'

'A girl I got hold of through a marriage bureau.'

'Oh?'

'She's Syrian.'

'Terrific,' Lorna said, but was disappointed at this relapse into fantasy. 'It's time you had a girlfriend.' And she added carefully: 'I was afraid it might be another bill for books you'd ordered.'

He ignored that.

'They gave me a choice of three, but I chose her because she's Moslem. We plan to marry and have three or four children.'

'So you've already met her?' It was the extent to which he was so ready with these details that was unsettling. And yet you couldn't think of his stories as anything but fantasy since he didn't change the tone of voice to suit the subject, to address her, to show enthusiasm. He didn't appear to be aware of any need to overcome his listener's surprise to have you believe certain things. He was so sure it would all seem perfectly reasonable. Because he believed it so completely himself of course. In the moment he said it.

'No, only corresponded so far. But all good Islamic girls want children. It's Allah's plan for mankind, the family, it can't be shirked. Anyway, the data from the bureau said she did. I have her photograph somewhere. Nicish body.'

But Kirsty had made a break for the astrologer now. With a toddler's eagerness she tried to grab a fluttering hem of gown.

'Your birthday, my little girl. Time and date. Let's see what the future holds.' The tatty man was reassuringly avuncular, like some friendly headmaster, but Lorna snatched the child back.

'No thank you. I'd rather find out as we go along.'

A tram squealed by. The astrologer's torn gown flapped hard and he had to grab at his mortarboard in a wind that sent litter scrambling along the duny beach behind. 'Forewarned is forearmed,' he said, more ominously than he meant.

'No thanks, sorry.'

'As do all good girls,' Raymond was saying, mouth wide in that tubby, stuffed-cheek grin which never quite seemed intended as a form of communication, but more as if half dead nerves had been randomly galvanized by some not quite tranquillized impulse. His brown eyes were glassy. 'You should have more children yourself. Though not with your present husband. I think three children is a minimum to fulfil your role as a woman.'

'Do you indeed?' she laughed. 'And why not with my "present husband"?'

'Genetic inferiority. Low IQ rating. Birth sign not . . .'

'Oh come on.'

He looked at her with what might have been a genuine desire to be frank. 'I know what I know about Americans.' He tapped his nose. 'They're all the same.'

They negotiated an area where the pavement was being dug up. To their right, for some reason the sea was suddenly louder and the air flecked with spray.

'Well they can't all have the wrong birth sign.'

'I know what I know what I know,' he insisted.

To cool things, she said, 'Kirsty love, would you like a little brother or sister?'

'I've been there. I saw what I saw.' He thrust his chin forward and upward above a bulging neck.

'No,' said the girl flatly. 'Kirthty want eyth keam.'

'And what if I don't want any more children?'

He shook off her arm and pushed his hands in his pockets. Dropping his chin now against his chest, he kicked at a pebble. 'Oh yes,' he said disconcertingly, as if to someone else, and then to her: 'Women obey.'

She tried to laugh again. 'You sound like Dad now.'

Raymond muttered to himself. They passed the sea flats and the two big sand pits they had raced between as children. The advancing tide frothed in the flat between them, just as it had so many years before. Which somehow prompted her to ask point blank: 'What did you see in America, Raymond? What happened,

217

I mean, before I came down to visit you that time? What was it?'

He kicked much harder at another larger pebble which flew over the parapet and down to where brave bathers were determined to be on the beach.

'Don't! Raymond!'

'Krauts and niggers, Jews and Spics,' he said, and she became aware of a new, fiercer tension in his body, the hands thrust harder into pockets, chin pushed harder on the chest. 'Genetic crap.'

'That's not a very nice thing to . . .'

'In Europe they fuck right enough, but in America they castrate you. I'm telling you. You should watch out.'

His head jerked back and nodded two or three times with an exaggerated backward and forward movement. Lorna felt her own grip tighten on Kirsty's wrist. She lifted the little girl into her arms.

'They castrate you and feed on your blood and sperm.'

'Blud an spum,' Kirsty sang, being at the repeating age.

Which transformed Lorna's embarrassment to anger. 'Not in front of Kirsty,' she snapped. 'Don't say those vile things.'

Surprisingly he responded, became meek: 'No, of course.' And then said in a mutter: 'I'm so confused, Lorna, I'm so ill.' His voice disintegrated into a wail. His head was in his hands. 'They've made me so confused. Help me! They're shining sounds in my brain. And the gas. They know I've found them out.'

Two passers-by turned their heads. What could she do but put down an alarmed Kirsty and stretch an arm round her brother's shoulders? 'Just try to get well, Ray. I just don't want you to say bad things in front of her, that's all.' But he was sobbing, shaking. So that without thinking, she asked: 'Did we give you your pill this morning? Did you take it? Is that the problem?'

He stood up straight and was suddenly completely cold. It was so disconcerting the way he could metamorphose like this, so that you never got a grip on him before he had wriggled chameleon-like into some other animal. When their eyes met it was as if he was seeing her for the first time, without a trace of recognition, and in a situation where he, not she, had complete authority; he had no memory whatsoever of those last few confessional moments.

'I know all about those pills and shan't be taking any more

of them, thank you very much. I am well aware that regular administration will destroy my internal organs, beginning with the liver and renal functions, and I know that this is being done in order to prevent the children of Allah from coming into their inheritance. So I shan't be taking any more, and that's final. According to the Royal Pharmaceutical Society's monthly . . .'

'Raymond,' she interrupted what was beginning to sound like a speech read out in a monotone, or as if somehow he were the mouthpiece of some other creature. 'Raymond!' But he kept talking over her.

' . . . and you thought you could all fool me there and induce premature sterility through the application of . . .'

'Nobody's pretending they're good for you in the long run, but you're supposed to reduce the dose gradually. Otherwise the whole thing'll begin all over again and they'll put you back in a home and . . .'

'Fuck off!' he suddenly shouted. 'Everybody just fuck off! Come on. I know all about you,' and face ablaze with excitement now as one or two people turned to stare, he burst out laughing, then, clapping his hands, began to chant. 'Fuck off, fuck off, fuck off . . .'

Lorna picked up Kirsty again, who had also begun to chant her own version, and turned for home, but he grabbed her shoulder.

Rather than stopping to watch, two middle-aged women were hurrying along all the faster now. An older man hesitated, embarrassed, but couldn't decide, a crumpled newspaper in his hand.

They were standing together on the pavement by the parapet with only dunes and white-capped sea behind.

'And if you tell Mrs Baldwin, I shall know what steps to take. Okay?' He was shrieking.

'Tell her about what?' Pulled up close to his face, his hand twisted into the shoulder of her jacket, she was again appalled by the fact that her brother was still to be found in those tense inflamed features. You forgot the real old him, the simple, generous, boyish features, then saw, or rather glimpsed him, one fleeting glimpse, but just enough to make the whole thing so much worse. She felt a desperate urge to run, but his grip was fierce.

'About Aziza.' He was breathing heavily.

'Why not? It's nice that you've got a girlfriend.'

A gust of wind wrapped her dress round her legs.

'You mean you don't know?' And as if to somebody off to the right, he said, 'You mean she's not in on it? Well now we'll see.'

'Raymond, listen, you're hurting me, for Christ's sake, let's go home.'

Although how that was going to improve things wasn't exactly clear.

'Of course, Lorna,' he was suddenly rational now, even condescending. He let go of her shoulder. 'Of course we'll go home. But not before you promise not to tell.'

'Okay, I won't.'

Now he had come down to almost a whisper, conspiratorial: 'Because I discovered some time ago that there has been a plot to prevent me marrying and having children and a family, or even a girlfriend. They're punishing me for fucking Mother.'

'What?'

He looked at her as if puzzled by this interruption. He hesitated. Then said, explaining carefully:

'You are married. Graham Ali and Garibald have girlfriends; so it is quite clear there has been a plot to throw a spanner in my works; because the Yanks and Jews don't want anyone who shares the Islamic faith to procreate. They don't want Allah's plan fulfilled for me. And then Father has always liked to keep me round the house to do the dirty jobs for him, to have cheap labour. So they wrote to Fadima and told her a lot of lies about me. Otherwise she would have come. She had promised to come. Fred sent the letters to her because they thought she would believe him more easily. Anyway, Fred was only brought into the family to control me after I became Moslem and . . .'

'Okay, let's go home,' Lorna said firmly. 'I won't tell anyone.'

'You swear.'

'I swear.'

'You see' – he still wouldn't budge from the slightly crouched stance he had taken up by the parapet; the tension in his body was a soldier's before action. 'I knew you weren't involved.'

'Good.'

'You were just their stooge. When Gaddafi . . .'

'Come on, Raymond, let's go home. Kirsty needs her tea.'

And then at the top of Broughton Street, having fallen silent for a good five minutes as they walked, he came out with something which she found rather beautiful: 'Standing bell, a little black.'

'Sorry?'

'Standing bell, a little black.'

She looked at him. All the agitation of a few minutes before had passed, the tiny beads of sweat, the intensity and glassiness of the eyes. He just seemed terribly amused now, and somehow pleased with himself.

'Standing bell, a little black?' she asked. It sounded vaguely poetic.

'You mean you don't know what it means?' He obviously found this hugely funny.

She smiled, in response to his laughter rather than at any humour she could see: 'No, I don't. Is it a quote?'

'You wouldn't,' he said, then turned and hurried to the door ahead of her, dragging a large bunch of keys half stuck in his pocket as he went.

SOLUTIONS?

'Aren't you going to open it?'

When the letter arrived with the other letter inside bearing the red Algerian stamp and addressed in Father's handwriting, Lorna hoped against hope that this might finally be the occasion to surprise her mother out of her long silence. But not so. Mrs Baldwin took one look at it and shrugged her shoulders, as if to say it held no interest for her. For Lorna had noticed that her mother's silence did not preclude communication through small gestures here and there, a nod or shake of the head; nor was she actually mad in the way her brother was, for she would occasionally do a bit of housework, make herself a cup of tea, feed or fondle the cat, watch the black-and-white television Uncle Harry had lent, turning it on and off at the beginning and end of programmes, and not, like Raymond, at random. No, it was simply that she refused to speak and refused to go out, or to meet anyone who came to visit: the psychiatric social worker, Uncle Harry (desperate to condole and find out more), and once the local vicar. She sat and appeared to observe, though without a great deal of interest or hostility, her son and daughter moving about the house, Raymond using the bath rug apparently as a prayer mat, Lorna coaxing Kirsty onto the potty. She watched but seemed to be willing herself out of existence, her body shedding all its boisterous presence, her face all its rapid vitality. She couldn't not look, not hear, not breathe, but she could not speak. She sat silent, gazing or vacant, the only flicker of life coming when she bent forward to stroke the cat, to draw the animal to her lap, the only initiative when she went to the kitchen to pour milk into a saucer, as if this simple unambiguous representative of animal life was all she could trust or wanted to.

Curiously, despite a week at home now, Raymond seemed

hardly to have noticed that his mother wasn't speaking, and indeed had made no mention of it to Lorna, as if the woman had been dumb all her life, or as if, could it be?, he understood this change in her behaviour perfectly, knowing what lay behind it. In any case, Lorna thought his docility so far was quite probably at least partly due to the non-interference from Mother, to the fact that she was not there haranguing him for anything less than total normality, trying to force him, as she had for so many years, to be the boy she loved.

'Aren't you going to open it?' Lorna repeated.

Now, at eight in the morning, Raymond was still in bed.

But clearly the older woman was not going to open it. She had had enough.

And so, even before looking at Fred's, Lorna did, and began to read out loud.

June 5th   Bougaa

Dear Brenda,

I hope all is well with yourself, Lorna and Fred and that little Kirsty received my birthday card. You will remember I said I would let you know when it was safe to come back; well, I did phone a number of times actually, but never managed to get through. Anyway, as you will have guessed from the envelope, circumstances have now changed some-what. I am writing from Bougaa where I am staying in the Commodore Hotel, in the same room you used to watch the cranes from actually, when they nested on the post office roof that year. In fact I'm enclosing the village's one postcard, of the mosque, that we used to send to everybody. It hasn't changed and I hope it will make you at least a little nostalgic because I'm now asking you to come back here. You've been bellyaching for months about my taking retirement too soon when I could have been earning more money to give to the children. So here I am. Just a week or so after you left, TCI wrote to ask me if I'd like to do some consultancy work for them. Trilling, poor chap, went and died of a heart attack and they were short of people who knew the job and the

226

score with the natives. I decided to take them up on it. My reasons were as follows:

a) Garry is short of money and needs help, as you never let up reminding me;

b) Ditto Graham if he is ever going to marry and buy a house;

c) Doing up Fleetwood Street is going to cost far more than I imagined. I had reckoned without the absurd inflation in labour and material costs. Then in my present physical and above all spiritual condition I am not capable of doing the work myself, nor is Raymond really capable of helping;

d) Raymond is never going to allow us to enjoy a happy, peaceful retirement, so what's the point? Here I reckoned without the ludicrous rules on committal;

e) I was very disappointed that none of the children showed any interest in visiting us, except Graham, and he only wants to check that I write my will the right way and don't spend all my money before I die. In short, the much celebrated joy of being near one's beloved offspring has proved to be another will o' the wisp;

f) the psychoanalyst advised me to discontinue the sessions with Raymond as he felt they were useless and perhaps even counterproductive; he suggested we both break away from Raymond definitively so as not to go on giving him an object for aggression; he claimed that in trying to improve his behaviour we only fed his persecution complex and that often he didn't behave normally precisely because we tried to force him to do so. Who am I, I asked myself, to contradict the opinion of a paid expert? Obviously you are perfectly at liberty to go and talk to the man yourself if you don't believe me.

Having read through these points and weighed them up I'm sure that you will now acknowledge that I did the right thing accepting TCI's offer. However, I chose not to mention this to you before coming out here, since I thought I might as well check out the situation thoroughly before bothering you with a difficult decision. To cut a long story short, I took advantage of your being away and having no special need to contact me in order to reconnoitre and ascertain exactly what was being offered.

As regards which, the situation is as follows:

TCI have signed a contract with the Algerian government to build a second cotton mill in collaboration with two Algerian companies about 70 miles to the east of the first mill. They want me to advise on and effectively be in control of site administration, but without actually having to give the orders and tell people what to do. There is a new site manager for that who is supposed to be learning from me. The contract is for four years, extendable to six depending on progress, hitches, unforeseen developments, etc. That is, it's for six years. We, if you come, will be living in what used to be a French missionary's house in the nearest village. There is running water, calor gas, plus a few basic shops nearby, certainly no worse than some of the situations we've been in before.

As I said, I have chosen to accept the offer. You have the alternative of coming out here with me, or staying behind to look after Raymond. I sincerely hope you will choose the former as I do not want to be here entirely alone, nor to have to eat in the canteen, and then I honestly think it would be better for you. Quite apart from which, the psychoanalyst made it abundantly clear that such a solution would be far better, therapeutically speaking, for Raymond, who, he said was oppressed and obsessed by a dominant mother figure. If we leave him on his own he will be forced either to be independent or to accept that he must go into care voluntarily on a permanent basis. Whichever turns out to be the case he won't be able to go on ruining our lives as well as his own.

So these are your options; however, please do not try to come out here <u>with</u> Raymond, or even so much as let him know where I/we are, because if you do so I shall disappear definitively. And I mean that. Quite soon after you left I realized that I had reached my breaking point as far as

Raymond is concerned. On two occasions I went to the police and informed them that if something nasty happened either to him or to myself then the authorities would have only themselves to blame – I must say they were very understanding about it, they've seen other cases presumably. For my part, I have put up with Raymond's madness for nigh on ten years and I will not, shall not, cannot, put up with it any more. I am sorry but I do not share your morbid determination to love him at all costs. I feel I have done my duty and that is enough.

So far I have written in a deliberately cold tone, because I want you to appreciate how clear-cut the decision facing you is and how rational I am being about it. But now let me say what I really feel as husband to wife. Brenda, you and I are both old enough and unwell enough to deserve retirement and a rest. However, our children, all of them, are proving to be only a burden to us and not the support we once imagined – I seem to recall this being the argument you repeated at the beginning of each new pregnancy: that our children would be a support to us in future years, that you didn't want to grow old without having children around to make you feel part of life and help you stay young. However, I must say that I personally have never felt older and deader and more utterly without hope than when in Raymond's company, nor more put upon than when in Graham's, nor more needled than when reading Lorna's letters, or waiting for Garry's. Being back here in the harness so to speak will, I can assure you, be a rest compared to being in Cleveleys with the Albatross round my neck and trying to make all the improvements you are so set on with just our meagre savings; why everybody always assumes I'm rich just because I have the bad habit of being generous from time to time, I really can't imagine. Anyway, since I arrived here I am happy to say that the stomach disorders that were giving me so much trouble have completely vanished.

We both pinned a lot of hopes on our retirement, Brenda. We drew pleasure from a picture of ourselves happily established in the big house with Raymond either miraculously recovered, or at least rendered innocuous thanks to the ministrations of the National Health. In this picture our other children visited with some regularity and problems and decisions were a thing of the past. I for one had become sentimentally attached to this vision of affairs. I now realize, however, that we should have thought less of this attractive mirage and more about the actual day-to-day reality of our lives, since retirement, with Raymond, is not for us. In brief: I used to nourish the illusion that life was about building something up for one's retirement and one's children, establishing something which one could then sit back to relish and enjoy. Now, however, I have come to the bitter conclusion that on the contrary life involves going on and on, liking it or lumping it, meeting people and letting them go if necessary, even your son, even your wife (children should be enjoyed when young, not counted on for when one is old). Most of all it involves always attempting to have the best possible time in the present. Because even if one does succeed in building up wealth of whatever sort, life does not freeze to let you enjoy it, while one's children don't deserve it and are hardly thankful when they get it. Indeed often I think of my children as rather less well disposed to me than the average stranger.

Despite which, I will wind up this sad but make no mistake resolute letter with the following generous recommendations for if you should decide to come out here; if you don't come you may do as you please of course.

1. Raymond gets the Broughton Street flat and the rent from the sea flats; let Graham handle the administration seeing as he likes to be so meticulous about money;

2. Sell the main house, which is yours to sell, and share the proceeds between Garry and Graham, after Graham has taken £1000 plus interest which I borrowed from him;

3. Give Lorna and Fred my best regards, but I don't think they need any money. I am very disappointed in Lorna. She squandered an excellent start in life and always gets her hackles up every time I try to tell her a home truth

or two. Doubtless in time she will appreciate her father's wisdom.

I hope I will see you here soon. If not, Brenda, the best of luck and no regrets. Obviously if you don't come I will send you an income as I always used to. Either way, I know now that I personally am destined to end my life far away from Cleveleys and from England.

Love,
Frank

PS. At the risk of repeating myself ad nauseam, allow me to make it quite clear once and for all that I am washing my hands of Raymond. He is not my son. My son Raymond died in those three months we know nothing of before we heard he'd gone crazy. I think you will find that that is the only way to look at it.

Garry had managed to work himself up into a fever. A glimmer over 99 to be precise (he had checked, more than once). Wearing Raymond's grey wool suit, for he had no other, un-ironed since its trip in the post five months ago, he had twice now stood in the entrance hall of Prestwick House on the Harrow Road where Softway had their offices on the 5th floor, twice tried and failed to take the job they had offered him. Once he had taken the lift, only to ride it straight down again. The first time he had walked directly out of a service door at the back.

And now the mental obstruction or block, or whatever it was that always prevented him from actually doing anything with his life, and so from ever really being anyone, had begun to take on a tangibly physical presence. It was not like that wild evening when he had spilled the aspirin out amidst pie crumbs on a plate and acted out for himself his own desperation, even watching himself in the tall black mirror a window made – that time seemed almost innocent now – but more as if, inching in the pitch dark, one were to blunder against a wall, but a wall so smooth and cushioned, so utterly without edges or corners, you couldn't even hurt yourself on it, which might have been all he wanted, a wall so compact you couldn't find a fault or grip, could never imagine smashing it or climbing it, or digging under it, a wall whose extent, whose composition, whose purpose one could never know.

And yet he'd always felt he was meant to be a carefree person. Certainly he was handsome, dressed well, knew how to tell a joke.

Sometimes, as when he had put on the suit the first morning, whistling happily, playing a part, or again the second time when he had just walked straight across the drab entrance hall into an open lift, pressing button five and exchanging brisk words on the weather with a tartan-skirted secretary who tapped a roll of photocopies against her dimpled chin – sometimes it did seem that the obstruction was only a fog, could be breezed through just by stepping out. And yet something in the centre of that fog, something lurking there in this dark confusion of vapour must have frightened him – or it was as if, picking up warning signals, some pre-programmed automatic pilot in his brain, some impulse that was quite definitely beyond the conscious control of Garry Baldwin, decided to take over and inevitably turned him back. The secretary got out and he pushed the button that would take him down. The wall was in himself.

So he stood on the uneven grey pavement outside a building of stained concrete, sucking through his nostrils as if he had never smelt rainwashed London streets before.

And went to telephone Amanda.

'Johnson,' she answered with her husband's surname from her husband's house, and since the box was wolfing fifties (he said) she called him back.

'I think I'm ill,' he told her.

'I think you'd like to be,' she said.

And after he'd talked for a while, she said: 'I'm not a shoulder to cry on, the only thing I want to hear from you is yes or no.'

'You know I wrote you such a love letter a while back, I . . .'

'Well I never saw it.'

'I didn't send it.'

'Oh great. Why not?'

'I felt I couldn't.'

'Why not, for God's sake?'

'I don't know, I just couldn't. It was too intimate, too confessional, I . . .'

'Thanks a lot.'

And she hung up.

But then the phone started cricketing again, just as he was closing the door.

'Garry?'

'Yes.'

'Just send the letter now. Better late than never. I love you, Garry. We've made a terrific cock-up, but I love you.'

'I haven't got it, I . . . tore it up in a rage, with myself.'

'Then write it again.'

'Yes, Amanda.'

Then after a long pause, during which it seemed one of the two must be crying, she said.

'This is too heavy for me, want to tell me a joke? Or we could talk about the weather.'

'Pissing down here.'

'Ditto. So that's exhausted that.' And reverting to brazen practicality: 'Look, mopey, yes or no, okay, but don't waste my time. Okay? I already feel stupid. I'm supposed to be here picking up my stuff, but I've been more than a week about it already and you never know I might just stay. So yes or no. Give you till Saturday.'

Garry stared at his handsome, not even haunted face (at least appearances were in order) in the polished glass of a new British Telecom box. Which made him think of Graham, always ready with some urgent talk about the stock exchange or the family's troubles. Either would do. And he dialled from memory.

'Leeds Access, can I help you? Mr Baldwin was that? From? Sorry? His brother. I'll just check. I'm afraid Mr Baldwin's not available just at the moment, sir. In a meeting. No, I don't know when he'll be available, I'm afraid. Sorry I can't be of help, sir.'

There was the cold tone of a definite put-off to her voice. And one which had cost him 20p.

Then the following morning, sweating with funk fever again, after three sessions on the bog, and thanks to the humiliating ministrations of Mariangela who pulled him through the door and into the lift ('do the man!'), and whose great round eyes in his back propelled him down a carpeted corridor and through a yellow swing fire door to where the Softway receptionist was twining hair round a silver pen – at the third attempt, and thanks, or rather no thanks, to Mariangela, he made it. And ushered into a nondescript office was at once explaining, perfectly lucid, perfectly eager, bright-eyed, urgent, as if there were nothing he wanted or valued more in the world than this marvellous job, how he'd had to go to Algeria where his mother was dying, had actually died now, yes, of leukaemia – Donald Benbow was duly sorry – and the moment he got back and saw those letters, realized they'd been sitting there a month and more, well, he rushed right over and here he was . . .

When Benbow said, no problem, he felt euphoric.

And yet realized in bed that evening, eating late night snacks she brought him (Bel Paese and olives on Ritz crackers) with Parkinson grinning over the foot of the mattress – realized that he hadn't in fact crossed or smashed that black wall at all; he had just moved it, stretched it a little, pushed it back. But it was still very much in front of rather than behind him. Because any and every day he could change his ambiguous mind, find an excuse, a stop-gap. Every day he would have to renew his intention, to force that black fog back, every day decide, if only because he was so lucidly aware that this was not what he had intended for his life.

So that it crossed his mind a moment, was this how his father felt? How his father lived? Had this been his state of mind every time he changed a job? A destination? A plane?

On reflection, probably not. For the extraordinary thing about Father had always been his mutton-headed self-confidence, the crass conviction of his selfishness. In a way Father was perfectly consistent in his wiliness. He knew what he wanted. For he had no dreams of being somebody else. Which was what, Garry thought, made him definitely inferior, himself superior. For what that was worth.

Parkinson leered, discussing someone's stage career. Mariangela, stretched on her stomach, feet waving in the air, licked her fingers in her theatrical way, sucking and popping. 'Mmm,' she cuddled up, 'this is really nice, this is 'ome. I am so 'appy.'

Next thing, he thought – her hand was in the back of his jeans now – she'd be announcing a baby. And when she went out to see what the Kilburn High Street Paki's had in the way of champagne, he banged himself a quick wank just to spite her.

'You really got off on the letter-writing bit,' she had said.

He could hear her voice now, teasing but definitely distant. Yes, she had put up a great show of being in the best spirits and having no time for lovey-dovey confidences or clear commitments. She could be like that from time to time. He'd seen it before.

Fred analysed. Was it wrong of him to have been proud of that letter? Did that mean he hadn't meant the things he had said: 'Domesticity, family, is the great adventure'?

'The great illusion, buddy boy,' she had laughed, taking off his accent. 'Look at me now: silent mother, schizo brother, kid with diarrhoea, one cat in heat. Great adventure.'

Why had she done everything to elude him on the emotional level, and on the practical level too, leaving questions like, when she was coming home/if she was coming home/on what terms she was coming home, unanswered?

But then without any threats either. Bright, busy, tactful and a little nervous about the whole weird situation, but giving nothing away at all.

So, a fruitless weekend really. Apart from getting on surprisingly well with Raymond – why hadn't she told him he was there? To stop him worrying? To stop him demanding she come home? Was that why she hadn't wanted him down the previous weekend? Anyway, he had proved a complete paper tiger, very sheepish about his badmouthing letters, he'd even offered to write an apology to the head of department ('Oh I don't think that will be necessary' – just to show him the thing had made no impression). And capable of an almost coherent conversation on linguistics. Hardly mad at all, more eccentric rather. Which only went to prove, though he would be the last person to actually say told you so, how much Lorna and Graham loved to dramatize. The guy had smashed up the apartment, sure enough, which was all it deserved as far as Fred could see, place was the pits, but he hadn't hurt a hair of anybody's head. The wrist-breaking and axe-wielding was just fable. Raymond was okay.

Otherwise, emotionally, a completely fruitless weekend, during which he had constantly been made to feel left out, and then, when he complained, ridiculous for imagining any such thing. As well as generally patronized. For example, when he suggested in an undertone that Mrs B should really see a specialist, and fast, Lorna had gaily said out loud, 'Oh Mum's all right, aren't you, Mum?' although this was exactly the opposite of what she said when she wrote. And Mrs Baldwin was very obviously not all right, had aged a decade in a couple of weeks. Not to mention those weirdly dull eyes. Indeed, if anything she was in rather worse shape than Raymond.

Did a guy who'd written a letter as nice and concessionary as his deserve to be treated like that?

At night, from a sleeping bag on the floor, when she'd protested she couldn't possibly leave them both and come home just yet, he'd said, 'You did read my letter, Lorna? I did say I'd be happy to have your mother with us.' And she condescending: 'You really got off on the letter-writing bit, didn't you? You really enjoyed it.'

What was the formula that decided that some phrases would lodge in the mind forever, unbudgeable, echoing back to humiliate at the most inopportune moments ('You really got off . . .'), the way some wounds, however innocuous (or otherwise) will scar and their scars sing and tingle years later to remind you of a stupidly broken glass, a moment's absurd clumsiness with a penknife?

('I leave it to you to decide all the ways in which that simile doesn't hold . . .').

Yes of course he had got off on the letter-writing bit, somebody like himself, so involved with words, was bound to (perhaps a bit silly to have gone into one of his metaphor routines though. She was tired of that, and fair enough). But did that mean he hadn't meant what he said? For her next words had been, though without malice: 'You're so proud, aren't you, of being able to capitulate and have ideals. So proud of all your concessions.'

Why shouldn't he be?

But, to give her the benefit, did he feel the things he had said then now? Was it only, as she seemed to be hinting, a question of working yourself up on paper and then walking cold away from it?

Fred examined; and decided that right at the moment he felt very much as anybody else would feel, riding down the M1 after an unsatisfactory weekend and in a hired car that steered heavily to the left. He felt tired. He felt eager to get home. He felt pissed off at being flashed at by people with faster cars, overtaken on the inside, obliged to brake when trucks pulled out without warning. He felt he needed a drink, a bite to eat, a shower. He felt he needed a leak, dammit, in fact one that couldn't wait until the next service station.

Then because there was still the last of summer twilight, Fred pulled up under a bridge and went behind a pillar to piss. Where he was shocked to see human turds, disposable diapers, a knotted condom. Pissing was one thing, but . . . and why on earth did they bother to knot them? Did the Family Planning Clinic advise it? Was this the new AIDS consciousness? And how on earth, in moments and in circumstances like this, or even on ordinary days when he rode the subways and gave lectures, could he expect himself to feel what he had written in that letter? No he couldn't. No one could. But the important thing was that he had felt that way once, had been able to work himself up to make those very real concessions, could feel the same way again now if he concentrated, and had never done anything to betray that feeling, nor more generally his faith to Lorna, with no lack of opportunity among his students either, and without any fear of getting mixed up in any of the old-fashioned shit suggested in Raymond's cretinous letter.

And this was what making plans was all about, wasn't it? You based them on some moment of truly felt emotion and you stuck by them. You trusted yourself. You trusted somebody else. You trusted life.

Fred climbed back into his car, casually glanced at a slope of yellow alfalfa in fast fading twilight, the contour of the low hillside poignantly sharp against a luminous dark-blue sky behind, and suddenly, to his own immense surprise, found himself in tears. His heart rose quite terribly to the surface. This constant awareness of the fragility of all he hoped to care for, this constant sense of tenderness, of passing beauty: it was too much.

Or was that in some way what she'd been trying to tell him? That it was all too much.

He wiped a sleeve across his face and pulled out onto the road.

One of the four times he'd tiptoed back from the john, past Raymond and Mrs Baldwin's doors, Lorna had whispered through the darkness: 'Want some action, keep the old seminal fluid on the move as the man said?'

She was jokey. But, still being embarrassed about it all, feeling laughed at, he had transformed his embarrassment to anger.

'No thanks. I wasn't planning to use you as a chamber pot.'

'Suit yourself, but I feel hot for it.'

'The only reason I want to make love to you is to have a second child.'

After a moment she said: 'Poor Big Fred.'

Which only made him more furious for some reason. 'Fuck off,' he'd said, and she, after another pause:

'I do appreciate your love, Fred. But don't get off on it too much. Don't make it another form of coercion.'

'It wasn't me asked for sex,' had been his retort then, with that illogical, dangerous determination to have the last word.

And she let him.

But now, cruising past Hemel Hempstead, on the last stretch more or less, it occurred to him that perhaps this was what she meant, what she had been meaning with her gestures and behaviour all weekend – because women did have that gift for communicating complex things through the way they moved and spoke and smiled and grimaced, the way they were, whereas he was always torturing words and sentences and punctuation and nuances of metaphor and simile into that thing that was to be expressed, and was so busy at it he wouldn't notice how someone else was saying something a different way, with a brisk movement of the arm, a raising of eyebrows, a shift of posture.

What she had meant, perhaps, with all that sparkling, wilfully superficial behaviour, despite the heavy situation, was: 'Don't be a moral megalomaniac, Fred, with your love and ideals and concessions, don't crowd me out, don't steamroller me, now I've dared to tell you I'm unhappy. You can't make me happy from one moment to the next, swapping one set of plans for another, showing how sentimental you can be with your home-sweet-home visions of the future. Remember that what you want hangs on the thin thread of my initiative, depends on my wanting, if not the same thing, then at least something compatible.'

Or perhaps it was more complicated than that; there'd been something very slightly mocking in her eyes as she handed him his breakfast coffee. Something teasing. But he wasn't far off now.

Wait for me, Fred, she was saying. Don't do it all on your own, with your fifteen-page letters. Wait for me to decide when I want to decide.

So that he realized now, and with some relief, though not without trepidation, that all he had to do, all he could do, all she wanted him to do, was wait. Till she acted.

Like sex perhaps. Don't do it all, she was saying, let me . . .

Unless he was fooling himself and it was just the brush off of a woman too scared to come out with the truth of how . . .

'Sorry to disturb you, sir.' A man stepped from the shadow of the porch as Fred quietly clicked the car door closed in a sleeping Fairfield Close.

'Yes?'

'Inspector Fowles, Scotland Yard. Anti-Terrorist Squad. Would you mind answering a few questions.'

He collected himself so quickly.

'As long as they're not about my love life.'

'If you'll just step this way into the car a moment, sir.'

And he felt elated for some reason, to have to face such a simple problem.

'Don't tell me, you've had an anonymous letter.'

'Phone call,' Markham's partner at the wheel corrected.

Yes, for some reason Fred really did feel immensely pleased, even complacent. He was being long-suffering and wouldn't even tell her.

Lorna to Garry

June 23rd   Broughton St

Dear Garry,

I spoke to Graham on the phone yesterday and we agreed
that one of us must write to you seeing as you never phone
him. Which meant me of course, since he's too busy as
always. Anyway, I get the feeling he's more or less washed
his hands of you. He seems to feel you won't respond to any
persuasion and may just as well be left out. Please prove him
wrong, if only to give me the pleasure of telling him told
you so. He's getting to be pretty unbearable these days, in
his own sweet way.

The big news. It turns out Father's gone back to Algeria
to do his old job again, and he wants Mum to go and
join him, but NOT Raymond. Nobody wants Raymond,
although actually he can be quite sweet sometimes. The
trouble is the awful way he attaches himself to you and won't
let go. I see now why Dad used to call him the albatross.
From the moment he wakes up to the moment he goes to
bed he just hangs around me, fidgeting and pushing his hair
back over his eyes and insisting on these impossibly heavy
conversations which are either about sex – 'How many
times do you do it? What method? What about Garry and
Mariangela? I bet Sophy's a prostitute, that's why he never
brings her over', etc. – or international politics – 'Long live
the Shiite revolution, down with western imperialism', etc.
etc.; this while I'm trying to prepare dinner (he eats like a
horse), or do the dishes, or wipe the table, or sort out the

washing. It's wearisome. The fact is though that while it's all very well for Father and Graham to talk about forcing him to live alone, I don't think he'll ever be able to be independent. He's incapable of really taking initiatives or dealing with people in any normal way. For example, while he was in the home he'd written to a marriage agency, or whatever they call themselves, to find a girlfriend (that's initiative, I suppose, but he obviously feels safe behind the personae of his letters, which is maybe why he writes so many – he wrote to the Pope last week, amongst others, a long thing about why Moslems reject celibacy). Anyway, the agency came up with this Syrian girl, apparently because he'd specified a preference for the Moslem religion. I thought it was all the usual fantasy at first until one evening he got terribly agitated and insisted I iron some clothes for him because he had to go out: he'd dug out an ancient three-piece from the back-room, he could barely fit into it, you know he's so fat now, plus he wore a white shirt, one of Dad's ties, a handkerchief in his pocket and the best part of a bottle of aftershave on his neck. Then, having dressed to the nines like that, he just loitered about, flicking back his cuff to look at his watch every thirty seconds, until finally he told me he had an appointment with this girl in a pub in Blackpool for 7 o'clock. It was about ten to by then. I told him to hurry, still thinking he'd invented it all as usual, but he just started going through one of his worst fidgeting routines, pushing back his hair, biting his thumbs, etc. There's a new way he's got of simply shaking and shaking his left hand, as if it were a rag, or something clinging to him he wanted to be rid of. It's incredibly unnerving. Anyway, after about five minutes of that he finally said he wouldn't go unless I did. He said it was a custom when Moslem couples met for a relative to introduce them, which was probably patent codswallop, I don't know, but it was a nice evening, so for a laugh, and to humour him, I put a pully on Kirsty and we caught a tram, me in my scruffiest old shirt and him in that drainpipe three-piece with the fly that wouldn't even pull up to the top.

The first surprise was that the pub did actually exist, the

Polar Bear, in a backstreet off South Shore before the Golden Mile; God knows how he knew about the place, seeing as he never goes out on his own.

But now the problem was he wouldn't go in. It was like trying to get Kirsty into the nursery Monday morning. He was in a complete funk. Quite a wild look comes over him when he's like this. As if I'd instigated the whole thing and he'd been against it from the start, as if I was trying to hurt him. Anyway, it was a tricky situation because of course I couldn't go into a pub with Kirsty, and so in the end I did a completely stupid thing. I told him to stay with Kirsty for a moment while I popped in to see if the girl was there, fully expecting that she wouldn't be, that no such person existed. And then he's been such a lamb with Kirsty these last two weeks, I thought I could get away with it, for like just one minute.

I told him to look after her and went in and there the girl was, you couldn't have mistaken her, on a stool at the bar trying to ignore an ogling group of boozey young builder types and staring at the door, since Raymond was a good hour late by now. I said, would she like to come out to meet my brother, not explaining anything, and she said yes. And then when we got out of the bar, he wasn't there. No sign. For a moment I panicked, I was terrified he'd taken Kirsty away, I started hunting and shouting and screaming – the poor Syrian girl must have thought I was out of my mind – but then I found her almost at once, gambolling along in the middle of the next road if you please, just round the corner, perfectly happy to be out past beddy-byes time and oblivious to all danger. No Raymond though. I can't tell you how furious with him and how sorry for him I felt at the same time – which is one of the major problems with Raymond, the way it's hard to have clear, unconflicting feelings about him. He obviously yearns to have relationships, but is so hopeless at being with people.

Anyway, the girl had come all the way from Bolton, so I bought her a Wimpy and explained and walked her back to the station with Kirsty on my shoulders. She was quite an attractive girl, with classic Arab features and raven hair, big dark eyes, full sexy lips, cheerful to talk to. I couldn't understand why she was having to write to agencies. But she said she was 29 and there weren't many other Syrians in Bolton. All the Indians wanted to marry Indians and all the whites wanted to marry whites, and she desperately wanted to marry anyone and have a baby. I told her not to be in too much of a hurry for that, as she might be better off single and childless, but she obviously didn't believe me. The fact is, I think, girls either want babies or they don't, it's got nothing to do with a rational weighing of pros and cons. So there's really no point in trying to persuade anybody either way. Which goes for lots of other things as well as babies, of course.

Anyhow, Raymond didn't come back that night, nor the next. In the end the police picked him up on Friday. He'd been bumming around the station for a couple of days trying to sell things to people for food. He'd sold his shoes and his jacket and he stank; when the police picked him up it was because he'd stolen a copy of some porno-mag from the kiosk; and then the first thing he did when he got home was to accuse me of having warned the girl off him. He'd invented a completely different story about what happened and believed it 100%. I'd warned her off, I'd deliberately abandoned him, I'd bolted the door at home so he couldn't get in, I'd sent the police to arrest him . . .

What I'm saying, though, is that this seems to be the score with Raymond: either one of us holds his hand day in day out, never letting him out of our sight for one moment, in which case he'll remain about half human; or we all reject him and he becomes a bum. I've realized, I suppose, that that's who bums and tramps are, or quite a lot of them, and every time I see one now I can't help thinking, that man has a brother or sister who disowned him years ago, obvious, that's how it is. The upshot being that it's no good Father and Graham going glibly on about the State being obliged to assume its responsibilities, etc. etc.; the reality is that if we disappear, Raymond will go downhill; he's never going to take his pills for more than a couple of weeks out of hospital, quite simply because he's been smart enough to read what's in them and find out how bad for him they are. He'll go downhill, he'll try to crash in on us, we'll refuse him, the police'll pick him up in a piteous state in a station or under a bridge or trying to steal something, they'll send him to a home where they'll force-feed him sedatives for a few days until he's sane enough to be let out, and then the whole thing'll begin all over again. Not to mention smashing up the flat here again, plus the other property too maybe, just so as to attract someone's attention – which he's determined to have, even if he doesn't know what to do with it once he's got it.

The fact is there's a responsibility vacuum here. Nobody is responsible for Raymond and he's incapable of being responsible for himself. So the only people who have any motive for helping him are those who remember with affection what he was like in the past, when he used to make up games for us, or fix intercoms between our rooms with old radio loudspeakers, remember? Or beg the money off Mum to take us to all those endless cowboy films they used to show in Beirut – what he was like when he was Raymond.

What I don't know, and I don't think anybody else does either, is how far that affection could or should go. I remember a time Raymond carried me piggyback in Lebanon when I'd cut my foot on some glass. He must have carried me the best part of half a mile from the harbour to home in burning sunshine. He was singing that Beatles thing, 'When I'm 64'. I think he must have just borrowed the record or something. Anyway, if I close my eyes I have a perfect memory of jogging up and down on his back and him telling me to hold on tight round his neck. I even remember the smell of his hair wet with sweat, how proud he was to be helping me, how happy I was to be helped. I remember him laughing at a dog that snapped at us. It's a wonderful memory. But is it any reason for being here with this creature now?

However, before I went off on a tangent, this letter was basically to say that Graham and I have agreed to have a major family pow-wow next Saturday 30th, when we're going to decide what to do about everything: Raymond, Mum, houses, money, etc. I want us to take turns keeping Raymond, what do you think? And the bottom line is, you'd better make it up here this time, otherwise you might not get your slice of the cake, as Graham likes to put it. Is that enough of an incentive?

It better be.

Though I do understand your reluctance.

Love,

LORNA

Oh, sorry, the other thing I know you'll be dying to hear is, I've seen — no, don't faint, hold on to something solid — Sophy. Yes, Graham's Sophy, in the flesh. She really does exist. The other afternoon, with Raymond bothering me with his politics again while I was baking and Mother in her room staring away the walls, a knock comes on the door and it's her. Her mother had been helping with some handicapped children's outing to Blackpool or something and Sophy took a place on the coach and the opportunity to drop in on us.

Quite unbeknown to Graham, I don't doubt, who would certainly have tried to put a spoke in her wheel.

Because the incredible thing is, she didn't know anything, absolutely nothing. She didn't know Father had left, didn't know Mother was like she is, didn't know I was here, didn't know Raymond was here. Zilch. She was expecting to meet Father and Mother for a cosy chat, because she said she thought it was a shame the families had never got together; her father had told Graham to accept the invitation from Dad, but somehow a date had never been fixed, i.e. Graham didn't let on. She obviously had no idea Mother had been to Leeds to stay and was shut up in his room while he ate at their place.

So apparently poor Graham is hopelessly ashamed of us all. Outrageous, isn't it? Still, I didn't tell her the half in case it put her off him for good. And then who would take him off our hands?

Or maybe – it's only just occurred to me – maybe he's ashamed of her and that's why he was trying to keep the two parties apart. We'll never know, will we?

I said: 'Actually, we're all wondering when you're going to get married.' And she said, 'Oh, I thought it must have only been Raymond he hadn't explained to. Just as soon as my divorce comes through.'!!!

In short, a completely different creature from the picture Graham paints; she was a primary school teacher apparently, made redundant, and she's doing the OU English degree to try and get a post at a comprehensive school. I bet she never has bad period pains at all.

Unless she's lying of course. Since I suppose you never really know what's going on with people at all. You just have to believe what you're told, and of course so often the stories don't tally, like a vast, complicated game of Newly Weds with no one scoring any points.

De te fabula!

Hey, Garry? Or didn't they teach you any Latin in Ecuador? Remember we expect to see you next Saturday, for the showdown.

Love again,
Lorna

PS again: Amanda also dropped in a couple of weeks back and mentioned she might be leaving her husband. Not because of you, I hope. I didn't say anything about Mariangela just in case.

Or why not try Raymond's Syrian girl? I have the address. Only then he really would be sure there was a plot against him!

Garry to Mariangela

Dear Mariangela,
    I've gone. Permanently. I'm not coming back. Don't try to find me or ask any questions. The best thing you can do is go home.

Forgive me,
GARRY

PS. Don't worry about the rent. I paid him yesterday and told him we'd be leaving this weekend.

Graham left early to arrive early. He hoped to be back the following morning in time to drive Colonel Gascoigne and his wife to church as he always used to before the return of his family had upset the happy rhythm of his life. He felt so relaxed, so right with the Gascoignes. Dressing at first light, he chose his office clothes, perhaps in the hope that the executive aura of self-assurance they lent him at the Leeds Access would spill over into his less confident private life. For if he had learnt one thing from Webb in Sales, it was that the more assured one felt about the rightness of one's own self-image and appearance, the more likely one was to get one's own way. Which was why it could be so important sometimes to adjust one's posture, straighten the tie, square the shoulders and breathe deeply, before tackling a particularly difficult phone call.

And why he was so satisfied with this neat little moustache he'd grown, which lent an air of experience and power; whereas Garry, as he remembered him, merely looked baby-faced and unshaven, both at the same time.

And why an expensive cigarette that gave tone, with little gold rings like military stripes, was an investment really, whatever the government health warning said.

What there was to be learnt, he reflected, had so little to do with what parents and schools and colleges and universities were bent on teaching you. He had done well to get out.

In Cleveleys before nine he stopped at the Better Snack to review his plans and flick through yesterday's stock exchange report in the *Telegraph*. All more or less satisfactory there – thanks to Maggie's splendid majority. Nothing spectacularly up or down; obviously he had applied for just the right amount of British Airports if the Investors' Advice column was anything to go by.

The thing now was to sell up and go for the mortgage at just the moment when the interest-rates/house-prices ratio was at its most favourable.

Holiday time mightn't be a bad moment actually. Less danger of being gazumped. Unless people were taking their holidays precisely to go around house-hunting these days – there was an idea. Put five grand down and mortgage yourself to the eyeballs. Once the house was actually there and they were in it the Colonel would be more or less obliged to help out.

Outside the Better Snack he crossed and walked down to the estate agents, where he gave the man the keys and asked him to proceed to a valuation of 11 Fleetwood Street.

'Completely detached, just a block from the sea, make an excellent small hotel, shouldn't be any trouble with planning permission. Room for development too.'

'If only the weather were such as to encourage tourists.' The agent was tall and leathery with what seemed like a wilfully Dickensian stoop and way of peering at what was in his hands, which, at the moment, was Graham's carefully typed description of the property.

'Nothing to be gained from defeatism.'

Said in the right jocular tone, this was another of Webb's worthwhile lines.

And sighing he added: 'If only the prices were comparable with the area where I'm planning to buy. Leeds, you know.' And he named one of the nicer suburbs.

'Oh aye?' said the old agent vaguely. His teeth were grey. Business clearly was not brisk in Cleveleys. 'Right then. I'll see to it.'

Which left Graham still time enough to sound out Lorna before his twin could hope to arrive.

If he did arrive. And if he didn't, all the better perhaps at this stage. Since the field was more or less free with Father gone and Mother mute.

Graham belted himself into his Escort. There must be some way to evict the tenants from the sea flats too, if only one put one's mind to it. Raise the rent for a start. No point in playing the martyr with them as his father had.

He slid the gears back and forth through side roads to Broughton Street, reflecting how much luck was involved in just where one's parents had been born or grown up. Equivalent property in London would be worth, what?, half a million? Or anywhere down south. He would be rich. Why, oh why did his stupid parents have to be northerners?

Such a bad habit. Such an unpleasant accent.

He would move south one day. Not now to be with Garry and pay his bills for him. They must be crazy if they thought he'd fall into a trap like that. But all in good time. When the Colonel died.

He climbed out of the car into a bright, calm morning, the trees breezeless (why was the agent moping about the weather?), the detached, orange brick houses cheerfully confident, apparently aware of and satisfied with their value, demanding a little respect from passers-by in return for beds full of flowers, predominantly roses.

Their own house must have been the only one in the row split into flats, for that had been Father's first idea for making money, before the travelling bug got him, before he was married: build flats, rent them out to the tourists who were just beginning to wander up from Blackpool.

And would that he had stuck to that scheme. For Graham's feeling was that Father had made a mistake travelling. Made a mistake because, for all the official salary might have been higher, there were real material advantages to be had in the long term from consolidating on a solid base in the one geographical location (so that perhaps he wouldn't go down south after all). With just a little intelligence Father could have developed a network of contacts who over the years would have given him steady business, rather than just collecting up one visiting card for every city of the third world and then stuffing them away in a drawer to gloat over as if they were a collection of postage stamps. He could have built more flats, got a grip on the tourist market perhaps, perhaps even become a local councillor with all that that entailed; it was only a question of choosing the right party and sticking around long enough; because if one stayed in the same place long enough, one could surely get one's fingers – and why not? – into so many pies, and keep them there. In short, you could really build something, not just earn a good salary and piss it away at the same time through constant moves, flashy generosity, bad administration and health services you had to pay for.

And if he hadn't got on with Mother, he could have divorced her for God's sake. No need to run away all round the globe.

Graham drew a deep suburban breath, filled his lungs, squared his shoulders, straightened his tie, patted a notebook in his jacket pocket and pushed open the wicket gate to 23 Broughton.

It was a shame having to surrender even this for a brother who was no use to anybody.

On the train, Garry clung to his *Guardian* as if he were falling and the thing must serve as a parachute.

Why would nobody advise him?

Or as if the Saturday Review and the opinion columns must stand between himself and the Furies, were all he had to keep them at bay.

He had rung Fred, told him all in a terrible torrent of confession, a perfectly lucid self-analysis, and Fred had said:

'Beats me. I've got my own problems. Anything. All your choices look good to me. You just have to decide.'

'But . . .'

'Give Lorna my love if you go. Tell her I can't make it up this weekend, but she can phone me if she wants.'

That is, he had simply refused to acknowledge the gravity of the situation. Had nobody told him his brother-in-law had taken an overdose once? Or was it that he knew and still didn't care?

And what did he mean he had his own problems? He was so cold and cynical.

The government was attacking the unemployed again. No sooner were they back in than they showed their true colours. Why hadn't people believed it when he'd been on their doorsteps telling them? Soon you'd have to accept any dumb job, like it or lump it. Or no dole.

Was there no end to it? The way people tried to push you into things.

His fine proud face, which it just seemed impossible for Garry to get away from, floated in the window as the countryside beyond flew by in bits and pieces. The earring winked, the nose was so straight and right, the hair fell so well. For a moment he stared, fascinated. But his self-love was exhausted now. He almost hated that stupid beauty. He really did. He would quite like to have smashed it in some way. As if everything that was wrong could be blamed on that. He was the victim of his own good looks was the truth. If he had been as plain as Fred, things would surely have been easier. He would have snapped up the first girl who showed any interest. And just to make some gesture, however tiny, to satisfy his self-loathing, he quickly unfastened the earring, glancing round to check that his fellow passengers hadn't seen, and pushed it into the back of the seat between the cushions.

Really, he would wring some advice out of Lorna if it killed him.

Or just take the opposite of what Graham would no doubt be only too eager to give.

Unless perhaps he should at least try and get some money for the thing from a jeweller's. It was gold after all. Amanda had bought it for him. She always bought expensive things. And forcing his fingers down between the cushions, he now tried to recover the earring. But couldn't find it. He stood up and pulled at the upholstery; it wouldn't budge. People raised their eyes. Managing to get a whole hand right down inside now, he felt only space. And promptly gave up. What a fool he was.

Lorna was in a crowded classroom doing an exam. Her pen was poised above her paper, but for some reason she seemed unable to write. And why was everybody else talking? Was she the only one who cared? She was chewing her lip, willing the pen to write. All her life seemed to be concentrated into that tiny suffocating space between face and paper. Her nerves strained. Waves of claustrophobia tightened her muscles, heightened her sense of failure. She would be sick if she couldn't write.

But at last it came to her why: she couldn't remember what language the thing was supposed to be in. She was supposed to be writing an essay, but she couldn't remember what language. Relief swept through her. All she had to do was ask the person next . . .

'Don't talk,' boomed a voice. Father's. Could it be Father moving through the desks collecting papers? Surely he would give her a few more moments.

'Excuse me, could . . .'

'Don't talk!'

'Dad!'

But no, it was Fred. How could she have made a mistake like that? Fred in his grey suit. For big lectures. He seemed so tall in that crowded windowless room, so tall his head was far above her. Even though the ceiling oddly seemed so low. She felt him bearing over her. And herself shrinking. Closer and closer to the grainy wood of this desk.

'Fred . . .'

'Don't talk!'

But everybody else was talking. The twins were giggling their heads off. How could this be happening? No rules, no discipline? She was going to fail. She had never failed before. Never, never failed. And why were all the others so relaxed? Could they really be that much better than her? Was it all so easy for them?

French. She was supposed to be writing in French.

The big classroom clock appeared to have stopped at a minute to twelve, but bells were already ringing. Her pen was slippery with sweat:

'Cher Fred,' she was suddenly writing – there were scratches and blotches, but she was writing – 'Cher Freddy, notre rapport est très important pour moi. Tu ne dois pas penser que . . .'

That's why it all felt so odd. Her left breast was leaking milk. Onto the paper. Hadn't anyone noticed? It must be past feeding time. Her tits were bursting with milk. And she hadn't written anything. How could she be expected to do an exam in this condition? Or were they all shouting and laughing at her? They knew she'd failed already. Raymond turned round from the desk in front, Raymond, frowning, opening his mouth to shout, opening it wider and wider, showing all his sharp fillings. Raymond! How monstrous he seemed with that gaping, savage, salivary mouth. What did he want? To be fed? His arm came up suddenly and . . .

She woke up.

Just a tiresome angst dream, recycling old neuroses.

Except that, moving to lie on her back, she was suddenly aware that Raymond was standing beside the camp-bed Uncle Harry had lent, right above her. She stiffened and jerked her head up, her eye moving quickly to where Kirsty was fast asleep on sofa cushions. But no, all was well. Another morning. And a nice one too by the looks, bright light flooding round flimsy curtains.

'Hello,' she said with the forced cheerfulness that was becoming a habit. 'Did you come to wake me up?'

He was leering rather unpleasantly.

He said: 'Has Fred ever taken any pictures of you nude?'

'You what?' For a moment it was almost as if she were dreaming again.

'Has Fred ever taken any pictures of you nude?'

'No,' she lied. It was pointless objecting that this was not the kind of question one really asked, not at any time of day, never mind first thing in the morning. For Raymond was simply not to be included in the category referred to when using the impersonal 'one'. And she had sensed over these last weeks that her brother had latched on to that, to the fact, that is, that he could now say anything to anybody with impunity; because he had nothing to lose; because he was not a member of acceptable society. It was a part of being mad he seemed quite perversely to recognize and to enjoy.

Which perversity was in itself a form of madness.

Because you could never say of anybody that they were mad on purpose, because that purpose itself would be mad.

And yet . . .

'Can I take some?'

'What?'

'Pictures, you know . . .'

'No you damn well can't.'

'I'm interested in what people look like naked.' He had his ridiculous, innocent-boy-experimenting look. Ridiculous because he had just turned thirty-three.

'I shouldn't bother if I were you.'

'I am your brother. We're supposed to be close.'

She said carefully: 'We are close, Raymond. But being brother and sister doesn't mean I let you take pictures of me naked.'

She was propped up on her elbow. He stood with his fat, odd smile, pushing a hand through greasy black uncut hair. His body, which always conveyed a sense of looming, of being something extra, unwanted, unwieldy, and hence menacing in a vague, yet pervasive, rather than directly physical way, swayed as he shifted uneasily from one foot to another. He was seriously overweight. The pills did it. Only she realized now that the fact that he was awake this side of eight o'clock must mean he had skipped last night's.

'You used to show me everything,' he said.

'Yes.' She was surprised at the simple appropriateness of this memory. His mind had its logic. 'But that was when we were small. And the twins were there too. Brothers and sisters do that when they're small. But not grown up.'

'What's a sister for then? When she's grown up.'

The question seemed to arise out of genuine perplexity, rather than any desire to insult, though she guessed from his edginess that he was on the brink of one of his difficult moods.

'I don't know. A sister's not *for* anything, they're just there, somebody you've always known, who's always known you. So you have a special relationship with them.'

'You're hiding something,' he accused. He began to shake his left hand. It flapped like a cloth.

'Not at all. Why should I?' She managed a smile. 'What would I have to hide?'

'Why won't you let me take pictures of you?'

It was getting tiresome. She was losing patience. His manner had had a certain novelty value at first which made humouring and helping easier. But this was wearing off. To be replaced by frustration.

'Because people don't. It's not done.'

'Why is that an answer?' he came back, the grin filling his cheeks again, the faint gleam of the clever pupil he had always been in his eye. 'We can do something different from normal people. We can be special.'

With his insistence she began to sense how easy it would be for him to bend down and rip the bedclothes away from her, could almost see him doing it, and for one instant now she had a vision of that open toothy mouth, that raised arm that had shocked her in her dream. Could he have been leaning over her then? About to do something? Was that why she had woken up? Would he do that? She didn't know. But then this was precisely the thing about Raymond. You didn't know. You couldn't. He was such a totally unknown quantity. Everyone was an unknown quantity up to a point, of course, how they would take things, how they would react. Who would have imagined, for example, that after sending his postcards every day for a week and more Fred would suddenly have stopped sending them altogether. Still, there was a kind of centre, or presence, with most people, certainly with Fred, that made you think of them as themselves: a Fredness, a Garryness, a Grahamness. But Raymond lacked this. Raymond was a complete unknown, unrecognizable from one moment to the next: weird, kind, violent, without any of the essential links. And this right in the family, where you counted on known quantities, where you would have thought that intimacy could go hand in hand with security.

'Come on, just one picture. Full frontal.'

'Look, I said, it's not done. I . . .'

'But why is that a reason?' he repeated.

'Because it is,' she said. 'It's to do with propriety. We're not kids any more to be going showing off our willies and bums to each other.'

'Just of your tits then,' he said in the tone of one who bargains reasonably. 'A close up.'

'I said no. Raymond. Enough. Come on.'

He stared at her. Under his gaze she was aware of how with lying on her side her breasts fell heavily against the material of the nightdress. But there was nothing lascivious or erotic about his attention. It was something else.

'No,' she said again.

'Dad had that photograph of him with those wog women.'

'Well he shouldn't have. He's a pig.'

'And Mum let me take photos of her.'

'Not nude she didn't.'

'Yes, she did.'

'Oh don't be ridiculous. You . . .'

'When she came back the other week. Before you got here and interrupted. You want me to go and get them? I've just had them developed.'

He turned to leave the room, already fiddling in his pocket for the key to his room, the key to his wardrobe, the key to a drawer inside. There was no end to his keys.

'No, I don't. For God's sake, Raymond, I've only just woken up.'

'And she wanked me off.'

It was the interminability of it, of his apparently wilful, hopeless strangeness that was getting to her.

'What exactly is wrong with you?' she said foolishly. 'Why don't you just tell me, if you know?'

'What's wrong with you, you mean,' he came back, petulant now. 'You're the one who has hang-ups about a couple of photos. You're the one who married an American.'

'Please, leave me alone and let me dress.'

She was aware that she would not have said that the first days. The first days she would have tried to keep him talking with gentler, kinder words. Soon, no doubt, she'd be showing her contempt as openly as Father always had. Yet how could you have anything but contempt for somebody who said these things? How long could you go on remembering someone he wasn't anymore?

'Go downstairs, okay. Leave me alone.'

Surprisingly he obeyed. He really was an unknown quantity. Except that at the door he came out with one of his pieces of gibberish: 'Giving today, giving tomorrow, goodnight to the players.' He said it in a falsetto sing-song.

'You what?'

He repeated, happy to have really grabbed her attention at last. 'Giving today, giving tomorrow, goodnight to the players.'

'And what's that supposed to mean?'

His grin was more accommodating now as he tapped the side of his nose. And it crossed her mind that he came out with these things on purpose, they were deliberately obscure, so as to have a secret. He was so convinced secrets were being kept from him, people were plotting against him, that he invented little codes and mysteries of his own.

Quite normal behaviour really. As when she would deliberately not reveal to Fred the contents of some quite inconsequential letter, so as to get him worried and jealous, or like her wilfully sibylline behaviour the previous weekend, which now she was beginning to regret. Why hadn't he written again?

And maybe nudity he saw as the ultimate secret, what everybody was hiding: their bodies, their selves, their sex lives; there was all the pornography he looked at and sent with his letters. And was it inconceivable that he had somehow managed to catch Mother nude, or force her to undress? Would Mother have done that if threatened, or even just asked? How far was she willing to go to humour him? Was that what she was trying to hide from her the evening she had arrived and couldn't get in, when she had been crying in the bathroom, 'Please be good, be my Raymond'? And could it possibly have been something that happened between them that had made her fall silent since then ... because if he saw nudity as the ultimate secret, then perhaps Mother's nudity ...

A moment later though, Lorna was reminded that it was as well not to try to rationalize the irrational. However strong the urge to explain things might be. In the kitchen he had turned the radio on full. And at the same time was chanting: 'Out, Yankees, out.' His voice raised to a yell. 'You fucking imperialists!' She heard him pick up something heavy and bang it down on the lino floor. 'Christian cunts!'

Rather than the fear she had felt at the beginning, she now registered just a straightforward acknowledgement of helplessness – it would be like this every day – which was immediately swallowed up by the practicalities of getting dressed. And on a piece of notepaper, while all the noise was going on below, she jotted down casually: 'Big Fred, I know I complained about you getting off on them, but that didn't mean I didn't want any more letters.'

For a moment then her heart fell. She felt absolutely terrified that her stupid sense of duty might trap her here for ever, while the boys escaped scot-free. And her husband ditched her.

It was the first time all four children had been together since Ecuador, the first time, three of them were immediately aware, since their characters had formed, or, in one case, disintegrated. So that they all felt slightly wary, ill at ease, with the memory of childish togetherness and nothing as yet to replace it.

They all picked up Kirsty and played with her, identifying the Baldwin traits. But it wasn't enough. There were silences and moments of embarrassment.

The twins looked at each other uneasily, so similarly built, yet no longer identical, holding their own stories in their eyes, the set of their lips, their posture and manner; they had nothing to say to each other. A year ago, they might have argued, and heatedly, about what each should do with his life, or about politics, they might have clashed, but now even that frankness was gone. They sat in their chairs and fidgeted, picking up a newspaper, talking to the child, both caught by surprise by this awkwardness; it hadn't been planned for. Lorna was luckier, being able to bustle about the house, the preparations for lunch, always an excuse for moving in and out of the room, simple questions to ask about who wanted what. Finally, a roast in the oven, she came in and sat down with them in the flat's small sitting room. The atmosphere eased just a little as everybody exchanged enquiries about health, comments about weather. Graham remarked that good weather always had a positive influence, all other things being equal, on the stock exchange. Lorna said: 'How about that,' hearing cynical Fred.

Then, as the one perhaps who had most reason to be nostalgic for a time when all was dream and potential, Garry was the first to recall the past out loud. He said: 'Reminds me of when we all used to sit around in Ray's bedroom trying to work out how much we'd get exactly if Dad died and what we'd do with it.'

This was a true memory, as they all well knew, discussing their parent's hypothetical death with adolescent sang froid, perhaps all children do this, but only Lorna smiled.

'And we two fought Ray for the slide-rule; remember those things. God, we always seemed to be fighting over something.'

The last part of this was just a shade forced, as if somehow he were obliged to do a little party priming, nervously aware of the space the others were leaving around his words.

'You wanted to use the money to buy a motorbike and drive from Alaska to Tierra del Fuego,' he told his twin unconvincingly. 'You used to be mad on motorbikes.'

They were sipping coffee Lorna had made.

But instinctively Graham wanted to stress the present, not the past, the new roles, not the old, since he sensed, or felt he did, how status had shifted from the co-identity of childhood, through the painful inferiority of university days, failed exams, to his hard-earned superiority of the moment, and future. He was impatient.

'Well, we're not playing now,' he said, with a grim briskness he was obviously learning to relish. 'We've only got today, I want to leave tomorrow morning, and I won't have time to be back here next weekend, even if anybody else will.' He put his mug down on a bookcase. 'We all know what the order of the day is, don't we?'

If childhood was only, or not even, a memory, Lorna thought, picking at skin around a nail, was family more or less superfluous now? For they had only exchanged quite formal embraces. Nothing very warm. Nor had this made her especially sad.

She watched Kirsty who was doing a small child's puppet-like dance around the central coffee table. Obviously you grew out of being a brother or sister. But perhaps that didn't mean one wasn't the better for having been and had one.

'Right, okay,' said Garry; there was suddenly a thin defiance in his voice, as though bravely accepting an unequal challenge. His eyes showed the strain of a sleepless night. 'Right, let's talk.'

But it was embarrassing. There was Mother in the room in her nightdress, the young grey cat on her lap, in heat, purring lasciviously as she was stroked, legs splayed out behind; Mother had always resisted change, and although she had apparently excluded herself from these decisions now it took a while to get the hang of simply ignoring her.

And then there was Raymond standing with his back to the jagged brick of the still unrepaired mantelpiece he had smashed. Were they to talk in front of him? He had been so enthusiastic these last few days about the idea of the children all getting together, but showed not a flicker of interest now, as if perhaps these were not the same children he had meant. He had wanted two boys in short trousers and South American suntans.

Or were they to chat idly until chance gave them a moment alone? Which was unlikely frankly. And idle chat such a heavy task.

Raymond's head loomed forward; he was rubbing his hands together as though cold on this bright late June morning that might have been the warmest of the year so far. Occasionally he stepped forward through where a ray of sunlight was boiling with dust over the threadbare carpet to take from the cake tin on the low coffee table. Kirsty took too, then, giggling, tried to grab a fistful of dust in the other hand. The cat watched indulgently. Mrs Baldwin did not. She fretted with the back of a wrist at the rash still spreading round her wrinkled lips.

So that once again Lorna's hope that some family event would prompt her mother to speak had gone unfulfilled. She glanced to Graham for guidance; how could they talk? What were they to do? It was all very well saying, right, we'll have a family pow-wow, but the actual logistics of it were far from simple. Perhaps they should have arranged to meet in a pub without telling the others, or . . .

But then all at once Graham's executive outfit (Lorna and Garry were both in jeans) seemed to be doing the trick; because now he said quite brutally to his elder brother, savouring the power as he made it grow:

'We're going to talk business now, Raymond. Would you mind going out for a bit. I take it you want to stay, Mother.'

Lorna was perfectly aware of course that this approach was wrong, that it could only feed Raymond's paranoia, his sense of others plotting behind his back. But her only reaction was to take a quick breath and turn her brown eyes away to smile at Kirsty who was now trying to snap the speckled dust in her mouth. For if Graham shared what had been his mother's notorious unwillingness to put on kid gloves for anyone, Lorna had just as surely inherited her father's moments of diffidence, his willingness, on just such occasions as these, to let things go, his easy tiredness.

And then they *were* plotting behind his back.

Raymond was petulant, as his young brother might have been with him twenty years before: 'Can't I stay too? I am the eldest.' His voice had a whine of lost authority. He said: 'I am bloody well staying, like it or not.'

'No, you're not,' Graham told him flatly. 'Out. We've got important plans to make. Come on.'

Mrs Baldwin didn't even lift her face to follow this.

'Perhaps it would be better if you sat out in the garden a while and got some sunshine,' Lorna tried, but faltering. 'We've got to talk over some boring money problems.'

Raymond appeared to hesitate, then, as so often when peremptorily ordered to do something, obeyed. With sudden decision, he moved quickly and angrily to the door, and, as always when he moved, head thrust forward, hands in pockets, elbows splayed, the peculiarity and repressed violence of his gait drew attention to his body as object, as problem. So that it seemed for a second as though his big shoulders might miss the space of the door entirely, as though he had been catapulted from a distance by some uncertain marksman. Because you simply could not think of him as a person, guiding himself as he went.

Instinctively, Lorna reached out to pick up Kirsty, but the girl wriggled away. And at that same moment, before Raymond slammed the thing behind him, the young cat in her first heat caught up with him at the door and slipped between his legs and out.

'Kittens,' Lorna thought, and after they'd successfully kept her indoors a whole week. 'Oh no,' she began, thinking to cheer everybody up, 'that's done it. We'll . . .'

But no sooner was the door closed than Graham was at once talking earnestly, ignoring whatever his sister had been going to say, brushing her aside as one brushes aside an irritating fly. He was so keyed up to get going. And leaning forward from the tall straight-backed chair where he had carefully chosen to sit, there he was now, already hurrying, explaining, persuading away, catching the others completely off balance:

'Because trying to look after Raymond is *like shovelling shit against the tide*,' he protested. 'Hopeless. Endless. Can't you see that?'

Talking, he lit a cigarette, the new moustache rising and falling, bristling as he pouted his mouth to suck.

'Because there's just *no point* in making such sacrifices, even if anybody wanted to, quite apart from paying for them. How can he ever get better? How can he ever even be made safe? And most of all, how can he be worth the time and attention of a healthy person? It just means throwing away a life to sustain . . . a monster really. When we all have our own lives already. When none of us could possibly afford to come down and look after him without ruining all our own plans. Why should we do it, who's going to make us?'

He gestured smoke away from his eyes, the thin gold band, well worth it, winking along with the milling dust in its girder of light. In full flight now.

'So when they put him in a home next time, and they're bound to, the way he's going, we sell up everything while he's there and' – blowing out smoke through fleshy lips – 'that's the end of that. Right?'

But now he was caught with a drooping finger of ash on his cigarette. Where to tap out?

'Sorry, could someone get an ashtray?'

He had done right to sit above them in their armchairs, another thing Webb had wised him up on. He was doing everything right. This . . . Had somebody objected?

'But no, Lorna, I'm afraid that's precisely what we can't do, you're only delaying the crunch with makeshifts like that. Try to think of it in practical terms. Try to see the reality.'

And ever more animated, Graham went on talking and insisting and persuading and explaining and insisting again; five minutes, ten; because he knew if he could only get his way now – and anyway he sensed this was his ascendant moment, he was the family leader, the family chief, even as he broke the family up, he was the family receiver, sorting out debts, and at the same moment the main creditor surely – yes if he could only get his way now, with the opposition so weak, then that would be it, everything settled once and for all – and settled, this was the ridiculous thing, to *everybody's* advantage – he really honestly did know what was best, so why should they fight him?

'Because it can't make a jot of difference to the quality of his life whether he's abandoned or not, since he lives in a world of his own that has no reference to anything you or I do or think. He doesn't appreciate or even recognize affection. He doesn't . . .'

'Hang on a mo', I'm not sure I agree.'

Lorna had imagined it would have to be she who finally interrupted this remorseless onslaught, who put up at least a token fight for family solidarity over selfishness and this urgency to snatch the loot, though she was shamefully ready to submit to a democratic verdict when it came to it, since like her father she'd had enough, and after a much shorter time too.

But in the event, with Kirsty crawling all over him – obviously he was her favourite uncle – it was Garry who spoke. Perhaps it was the spirit of contradiction his twin brother always roused that finally did it for him, perhaps the idea's sudden obviousness, even attractiveness, as his personality teetered on the brink. For it would be some kind of purpose, even if not remotely what he'd been looking for. In any event, it was with a peculiarly inspired confidence that he heard himself saying:

'No, I'm sorry, I don't agree at all, Graham. I'm perfectly willing to share looking after him.' He turned to his mother: 'And since I've got nothing to do just at the moment I may as well be the one . . .'

With a loud crack Raymond shoved open the door with his butt and backed into the room, bent forward over something he was holding hidden from them.

They turned in irritated, embarrassed silence, with more than a slight feeling of being caught out. But what could you do? They had to discuss this.

And as they turned and he did too, they saw it was meat he

held on an Ecuadorian souvenir plate of beaten brass. One of Father's trophies.

Or rather it was the cat, chopped into head, torso and haunches.

'The division of the spoils, sister and brothers.' He stepped forward with a perfectly knowing grin to lay this small horror on the coffee table between their chairs.

'Your inheritance divided into three parts. Shem, Ham and Japheth. I shall keep the memory of the cat.'

There were twists of blood-matted fur and the mouth was open showing teeth.

Involuntarily, Lorna screamed.

Kirsty shouted, it seemed with glee, 'Pussy!'

And there were other voices crying, 'Raymond!'

But the loudest voice of all was Brenda Baldwin's. And likewise her body was transformed from weeks of determined passivity to sudden movement, springing the three paces or so across the squalid room. Her breasts swung in the crumpled nightdress. Her big feet thumped on the carpet. The room appeared to shrink into the suffocating space of a nightmare.

'You can hurt me, you can shame me, you can rape me,' she shouted, sharp and staccato, 'you can do anything you damn well want to me, but this' – jabbing in his face the small cake knife that had appeared in her hand – 'this is disgusting, this is vile, this is the end, damn you, I hate you.'

And jabbing still and thrashing now with him on the floor, she continues to bellow and shriek in much the same way. Until Garry manages to separate them.

Graham is still sitting paralysed on his tall, straight-backed, authoritative chair.

Lorna has dashed out, clutching Kirsty, to call an ambulance.

Lorna to Fred

July 3rd   Cleveleys

Dear Fred,

No, don't worry, I'm not writing to say I've changed my mind. I'll be back next week as planned (they're taking Mother down Thursday). No, I just thought I'd take the opportunity of this distance, while it remains, to say the kind of things one can't say so well face to face, or at least I can't, nor when British Telecom is paring away one's coins in a box. In fact I don't see how anything of importance can ever really be said on the telephone. But I suppose that depends on what one means by things of importance.

You can accuse me of getting off on the letter-writing now.

But I want to be serious. God knows I should be with all that's happened, though I feel like giggling.

Fred, you said all sorts of true as well as all sorts of silly things in your mega letter. One thing you said stuck. You said I was diffident about family because of what I had seen happen to mine. This is fair comment, Big Fred, and I suppose it didn't need a brain the like of yours to tell me that. But then you said that really I was only using my old family as an excuse for deserting the new. And that I don't think was fair. Then with your eager, dramatic, all-male, all-American love, which you are as determined to keep on course as your career, you drew the inevitable conclusion that I should just stop worrying about the Baldwins and get on with producing the Shakers, come what may.

All I want to say is, I came back here because I felt I had some sort of duty to fulfil towards my parents and brother and because I was furious with the way you seemed to think you owned me. I remembered there was part of me that had nothing to do with you or your plans at all. What I found when I arrived was that two members of my family had really ceased to be who they had been, had become nothing more than awful practical problems, though always sufficiently ghosts of the past to make you shun the mere practicality of it. And this may well happen to our children, Fred, or indeed to us, who can say? We are all headed for emptiness one way or another. But just because a person has been transformed in this way, I still believe we have some sort of a duty to them, even if based on nothing more than fond memory. And if that duty is incompatible with one's own life and set up, I don't think you can just sit back and say too bad for them, or at least not right away. I think you have to suffer that incompatibility and make sacrifices. You can't just put together your plans and stick by them willy nilly. Because otherwise you would lose some image you have of yourself and of your future relations with the people you're with now. Fred, you said one shouldn't accept responsibility for the unsolvable – shouldn't it be 'insoluble'? – but I feel that maybe a lot of life is about doing just that. Certainly that's what my mother has been doing ever since Raymond fell ill, and certainly it was that that destroyed her in the end. A recipe for tragedy, you said. But is that any reason for saying she was wrong?

Perhaps I'm just trying to say, if some problem comes up again, I'll do it again. I'll go and help again. Since that's the only kind of basis I can see for having and being part of a family. And maybe, in a way, going back to be there, I wasn't deserting my 'new' family at all. Maybe rather I was looking to see if it really had any foundation apart from your carefully drawn up plans, your lectureships and bigger flats and ideas about the ideal number of children. And I haven't come up with an answer, Fred, I'm not sure. I don't know if what we're putting together has anything solid about it at all. Even after your letter I'm not really sure. You said it was a great adventure. And I think you're right there; if only because we will need so much luck and so much love to avoid its being a recipe for tragedy. But don't get obsessed with plans, Fred. Don't bank everything on some job or contract or piece of property or prestige. Remember that at any moment anything may happen. To anyone. Perhaps it's my childhood, I don't know, or simply this business with Raymond, but I feel that so strongly, so continuously. Which is why perhaps I go to the opposite and, I admit, equally negative extreme and never seem to make any plans at all, because I never feel confident that things or people will remain the same or in the same place for very long. Be ready for diversions and losses, Fred. Be ready to write things off.

But in the meanwhile, as I said on the phone, I'm throwing in my lot with you, disasters or no; because I can think of no alternative, and because I do love you and I can't bear to think we should have failed so soon in our adventure, and then because I've sworn I won't be so pushed around as I have been in the past and frankly I want to see if I can stand up to you. So prime your prostate, buddy boy.

Or let's say, you make the plans, okay, and I'll ruin them. What about that for a deal?

See you soon.

> Love,
> Your Little LORNA, soon to be big.

PS. We were quite wrong about Garry. He's been a real darling. He's been to visit both of them everyday (they think they're going to save Raymond's eye) and has done a lot to improve the appearance of the flat; 'there are worse ways of throwing away one's life', he says. Certainly without his help I couldn't have dreamt of coming back so soon.

Left on the kitchen table in Fairfield Close.

LORNA,
   THEY'RE TAKING ME TO THE ROYAL FREE. I THINK
THEY'RE GOING TO HAVE TO OPERATE. I'M IN AGONY.
NO METAPHORS TO DESCRIBE THIS ONE. AGONY.
   COME AND VISIT AT ONCE. PLEASE.
   FRED.

⚓

Graham to Lorna

September 10th

Find enclosed one housewarming/engagement party invitation (as promised on phone).

One thing though. It really irritates me to hear you constantly praising Garry. He only decided to take on Raymond because he couldn't be bothered to find a job and saw it as a way of getting easy money at our expense; he has twice written asking for sums in excess of £100 to pay for damages Raymond <u>apparently</u> caused to a neighbour's property. But how can I check that the money really was used for that? What's more, when I last phoned Uncle Harry, he said Auntie Mary had seen Raymond ferreting in a bin at Talbot Road Bus Station barefoot and unshaven. So I have my doubts about the value of Garry's care – and if he walks out one day, are you going to go back up there to take his place? I still believe my own plan was and is the better policy. This way the whole story will just go on and on.

The irony is, of course, they committed the wrong one: Mother isn't mad at all; actually, I was wondering, do you think it might still be possible to formulate a rape or at least indecent assault charge if she testified?

Best,
GRAHAM

PS. I've sent an invite to Dad, if only in the remote hope of a present.

PS. again. I think adoption is folly, frankly, but then nobody

ever listens to my opinion. Anyway, you more or less have
to adopt an 'ethnic', as they say, don't you? Just a con-
sideration . . . I feel we have enough 'aliens' in the family
already.

Garry to Amanda

September 28th

Broughton St
Cleveleys
Lancashire

Dear Amanda,

You'll be wondering what happened to my famous letter and why I disappeared from the scene for so long. The fact is we had something of a disaster/tragedy in the family. My mother went mad and attacked my brother with a knife and they both ended up in hospital. Seeing as my father has pissed off for good and neither of the others were willing to, muggins here agreed to be the one who stays up in Cleveleys to look after Raymond, at least for the time being, and not without great risk to life and limb may I say. When not defending myself and generally cleaning up after him – I do feel rather a hero actually – I'm writing a novel. Perhaps I've found my true vocation at last; I was always good at telling jokes, so why not stories; Raymond is certainly supplying enough of them; and anyway, it certainly beats nine to five.

But the reason I'm writing is to say, if you could make it over here for a day, I could at last take you out to lunch, since I have something in the way of spare funds now I'm not having to pay rent to anyone. I certainly owe you a meal or two I think. We could have seafood. There are some quite decent restaurants in Blackpool, believe it or not.

Look forward to hearing from you.

Best,
GARRY

Letter returned to sender, October 2nd.

277

Raymond to the International Court of Human Rights

Broughton Street
Cleveleys
UK

Honourable Sirs,

By the time you receive this cry for help and for justice, the voice that raised it will probably be no more. They are remorseless. Every colour has been stained to a foul-smelling graphite black. This is most notable on the inner lining of my skull and in the lymph. Half my keys have been taken from me and many of my books; usually it happens while I'm sleeping. The most recent turn of the screw is their acquisition of high-tech, pin-point, long-range nebulizer spray equipment for introducing the most refined and in many cases odourless poisons into my immediate vicinity. In this way I have already been deprived of a number of vital psycho-motor faculties: for example I have a very severe limp in my left leg and difficulty balancing when using a bicycle. Also my head tends to fall heavily to one side. But no doubt you will have heard other reports of such developments from other quarters. You will not be without your informers. I myself refer to this new generation of weapons as Blind Green Psyche Super Poisoners (BGPSPs), and I think you could do worse than to adopt the term. What does surprise me about this turn of events is that such loathsome worms as my oppressors should have access to such extraordinarily sophisticated technical know-how. The Americans will be doing their part no doubt. My one consolation is that a cause

278

which has raised the combined opposition of the infernal services of this and quite probably other worlds too must be a just one.

A raised fist and a proud heart will be the treasure of my last agonizing apocalyptic seconds.

The specific reason for my writing, however, is that I wish to draw the Court's venerable attention to an utterly revolutionary subterfuge, of which you may well not as yet be aware. The truth is that I myself only stumbled across it very recently: they have been substituting the members of my family with other beings; indeed it has now reached the point where not one of them is the same person. Obviously the scope this gives their organization for close observation and refined torment is immense.

The proof: I must confess that I have not as yet managed to get hold of documentary evidence pointing to the exact time and place of each substitution. The more I think about it, the more I suspect that the first substitutions probably took place long before I had any idea of what was going on, perhaps many years ago. But that is a matter for further investigation and study; what follows is a series of facts which prove beyond all reasonable doubt that those masquerading as my family are not who they pretend to be:

◊ The first and most devastating proof is quite simply that none of my 'family' behave as if they were in any way related to me, and when they do attempt to do so their simulation is nauseatingly evident. I appreciate, however, that such evidence is difficult to present in concrete form, so from now on I shall stick to the demonstrable details.

◊ On January 19th 1987 my 'mother' returned from a short shopping trip with blonde hair and ringlets; in the past her hair had always been dark brown and wavy. I put it down to poor homework on the part of the infernal services (there may even be some suggestion of colour blindness). When 'she' realized I was on to her, she stopped speaking entirely so as to cover her tracks; this also was very uncharacteristic and a considerable blunder; I laid low pretending not to notice; later, in desperation, she attacked me with a knife and went for the eyes, attempting to blind me to the obvious physical anomalies that I had previously tricked her into revealing (sagging breasts, flab, severe varicose veins on the inner left leg). When the attempt failed, the services removed her to prevent further embarrassment. No doubt she, if one can really talk of sex here, will have paid the price for her inadequate disguise and I can't say I'm sorry. My real mother, I might add in parenthesis, was an exquisite woman, affectionate, practical and above all physically beautiful. I feel deeply ashamed that I did not register her substitution at once. But of course they count on your not being ready for such radical infiltrations. Every day I mourn her passing. Who knows what awful death she may have died at their hands. Anyway, I do not expect to see her again.

◊ My father recently disappeared and is obviously being substituted at this moment. I look forward to spying out the small differences when 'he' returns. I have photographs to compare with. Why, however, they should have bothered substituting someone who was already an accomplished tormentor in his own right and long in their pay is a detail that must remain obscure.

◊ My 'sister' not only married an American but has been spreading evil rumours about me to police and other authorities at both national and international level. My real sister would never have dreamed of such betrayals. Being a prostitute and a masquerader, the present 'version' has more than once refused me permission to inspect her naked body for fear that I would find out the truth. Not unexpectedly it now appears that she has produced a baby of inferior genetic, probably Negroid origin. Need we say more.

◊ My 'brother' Graham Ali was obviously substituted some long time ago, I am sure he was the first. His physical disguise is excellent, but never was behaviour less fraternal. As to his character, it bears no resemblance to how he was as a boy. He smokes American tobacco and openly supports the Thatcher-Reagan coalition of death.

◊ I am presently forced to share my prison with the being who likes to pass for my once beloved brother Garibald. Activities indicating surrogate, if not robotic status are: frequent writing habit (taking notes and making reports on myself – he refuses to let me see what he has written); constant stealing from myself of keys, scientific publications, my interstellar bleep pen, to mention but a few; frequent and unfraternal resorting to violence in any kind of remotely confrontational situation, such as when he insists on taking away my clothes on the flimsy pretext that they need washing. The real intention, as reliable sources have been able to inform me, is to check for corporeal secretions. The absence of his girlfriend of long-standing is another suspicious factor. Like the others he regularly refuses any clarificatory physical inspection.

These then are the incontrovertible proofs. The result is that I am being tormented on every front and plane and level, physical, psychological, emotional, spiritual. Above all, the girl who Allah planned for me to marry has been raped and killed, her flesh tossed to the vultures of the desert. They have been putting nails in my shoes, poison powder in my clothing, acid solutions in my eyes. But I shall not take my life as they intend. I shall go on living at all costs, if only in honour and memory of my own dear family, all of whom I now must accept are dead. It is a great burden to me to think that I alone am left to preserve the memory of the wonderful people they were, the wonderful times we had together when we were younger.

To conclude my letter, I should like to appeal to the Court under the terms of the Helsinki Accord on Human Rights, to intervene to end this hideous nightmare and to bring its evil perpetrators to justice.

Faithfully,
RAYMOND BALDWIN

encs
◊ Translations in French, Spanish, Arabic.

◊ Evidence: a) piece of paper towel I believe bearing specimen spermatozoa of the Garibald substitute; could you please use your laboratories to check if this is human; b) photographs of my mother before and after substitution.

Postcard of Blackpool Illuminations

Sorry, Lorna, could you rush off £80 or so: Ray's thrown brake fluid over Mrs Howarth's son's new Datsun and it needs a paint job. Sorry to be so demanding, but you know how it is.

GARRY

Lorna to Mr Baldwin

May 5th

Trysting Road
Tolworth
Surrey

Dear Father,

Are we to lose touch entirely then, or did you think we already had? I send you a huge letter with all the news, important news – how could it be more important? – and all we get from you six months later is a birthday card for Kirsty with a £20 note enclosed. Is money the only thing that attaches you to people, the only part of yourself you can give?

But I don't want to discourage you. Please write and defend yourself (note change of address above) and give us all your news.

We are all very well, and likewise Mother. Or at least she's improving. They now let her come over here at weekends. Fred hates it and shuts himself in his study to work. His next tome comes out in September.

Garry appears to be managing famously with Raymond. Apparently his Algerian girl came over, but then went away again. Who can blame her?

Best love, Dad.

Your disappointing daughter,
LORNA

PS. Seeing as birthdays obviously means something to you, remember that John's is August 10th.

This slim young woman with the creamy face sits a moment, turning her father's card with its three yellow elephants over and over in her hand. The elephants are dressed up as policeman, nurse and baker. Inside the card it says:

> 'Now you are three
> Whatever will you be?'

Indeed.

Fred says: 'If I were you I wouldn't bother, frankly.'

She says: 'I've finished now. I may as well send it.'

He says: 'The time would be better spent writing off for that job.'

She says: 'Yes sir, no sir, three bags full sir.' And she says: 'Fred?'

'Yes?'

'I'm not going to tell you whether I've written off for that job or not.'

At which this couple look at each other across a space of toy-cluttered table, seeing nothing as they search each other's eyes but blue and brown irises flickering over whatever lies behind. And how, oh how, in these circumstances, Lorna asks herself, can the necessary arrangements ever be made: children be brought up, homes kept and cleaned, holidays planned? She smiles. Thin wrinkles appear about his eyes, a twist to his wide mouth. Her smile broadens. For a moment it seems they will embrace, perhaps even make love, the children are in bed after all, but then Fred has his work to get back to.

HOME THOUGHTS

'For such a short book, Parks presents an impressive number of characters in full dress. There are well over a dozen, set in a plot of such convoluted intricacy it could fuel a soap opera for years . . . This is a startlingly sharp and impressive piece of work.'

New York Times

'No reader will feel short-changed by Parks . . . Between the orderly lines there are passions, betrayals, violent deaths – more surprises and revelations than one narrative could normally contain.'

Hilary Mantel, *Books*

CARA MASSIMINA

'An unusually classy thriller, true to life and not to be missed.'

Independent

'Tim Parks presents the real, virginal, boastful, cracked Morris lurking behind his own justifications as matters turn lethal and ugly. Clever, blandly humorous and utterly immoral.'

Sunday Times

'Better than *Silence of the Lambs* . . . macabre fun orchestrated with immaculate precision. It's a killer.'

Los Angeles Times

MIMI'S GHOST

'An unusually classy thriller, true to life and not to be missed.'

Independent

'Comparable to Highsmith at her best . . . Parks is a writer with real talent.'

Time Out